Sherlock Holmes

THE
KEYS
OF
DEATH

Forward by Mattias Boström

Gretchen Altabef

Hardcover ISBN 978-1-78705-887-3
Paperback ISBN 978-1-78705-888-0
ePub ISBN 978-1-78705-889-7
PDF ISBN 978-1-78705-890-3

Published by MX Publishing
335 Princess Park Manor, Royal Drive,
London, N11 3GX
www.mxpublishing.com

Cover design by Brian Belanger

Dedicated to my all-time favourite Sephardi couple, Morris and Rebecca Altabef.

"...it is only when a man goes out into the world with the thought that there are heroisms all round him, and with the desire all alive in his heart to follow any which may come within sight of him, that he breaks away...from the life he knows, and ventures forth into the wonderful mystic twilight land where lie the great adventures and the great rewards." – A. Conan Doyle. *The Lost World*.

NOTE:

This novel is a compilation of two graciously shared journals. Plus the inclusion of my notes on the murders that took place in Baker Street in the year 1880, brought to light by Mr. Sherlock Holmes. The journals to which I refer are Mrs. Hudson's journal, and one by her husband, Mr. James Hudson, posthumously published, here. We believe he looked to publicise under the heading: "Mr. Hudson's Garden." His complete monograph is to be found on Page 230 of this chronicle. For the pleasure of your reading, I have undertaken to keep the distinctions clear, with a subtle change of typeface for each voice.

John H. Watson, MD.

Table of Contents

FOREWORD

In the beginning, there was *one* Sherlock Holmes. That genesis was, however, just a short glimpse in time, and for ninety-seven percent of his existence in literature, there have been two of them: Original Holmes and Parallel Holmes.

Only a few months after the full-blown 1891 success of the Holmes stories in The Strand Magazine, other writers began using the Baker Street detective. Initially, these appearances were in parodies, as a direct reaction to the sudden popularity of Conan Doyle's invention. Many of the parodies in those early years were written by Conan Doyle's author friends, and they were appreciated and endorsed by him. Conan Doyle even inserted an early Sherlock Holmes parody by his dear friend J. M. Barrie (of Peter Pan fame) into his autobiography *Memories and Adventures* in the 1920s.

By accepting the parodies, Conan Doyle had, unintentionally, also left the door ajar for Holmes to appear in pastiches and as a minor character in novels by other authors. In the mid-1890s, after Conan Doyle had killed Holmes, that door was now wide open, e.g., when John Kendrick Bangs used a deceased Sherlock Holmes as a character on the river Styx in *The Pursuit of the Houseboat*, and the book was dedicated to, "A. Conan Doyle, Esq., with the author's sincerest regards and thanks for the untimely demise of his great detective which made these things possible." Even Mark Twain saw no problem with using Sherlock Holmes as a character in one of his novels. The copyright situation had become much more regulated at the end of the 19th century, but it was primarily seen as the copyright of texts and not a copyright of characters.

For forty years, Conan Doyle wrote about Original Holmes, now and then giving him new traits, or removing old ones, but pretty

1

much preserving him as the character he had been since the first novels. There was of course a leap between *A Study in Scarlet* and *The Sign of the Four*, a leap in which Holmes matured and became less odd, but after the latter novel, he more or less stayed the same, a gentleman detective with some spectacular add-ons.

At the same time as Conan Doyle preserved his original character, the development into a world-famous popular culture icon mostly took place in the forming of Parallel Holmes. While Original Holmes is Conan Doyle's creation, Parallel Holmes is how other persons changed the detective. And not just writers, but actors, illustrators, and many more.

To many people, this Parallel Holmes is often truer than the original version. Without Parallel Holmes, the detective would lack many of his most characteristic features: the deerstalker, the curved pipe and the line "Elementary, my dear Watson." The deerstalker was of course put there by Sidney Paget – and that's definitely connected to Original Holmes – but without the American actor William Gillette's use of it, Holmes would have had no characteristic hat, and his easily recognizable silhouette would be less easily recognizable.

When Gillette's play toured America and all over Europe at the turn of the century, newspapers calculated that more people had seen this Sherlock Holmes on stage than had ever read a book about Conan Doyle's detective. Even if Gillette's Holmes had lines and plot taken from Original Holmes, it was nevertheless Parallel Holmes – Gillette's own view of the detective. Gillette's Holmes play showed generations to come what could be done with the detective (e.g., his emotions towards Alice Faulkner) and how far away from Original Holmes he could be taken – while still being able to call him Sherlock Holmes. And remember, Conan Doyle had said okay to this whole transformation, Gillette had even read the manuscript to him in advance. Conan Doyle accepted that there was a Parallel Holmes, a detective that in many ways was different from his own creation.

But Gillette's Holmes wasn't the only forefather of future Parallel Holmes. The parodies of the 1890s had done as much to create that Parallel Holmes. They had sped up the plots and made Holmes's deductions faster and more impossible – and, of course, sometimes entirely wrong, since they were parodies. They had given Holmes even sharper features and a more insane personality. And they had spread and further established Sherlock Holmes's increasingly famous name among the readers.

These two early types of Parallel Holmes melted into one big category and formed what was to become the popular icon, Sherlock Holmes. Parallel Holmes was – and still is – the Holmes that most people know about. Much fewer have read the original stories. Original Holmes was the origin of Parallel Holmes, but Parallel Holmes was the origin of popular icon Holmes.

By dividing Holmes into an Original one and a Parallel one, it is interesting to look at the whole genre of newly written Sherlock Holmes stories. There is no need in coming close to Original Holmes in such a story unless you wish to create a perfect pastiche of Conan Doyle's writings. Instead, it just needs to be a good Parallel Holmes story. Many creators of such fiction are not satisfied with just playing the game, but are instead constantly adding to it, evolving it. It is sometimes the case that when Parallel Holmes gets even further away from Original Holmes, great entertainment is to be extracted, and new revelations regarding the detective's character are to be made.

I'm an Embracer. I think you can pretty much do whatever you want with Sherlock Holmes and Doctor Watson. You can't expect everyone to like it, but you are fully entitled to do it. And I will appreciate every attempt to do something unexpected, a new perspective, congenial or not. I already have the originals, now I want something else, something that will wake me up – no matter if I like it or not. Because if you do take risks and invest your intelligence and time in trying to do clever things with something that is so close to my heart, you will get my embrace. The opposite – i.e., if you don't do anything at all – is a much more boring alternative. So, shake up Sherlock, and I will give you, my love.

Mattias Boström

October 2021

Chapter 1
LAST & FIRST MEETING
From the Journal of Mrs. Hudson
"Garden as though you will live forever." – William Kent

21 September, 1880

My autumn London day began blue-skied and cold. Its capricious nature soon embodied my own state. Equinoctial winds whipped the trees and an hour's dreich downpour pummelled the city. Streets became fast rivulets, and rain thrust inside my coal-black cape. I arrived dripping puddles.

This was not what we had planned.

Inspector Lestrade met me at the mortuary, he hung my cloak and offered his arm, then coolly shepherded me down the grey hall he was used to treading. *I am desperate to find James. Yet not this way. Maybe they are wrong? Maybe it is someone else?*

I was keenly aware of the sharp astringent of the morgue as the inspector and I trudged the faded whitewashed hall. We turned into a white-tiled room, well-lit by gaslight. Beneath my capable exterior, a waif cowered. The coroner in lab coat and black apron discoloured with the blood and offal of his subjects, and a tall young man stood near. The inspector mechanically brought me to the table, nodded to the coroner and uncovered the head and chest of the corpse.

My husband lay naked on a slab beneath a sheet. So perfect, I was afraid to touch him. Afraid the mirage would break apart or fade. His wound was visible for inspection. His face was as beautiful as in life. I took hold of his hand. It was shockingly, inhumanly cold.

The young man rushed over as my knees gave way. The room was stone silent except for the clatter of his walking stick as it fell to the tile. His strong arms must have caught me before I hit.

"Lestrade, ammonia, *now!*" he called.

I awoke sitting on a bench in the hall with the sting of brandy on my lips and pushed aside the gently offered flask. The young man was very solicitous, a look of care on his thin, prominent, and handsome features. There was the young'un about him as if he had not yet grown into his nose, ears, or feet. The long, lean fingers of his right hand were warmly patting mine.

One bullet, a small internal explosion, a blemish on perfection. James' perfectly sculpted Adonis body rebelled at the very idea of death. Gods lived forever!

I thought, *Where was he now? James was so alive, lived every minute compassionately, joyfully. We married for life. How could I go on? This was not real. James was still alive. I knew it! I felt it! That frigid body in the morgue had no feeling, no life--it could not be James! What was I going to do without him? How could I go on?*

Someone coughed, and I realized I was standing in an open office with tears running down my face. I signed papers conferring my beautiful husband to the West London Synagogue for British Jews. The young man offered his handkerchief. But the tears wouldn't stop. A dam was bursting.

"His wedding ring, Inspector? I would like it."

"Jewellery is routinely removed. But he had none and no identification of any kind. The Jew, Dreyfus, identified him."

Like a bluebottle buzzing into my thoughts, Inspector Lestrade questioned me about my husband's involvement in illegal activities. I told him unequivocally that James never would.

He continued as if my words were meaningless. Realizing his horrible questions were tinged with that sneer usually reserved for those of the Jewish faith, I lost my fine senses and hollered.

"Are you, deaf, Inspector? James was as law-abiding as you!"

At this point, the young gentleman introduced himself as Mr. Holmes and offered his arm. He led me out of the morgue, into deep night and brought me home in a cab. I fumbled with my keys and unlocked my door. He hung up my wet cape, sat me down, wrapped a blanket around my shoulders, stoked the fire, and made tea in my kitchen. The dam had burst, and my tears were endless. He gave me another handkerchief, picked up the awful telegram from the hall carpet, and threw it in the fire. He wrote a message on the back and placed his card on the table.

Then he left me to the horror and regret of my grief.

22 September 1880

DAILY CHRONICLE
Murder in Westminster
James Hudson Killed in Baker Street

Tuesday, 21 September, 1880.
A young ruffian of the Jewish persuasion, identified as James Hudson, was found dead under circumstances that point to foul play. He was a member of the notorious St. James's Boxing Club. The coroner reported he was shot through the heart and died where he fell. The discovery was made first by moneylender Dreyfus' in whose disreputable premises the dead man was found. Inspector Lestrade, a new and promising member of Scotland Yard's Criminal Investigation Department, reported the dead man was built like a pugilist.

"I see it all the time. In his line of work, this is not unusual. Thugs like this specialize in assaults, intimidations and the like. They are hired by moneylenders to put pressure on clients or to collect on a debt. He may have simply met his match this time. It is an occupational hazard," the inspector said.

At least one other unsavoury-looking brawler was found lurking at the Baker Street windows with other gawkers outside the scene of the shooting. Authorities pursued the miscreant and were confident of a quick apprehension.

Let this be a warning to all citizens of our fair city--beware of devious associations and unscrupulous practices!

23 September, 1880

Mr. Holmes came again, always with staples, milk for tea, fresh eggs for breakfast. I went to unlatch the door and heard shouts on the other side.

"Tell your hounds this house is under my protection!" It was Mr. Holmes' voice.

I opened the door, and he was standing on my step dusting off his frock-coat. A little rumpled, Mr. Holmes entered and firmly closed the door behind him. Yet he had a triumphant smile and the air of one whose decision has been made. In my kitchen, he washed his hands, wrapped his handkerchief around the knuckles of his right fist, and put my kettle on to boil.

"Excuse me, Mrs. Hudson," he sheepishly said.

That was all. Mr. Holmes was a young man comfortable with silence. Then, as I poured the tea, he asked if my lodger had moved out. How he knew was beyond me, but I told him the rooms would be available at the New Year. He gave me a generous advance right then and there. Said he would take it. Then he warned me to keep my doors and windows locked, and left.

While washing the tea things, I thought about what Mr. Holmes had announced to all the ears of Baker Street. *Was he truly my protector? Did I need protection?* He thought I did.

Out in my garden, the trellised roses were blooming, most of the beds were now fallow, dried stalks, leaves, and marigold seeds to be gathered. My beautiful husband and I planted this crop. It had begun with hope and love. Provided for me throughout the season, and now was over.

Like so many comings and goings of my life, it was unusual that James and I had met at all. Being of an adventurous Scots disposition, I was attending the Lectures for Ladies at Newnham College, one of two women's colleges founded by Jewish and suffragist educators at Cambridge. No woman could achieve a degree at this time, yet we were now allowed to study the same subjects as men students. And the colleges were filled with the excitement of history being made.

A tall, young gentleman, with a musician's gifts, came into my life during the Peterhouse November Concerts. We discovered our many shared interests, and it seemed natural that we should court. One afternoon he steered me to Claridge's and over tea, he asked for my hand. As we were of different faiths, and both living in London now, our casually heretical wedding fete was held in the Summer Garden of the Imperial Theatre. The orchestra played, minus one French Horn, all morning.

James' parents had a unique openness toward their son and his exceptional choices. During his early years at the prestigious Priory School and later the intense focus required to achieve each stage of his Cambridge degree, his Jewish life remained in London. In this way, Rabbi Moshe hoped his son would achieve his goals bypassing the anti-Semitism that even now existed in many British communities.

James and I built a joy-filled life here in Baker Street. My beautiful husband. What do I do now?

Chapter 2
MR. HOLMES TAKES THE CASE
From the Journal of Mrs. Hudson

"Mrs. Hudson stood in the deepest awe of Holmes, was fond of him too, for he had a remarkable gentleness and courtesy in his dealings with women." - John H. Watson MD, "The Adventure of the Dying Detective."

5 November, 1880

Mr. Holmes arrived once again at my door. I was grateful for this friendship which had appeared at the worst moment of my life.

"Guy Fawkes day, Mr. Holmes. Come join me in some tea."

"Thank you, Mrs. Hudson. Will you be attending a bonfire? I understand such things can be healing," he said with a twinkle in his eye, as he removed his gloves.

"I do enjoy this rebellious holiday. We throw down the enemy within our midst and celebrate the preservation of the monarchy and our government. Living so close to Regent's Park it is hard to dismiss the aroma of the bonfires and the handmade fireworks reverberating down Baker Street."

"The wealth of research offered to the scientist by the park's Zoological Society and the Royal Botanic Conservatory are splendid reasons to live here."

With that, he handed me an envelope with the remainder of his first two months' rent and I gave him the keys to No. 221B. He attached them to a ring on a silver chain and placed them in his pocket.

"I noticed there is an empty bedroom on the second-floor. What would you say to my sharing the rooms at a rate that should cover your additional cost? Naturally, this would depend upon your approval of the gentleman I choose?"

"Of course, if he is a friend of yours, Mr. Holmes."

11

"Excellent!"

Mr. Holmes then dropped his playful facade, and his tone became quietly professional.

"Mrs. Hudson, I should like to inquire into your husband's death."

My sunny front fell into the angry greyness of my grief.

"If it will help you. Nothing like Inspector Lestrade's questions, I hope!"

He chuckled, shook his head and patted my hand.

"Mrs. Hudson, would I rent your upstairs flat and relocate my consulting detective practice under your roof if I thought that this was a den of illegal activities? I think you will find my art of Deduction and Analysis is far away from Lestrade's nonsensical stabs at the truth."

He lit a cigarette at the fire and measured his strides on my black and white tile.

"Your husband, James, attended the West London Synagogue?"

"He was very involved in the music program until his career took him away. Rabbi Moshe is always welcoming."

"Yes, it is a fine British Community. The rabbi has assisted me in my investigations before. Have you spoken with him lately?"

"Mr. Holmes, I very much doubt your investigation will lead to the synagogue. You will not find James' murderer there."

"It is his friends I am interested in."

"James played French Horn in the Imperial Theatre Orchestra." I picked up a freshly washed handkerchief from the linen I had taken in and folded it.

He turned round with an eager face. "A musician!"

"Yes, heart and soul, he was very good."

"Your home will welcome my violin, then?"

"It would give me joy, Mr. Holmes."

12

"It is a difficult horn to master."

"He was also a member of the Saville Club, but mostly for concerts."

He wrote it on his shirt cuff. I folded a towel.

"Family, friends?"

"James was in love with people, he had a lot of friends. Rabbi Moshe and Rifka are his parents, the Dreyfus' his aunt and uncle. An older brother, Adar. He is an adventurer, a pioneer. You would like him. He is presently in Palestine as part of a small advance corps for Baron Rothschild. They are searching for arable land and share the dream of building Israel in the desert. James and I were very proud of his trailblazing efforts."

"It is a laudable enterprise," he said. "Your husband was a fortunate man."

I picked up the handkerchief and dabbed my eyes, wiping my nose.

He stood looking down at me watching my ministrations. I think he thought, kindly.

"Mrs. Hudson, the Eastern Buddhists believe that living with death on one's shoulder as a persistent reminder of one's mortality is a way to an awakened life."

Drying my eyes, I said, "Mr. Holmes, I would give anything to be free of it."

"At the morgue, you mentioned his wedding ring."

"You are an observant gentleman, Mr. Holmes. It was missing. I do not understand it."

"Who would remove this ring?"

"I wish I knew. He usually kept a handkerchief and keys in his pockets, his pocketbook, calendar, and pencil. Always wore his watch, watch chain, and wedding ring. All good gold, and an amethyst tiepin. Was he murdered for such as this?"

He threw his cigarette into the fire, joined me, and sipped his tea. "Forgive me." He took my hand for an instant. "I must ask a few unpleasant questions. Did he have any unsavoury habits, drinking, gambling, opium? Was he in debt?"

"No."

"Any unsavoury friends?"

"Of course not!"

"Thank you. I am sorry to upset you. Would you like to continue at another time?"

"No."

He was ticking off questions in his mind. "Did he keep a notebook, diary, a commonplace book?"

"I will look in his study."

"I should like to investigate whatever you find if I may."

"He liked to fish for trout. My husband's fishing partner, Mr. Rosa, is just down Blandford Street, the blacksmiths."

"Thank you." He wrote on his cuff. "Your previous tenants, what were they like? Employment, habits, visitors?"

"My former lodger said he worked as a clerk in offices in Marylebone, but he always seemed low in funds. Mr. Fiant was a quiet man. Kept to himself most of the time. We shared tea once or twice. A good tenant at first."

"And then?"

"He changed, became secretive. Sometimes he would not take a meal I prepared and lock his door against me. He must have lost his position because he even stopped paying rent."

"Thank you, Mrs. Hudson. You will not encounter my locking you out," he said.

"We gave him every chance. It is the gamble we landlords take." I sighed. "The tenant before him was worse. He was a noisy young

Bohemian gentleman, Wilhelm, who threw parties above our heads at all hours, drank all the time and almost burned the place down." I watched him as he was jotting it down. "I am sure you do not have any unusual habits."

Mr. Holmes' hair had fallen over his forehead obscuring his vivid grey eyes. He was certainly an interesting young man and we have become friends in unusual circumstances. But there were times . . .

"Mr. Holmes, marking up your cuffs like that even with pencil requires the extra expense of Fuller's Earth to clean."

He moved his focus away from his shirt to my face. It seemed his intelligent eyes flashed humour for an instant. Then compassion filled them. He patted my hand, pulled out his pocketbook and continued.

"Do you have their forwarding addresses?"

"You certainly are thorough, Mr. Holmes. I will look in James' account ledger."

"Thank you. Mrs. Hudson, my next request may take some little time for you to accomplish yet might be exceedingly helpful to me. This is an unusual situation and your memory is our greatest asset. I would like you to create a calendar of how your husband spent his days during the last year of his life."

"That is no small feat, Mr. Holmes. But you should know there is something nagging at the back of my mind, something I am trying to remember. But I cannot reach it; it is like calling to a person who is moving away from you in the fog."

"It is better to try not to remember, Mrs. Hudson. Trust it will eventually appear. And please let me know when it does."

He moved to the hall, pulled on his coat and gloves.

Mr. Holmes' Montague Street landlord had only good things to say about the refined Mr. Sherlock Holmes. All the same, I wondered who this other gentleman boarder might be, especially since Mr.

Holmes had never mentioned him before. Two boarders were unique in my home, and I began to consider my costs.

He stopped buttoning his coat and looked out into the garden. "Are you burning leaves, Mrs. Hudson?"

I opened the backdoor and we rushed out to find an effigy burning from my planetree. Mr. Holmes threw his coat and scarf on a bench.

"Take the rake, Mr. Holmes and be careful!"

As he pulled it down the body of the thing separated from its head.

"Watch out!" He said as the dried stalks caught fire.

I filled a pail with water and doused it good. Mr. Holmes shovelled soil over the flames while I unrolled and turned on the hose. I wet down the planetree bark. A final wetting and the flames were out.

Then we looked at it. Like most of the Guy Fawkes figures, it was scarecrow-like and made of flammable materials. Moving like a magician Mr. Holmes plucked something from it and put it in his pocket.

"Mrs. Hudson, it seems Guy Fawkes has come to you." He attempted to laugh it off as we sat on the benches.

"What did you hide away, Mr. Holmes?" I held out my hand.

"Oh, nothing of consequence."

"Do not coddle me, sir."

He took it from his pocket, it was a child's toy horn.

"How horrible!"

"Mrs. Hudson, this event is not altogether useless for our purposes. The villain himself has narrowed my research."

We put away the tools; in the kitchen, we cleaned the soot from our hands and faces.

16

"Please lock all windows and doors and call me in if anything unusual occurs." He wrapped his scarf around his neck.

"You are welcome to bring your things in while I am away on my holiday visit. My house will be safer with you here."

"Thank you, a splendid idea, Mrs. Hudson."

"Do you think you could solve it, Mr. Holmes? It would give me some solace to know what happened to James, and why."

"I will do my best. One more question. Your husband lived a good life that many would envy, but who was his enemy?"

"I ask myself that over and over, Mr. Holmes. As far as I know, James had many friends but no enemies."

"The only thing I am sure of is James Hudson had at least one enemy."

No need to see me out, Mrs. Hudson," he said as he held up his keys. He firmly gripped the handle and opened the door. Head erect, he stepped out to Baker Street. I watched his shoulders straighten as if he now felt a certain sense of ownership and he securely locked the door behind him.

Who would do this thing? In time the winter bleak and bare planetree would shed its burnt bark. My constant November roses proudly bloomed in hardy contrast and gaudy rebellion against Guy Fawkes and his imitators.

Whoever or whatever this was, I would not be defeated by it. I placed the garden chairs with the sundial against the eastern wall. Swept the fallen leaves, tree bark, and ashes into my compost pile, separating out the tinder to dry. With twine and wooden stakes, I defined the new growing beds. Next, I called in the urchins who swept Baker Street. I paid them to bring in pails of fertilizer and pitch it within my set boundaries. I sent them to the stables for straw that was spread at a six-inch depth. This will keep the soil protected through the wet winter and ready for tilling in March. I was dishevelled, dirty, and satisfied.

17

My backyard garden now had a distinctly Baker Street aroma. It echoed with the joyful sounds of boys splashing in the tub of water I provided. Sitting with their boots at my fire, they were now enwrapped in towels at the hearth, and bawdily ragging each other over their meal. I turned back to the garden. It was no longer empty but alive with promise. I thought, *It is in your hands, James.* Then I entered the kitchen and paid my little helpers. They left clean, dry and fed.

I was more than intrigued and taken with Mr Holmes' energy and the fire in his eyes when he spoke about music or his new science. He would be moving his detective practice here on 1ˢᵗ January. This I thought was something to look forward to.

Mr. Hudson's Garden
The Garden Wall
An excerpt from Mr. Hudson's Garden monograph found on page 230

Summer 1880

You may be pleased to note that some roses are, in fact, evergreens. In these Isles, we celebrate roses in perfusion 'til December and beyond.

It is reasonable to dress our garden walls with whatever will make them look the best. For me, hardy varieties work well. We have trained Piccadilly and November Roses to climb as high as is possible and added clematis for early contrast.

Plant the November Roses at the wall. Train carefully. Bend only as each cane's direction permits and anchor them onto the wall. They will require pruning and redirecting. This process will take many seasons, yet its result is well worth the effort. Piccadilly and other varieties of climbing roses require less effort as it is in their nature.

Morning Glory and honeysuckle are other yet wilder choices. They will run up a wall of their own accord and will occur where they may. To be greeted by the brilliant, trumpeting Morning Glory is its own delight.

> *Note: Our upstairs lodger shows an interest in the garden. He watches me from his bedroom window. I will invite him to join me next time I need a hand.*

Chapter 3
SPIRITUAL QUEST
From the Journal of Mrs. Hudson

"She still remains a widow, devoting her whole life to the care of the poor and to the administration of her husband's estate." - John H. Watson MD, "The Adventure of the Dancing Men."

14 December, 1880

Widow to most was just a word, to me it was the grey land where I now lived. My grieving was spent questing for an answer to, *Where was James now? Was he still alive somewhere?* In my searches, I visited a young minister in his starched collar and ancient church, who had never been through it and had nothing real to offer me. That was the thing about grief you could see right through pretence.

He said we see our whole life on the other side, and we are judged by it. All I knew was grief thrusts us into a state of morbid alertness. I was faced full force with all the mistakes I had made in my life--all the regret, and shame over my imperfections, and my role as wife. All of it stared at me, haunted my dreams as if I were looking through Mr. Holmes' microscope into my very soul.

This was the place many got lost. They took to drink or worse in the attempt to kill it off. Some joined with their beloveds. It was a hard place to be, still breathing. Some steeled themselves and lived bitter lives, the awful pain of regret conquering their spirit.

Then a visit to my father-in-law, Rabbi Moshe, at the West London Synagogue who always gave me a secure footing. I entered in from the backyard portico and could hear his violin wailing sadly through the temple. My gift of James' roses were vaingloriously blooming on Rifka's table as if scarlet alone could heal all. I must remember to bring more.

"Rifka, thank you for your honey cake recipe. It is on my New Year's sideboard," I said.

"An old family recipe. I am happy you are sharing it with friends."

Once again, we expressed our mutual incredulity at James' loss and held on to each other. Rifka was so small and seemed fragile, yet I knew better the inner strength of this lady. I also knew she was sorely tested, as I was, with the loss of her son. She felt like bones in my arms. I thought of the goshawk's light, hollow, strong bones with which she soared across our island in search of safety for her brood.

We moved apart, and as she wiped her tears, she said, "The hardest thing about being left behind is that you're left to pick up the pieces."

While we prepared the tea, she continued, "You try and carry on as normally as possible, but very often it's not possible, so one has to give oneself a lot of space, a lot of sitting still, and a lot of praying to come to terms with it." Rifka looked to me, and I assented.

Then she shooed me into the sitting-room using the same gesture James' used. I complied with her wishes and sat in the library waiting on the settee.

Rabbi Moshe smiled and nodded to me as he ended the piece. He sat down next to me and took my hand. We talked as the afternoon settled into evening. He was a simple and direct gentleman, with humour around his eyes, yet I knew his simplicity was never simple.

"How are you, Marti? We are a family in mourning. What's to be done? But to go through it together." He shrugged his shoulders. "Rifka and I have missed you." He patted my hand.

"Rabbi, I do not think I will ever not be in mourning."

He sighed, "Yes, it is difficult to let go, for Rifka and me also. The shock is still so new. There is time to cry and wail." He gestured to his violin. "I have helped others pass through this valley, and Marti, you are not to hold back. Take the time you need: Cry when you must, pray, rail at the Almighty when you must. He is certainly hearing from me! But He can take it. Remember James. He was more than the pain

22

we feel over his loss. He was the love he gave us and the love we still feel for him." He patted my hand. "I do not believe that life is just what we experience here and now."

"So James is not really gone?"

"Do you still feel his love?" I smiled up at him. "What better proof than that? You are here, Marti, and there's a reason for that. You must accept it and live your life."

"Yes. I suppose you wouldn't know the reason?"

"I believe, like all of us, you are not here by chance. That your gifts are for the good of the world."

"Rabbi, my steps are firmer than I am."

"I do understand. But you will find your stability if you are patient. If only to honour James' memory. You are a lady of strength, Marti. Always remember that you have family here, and your life is not yours alone."

"Thank you, Rabbi. I can see something else is troubling you."

"It is the history of our London community and the changes ahead for us. We have always kept our own identity while at the same time being equally proud of our British heritage."

I nodded. "My Scots background allows me an understanding of your struggle."

He looked at me. "Yes, it does. We have built our dream in just forty years, one generation. And are now faced with a challenge that could utterly destroy that success. If James were here, he would speak for these poor emigrant people."

"Rabbi, if James is still with us, bring him with you to your council meetings. I have asked my new lodger, Mr. Sherlock Holmes, to attempt to solve James' mystery. I hope you do not mind. But what is your challenge? Maybe Mr. Holmes could help?"

He laughed and patted my hand, "Oh, Marti, if only he could! But this is my challenge, the Synagogue's challenge, and that of our friends at Bevis Marks Synagogue. Yet, you have me thinking. Detectives search for the truth and for me, this may also be a beginning. For you, Mr. Holmes is a good man and seems to have a gift for it. Please keep us involved in your quest." He took my hand. "Come visit us more often, Marti."

I hugged Rifka farewell and exited as I had come through the halls filled with Rabbi Moshe's mournful violin. Is there any question where James inherited his musical gift? Out the back door, I went, past the Marble Arch and into Hyde Park. My only thought was an echo of Rabbi Moshe's wisdom. *In James' name, what gift do I have to give the world?*

Walking head down through the park, I didn't look up until I reached the edge of the Serpentine. The sounds of holiday vendors were just registering at the edges of my awareness as were the geese begging for crumbs.

As a Scotswoman, I knew only too well what it meant to be a part of and yet separate from Great Britain. Here James' family was building their community without a country around them. Each person carried the belief of their land with them and was a strand in its weaving.

A call of, "Good day, Mrs. Hudson!" brought me from my reverie.

Mr. Holmes called from atop a gorgeous chestnut stallion. He dismounted, held the reins leading the horse as he joined me at the waterside.

"Lovely day, glad to see you out and about."

"Mr. Holmes! You startled me," I said.

"I ride here, it is the best place in the city for such things. And when things quiet down, it is a rare place for a gallop. How are you?"

"You own a horse?"

24

"*Equus ferus caballus* or English Thoroughbred. He is somewhat tall for racing at 17 hands, yet fine for me, and a sprinter."

"Does he have a name?"

"Forgive me, Mrs. Hudson, please meet my friend, Prospero. I call him that, it rhymes with his original given name. He was a gift and is kept with my client's horses; it is a lovely arrangement and all I did to earn these rides with my friend here," he stroked the horse's cheek, "was to prove a certain gentleman did not cheat at the races. A simple matter."

Mr. Holmes was exuberant with his exercise, startling to me who had only seen him more subdued. I patted the horse's soft muzzle and said, "Very nice to meet you Prospero, next time I will come prepared with an apple."

"How are the Rabbi and his wife?"

"As good as can be expected. Yes, of course, you would make that connection. It was good to see them," I said.

"I am glad."

"Rabbi Moshe posed the question, 'In James' name, what gift do I have to give the world?'"

"I imagine the Rabbi was considering the meaning of his own existence and the trials ahead for him. I doubt he meant you to take on his weighty thoughts, Mrs. Hudson. Yet, I am foolish enough to think you have already answered the question."

The horse whinnied and nudged Mr. Holmes. "Forgive me, but I must continue his exercise run. Take care, Mrs. Hudson and enjoy your outing," Mr. Holmes said as he stepped into the saddle and was gone.

I thought, *It seems Prospero is a match for the speed of his fast rider.*

15 December, 1880

The next day my search for answers led me to a medium. Yes, I know how strange this seems, maybe even dangerous. None of these cautions proved necessary. Ada was a very gentle person who had been through the shadowed valley my life had become. She knew all too well the place where I now dwelt, and she understood its perils.

"Marti, I am so sorry! The press is so unkind. How are you holding up?"

You must understand, I was desperate for anything that would grant some understanding of this sudden and terrible change. I wasn't sure Spiritualism was what I was looking for or how much I believed. Spiritualists saw their practice as a way of providing evidence of life after death and the existence of the soul. And I wanted proof. For me, it offered an answer I could find nowhere else. And like all religions, when practised with heart, it required belief and offered consolation.

Funny, she had a collection of stones on the table around which we sat: polished smooth, different colours, sizes, crystals. She called it an altar. But collecting stones was child's play, poor children with nothing else. I looked at her then, clean and starched, but her dress old. Her little room missing more than it had. Still, she offered tea.

I said, "But where is James? Did he go out like a candle? Could I have saved him, stopped him? Maybe if I was smarter, or sweeter, or surer? Maybe if I were like other ladies and accepted my place? Maybe I was the wrong wife for him? Why did I not know? Do we truly go on, or is this life all there is? Is his essence somewhere, and is he safe?"

Ada patted my hand and said, "Your remorse is natural, but his death is not your fault. You could not stop it, nor could you change it. But even though these thoughts seem endless, you are not helpless."

"But I deserve no better."

"Marti, here's something you can hold onto and believe. I know that your James is alive and where he is supposed to be. He is even teaching music, and waiting for you to join him when it is your time."

26

Ada shared her visions with me. It was curious when she went into a trance; her voice changed. She had warned me that this would happen with the voice of her guide. She could see James standing next to me, that he was surrounded by love. This idea allowed me to breathe and time slowly began for me. And in turn, I was able to aid her.

"Keep your private feelings in a journal," Ada said. "A place where you are exempt from the strictures of society. A sanctuary of sorts. To write in detail everything you need to say, all your feelings, including anger or even rage. We women are not supposed to have or express rage, but we do, and especially at times like these."

I learned that the guilt and regret of mourning were soul killers. Most of the pain of grief was caused by them.

"Do not listen. They are all lies," Ada said. "Hold to the love you had and will have again."

There is no magic answer for grief. It is a process of cycles. Some days are lighter and some darker. It takes time and care, acceptance, and as Rabbi Moshe said, rage at the Almighty.

"I surrender! Just let it end."

It was now three months from September, and I was about to walk into a new year. Yet, everything I did or thought about, my first thought was still: *When James comes home. Oh, please come through that door one more time.*

I do not know who I am without James. I do not want to know who I am without James! I was left, exposed, scattered, torn, a whirlwind threatening to breach every door. Day like night. Noise like sobs that came up from my core. Lost in the storm's crash and thunder, until it was all I was. Standing with my arms out, *Hey, wait, there is so much I did not tell you, give you--Wait!*

27

Chapter 4
FIRST-FOOTER
From the Journal of Mrs. Hudson

"All the detectives of fact and of fancy would be children in your hands. That's your line of life, sir, and you may take the word of a man who has seen something of the world." – John H. Watson MD, "The Adventure of the Gloria Scott."

17 December, 1880

I travelled to my Aunt Janet Fergusson's farm for the holidays. Yes, I believe we were distantly related to the poet. I was hoping to find the comfort of my childhood summers spent in her garden, fields and woods.

For generations, my family had raised sheep here in the Scots lowlands. They survived the expansion and croft clearances of the day. The Fergussons remained rooted, while so many friends, were ploughed under.

My Aunt Janet and her farm garden taught me about change, that it could bring variety and newness to life. But this was the change of progress that swept through our land uprooting generational crofter families, taking their land, and leaving poverty in its place. My distant relation, Robert Fergusson, put it this way, "And dwining nature droops her wings, with visage grave."

Christmastime has always been a joyous gathering of families from the area. This year's firesides were filled with discussions of the Highland Land League and political avenues to the reclaiming of their land.

Our holiday celebration became the noisy and necessary political arguments of friends bravely fighting back against the tide. For battle, there is nothing like a Scotsman with his ire up. Or a Scotswoman for that matter. This holiday was nothing like I expected it to be. Instead of the Christmas spirit, it was filled with the fierce spirit of a people for their land.

Things had quieted down as our guests left for the next hearth down the road. My aunt and I sat at the fire.

"Marti, our changes are hard on you this year."

"Aunt Janet, maybe I am broken. I can not get my mind around it."

"Not broken, just a bit overwhelmed, I imagine."

"I remember the summers we spent gardening. And riding the gentle and even Lady Annie your plough horse."

"Like Lady Annie, much has changed. Our neighbours fleeing to Canada, our focus on the battle over our land. But surely you can understand us?"

"Of course and support what I can of the legal battle back in London. You taught me we are a persistent and agreeable lot. And we know when it is proper to cooperate or to stand fast."

"But you were looking for some stability."

"Yes."

"It is Christmas Eve, let us have our own holiday, tonight?"

And with that, we exchanged wrapped gifts. We made punch and she brought out her plum pudding. Afterwards, we lit lanterns and walked to our neighbour's cottages singing carols. Each house brought us in with a drink and we picked up other carolers on our way. Back at the farm, we shared food and drink and for a few hours, we left instability behind and celebrated our friendship.

On the Friday, I wished them all exceedingly well and gratefully returned to the simple New Year's celebration I would soon host in town.

New Year's Eve 1880

From the dark, noisy, smoke-filled Underground, I ascended and blinked into brilliant, blatant Baker Street. At the corner, I purchased some rather expensive oranges, local apples, and chestnuts. I crossed carefully in between horses and carts, an omnibus, and carriages, the butcher boy's bicycle, the repairs going on across the way, the dirt, the smells. The postman, commissionaires, and ladies walking arm-in-arm. Past the post office, the bookshop, and the pub. Fashionable city gentlemen with their walking sticks in rhythm, barefoot dirty street urchins up to no good. And the last persistent holiday strains of a hurdy-gurdy near Regent's Park.

I have travelled back here alone, drawn by instinct, by memory, the certainty that our love still existed in our home in town. This city and this street and this house were who I was. I knew my destiny lay here, and that was something. I reached my presupposing door with its only distinguishing feature the unusual street number on our fanlight. And my key turned the lock.

Mrs. Turner waved from her doorway, "Welcome home, Mrs. Hudson! I have the desserts."

Inside, my house was quiet and cold, so I kindled a fire in the hearth, measured and placed the tea in the teapot my husband had given me last summer. *Thank you, James. You were always thinking of me.*

James and I had written to each other with plans for a garden. We talked about a huge garden, and we designed it many times. He wrapped his letters around seed packets. When we bought this house, our garden had a shape. Its backyard spoke of abundance to come—the abundance we had in each other. Around the planetree, we planted. And for three seasons we lived within our garden, some summer nights we even slept here, against all propriety. It was the last night of the year, and I was grateful to see it go.

There was just enough time to prepare for tonight's small gathering with good friends. And I set to arranging the feast.

The new portable cast iron stove that I had installed changed everything. It used illuminating gas and was much cleaner than coal. I no longer spend my time washing off soot. Yet even though it had a

30

temperature gauge, I still put my hand in to check. And when Mr. Holmes moved in, I looked forward to testing its back boiler for some assistance in heating the ground floor and the hope of an adjunct to my fireplace coal through the house.

James' friend, David Rosa, rapped at my door. Standing on my doorstep, he still wore his boots, hat, and carried his fishing tackle in hand.

"Marti, I hope these perch will add something to your celebration tonight. They are fresh."

"David, you are a lucky friend to me. Thank you, I shall prepare them right away and you will enjoy them tonight."

"No, Marti, I shall savour our friend's enjoyment, I never learned to like it. I love fly fishing, but I must admit, James' catch always included mine." He waved his fishing pole at me, "See you soon," he said. And turned for home.

He had gifted me with six fat perch. I boned them, pickled them in vinegar, with bay leaves, peppercorns, allspice, and salt. Sliced into strips, fried until the skin crisped, and served drizzled with lemon or Mrs. Beeton's Dutch Sauce. My menu included cold pheasant and spiced beef with mustards and anchovy relish, Mrs. Turner's Christmas pudding, mince pie, Rivka's honey cake, and the holiday bread I had baked at the farm.

This last winter evening of the old year, I set a great log-fire blazing in the hearth. Warming brandy and whisky readied for salutations. Chestnuts waited to be toasted and cracked with midnight's hearty banquet at my sideboard. Cheerful friends arrived, and I welcomed them to my hearth, where they joyfully chided each other over their new resolutions.

What resolutions could I make? At holidays everyone's grateful, and I was worse than Scrooge. It was New Year's right here, in our home, yet how was that possible? Time for us stopped September last; 1880 had brought me sorrow and loss. 1881 what would you bring?

31

Sherlock Holmes put his new key into the lock and opened the door. He was greeted with a glass of whisky and welcomed into the toast with three "Hip, Hip Hurrahs!" Mrs. Turner, Molly the maid, her beau, Mr. and Mrs. Rosa, and I toasted him. In the distance, Big Ben was chiming midnight and the back door to the garden was opened to let out the old year. My new lodger was quick and instantly realized he was our New Year's first-footer.

The first to step over the threshold of No. 221B Baker Street for this untried year, and of course, he knew what was expected of him. He filled everyone's glass with the whisky he had brought for his sideboard and was cheered again as the bringer of good fortune for the coming year. After feasting, he produced his violin and played, *In dir ist freude* ("In you is joy"), a Bach chorale prelude composed for a long-ago New Year. The piece had been transposed for violin, and Mr. Holmes played it up-tempo, more like a dance than a chorale. During his performance, I used my handkerchief, and Mrs. Turner patted my hand. Mr. Rosa helped him bring his belongings, which I guessed were the reason for this visit, upstairs to his first-floor flat.

My new tenant dropped off his things, ran down the stairs and out. My guests hugged me farewell and followed him. I stepped through the door and felt the crisp cold air; I looked up at the whirling stars of a new London year. Back inside, I locked the Baker Street door, pulled the garden door closed, and set my house to rights.

Chapter 5
NEW YEAR'S DAY
From the Journal of Mrs. Hudson

"Sherlock Holmes seemed delighted at the idea of sharing his rooms with me. 'I have my eye on a suite in Baker Street,' he said, 'which would suit us down to the ground?'" – John H. Watson MD, *A Study in Scarlet*

1 January, 1881

Noon on New Year's Day, along with a portmanteau, Mr. Holmes did bring another gentleman with him. Both bedrooms were now occupied, and my rent was secured by two honourable young men.

Doctor John H. Watson arrived bearing congratulations for the New Year. A large round of bread, salt, and coal. The traditional wishes for enough to eat, financial abundance, and a warm hearth throughout the coming year. He doffed his hat and bowed as Mr. Holmes introduced us. We were of similar age and Scots background, so of course, he was a true gentleman. He recently returned from the fighting in Afghanistan and was still recovering from his wounding. A doctor and war hero under my roof.

They spent the day setting up their rooms, and I produced a New Year's cold collation. Later we shared a dessert sherry while they showed me around their new flat. Their combined taste has filled my walls with framed landscape photographs and army trophies from the East. Doctor Watson added a portrait of Major-General Gordon. Mr. Holmes does have some feeling for art, yet the criminal portraits he hung in his bedroom would keep me awake at night.

They are getting along famously for two men who just met; their gentlemanly laughter filtered throughout the house as they hammered, climbed, and overflowed the bookshelves with all the volumes they brought with them. Mr. Holmes was usually reserved and refined, yet when he laughed, it was an invitation to join him, and impossible not to. It was good to hear the deep tones of gentlemen's hearty laughter reverberating in my halls again.

I granted Mr. Holmes and Doctor Watson access to whatever they could find in my lumber-room. In their exuberance, they traversed the stairs with that easy energy of young men levering the large pieces through the landing.

"Holmes, watch your head!"

"Thank you, Watson. I do not know about the armoire mirrors at the foot of my bed. Would you facilitate me in lifting it closer to the door?" They shouldered the heavy furniture.

"Use your legs, and watch your back, one-two-three, up and over."

"Yes, much better, thank you, Doctor. Do you require another hand upstairs?"

Doctor Watson rested an Afghan War trophy on the table. "Not at all. And I do not think we have the same taste in portraits, Holmes, or in hideous arrangement." They laughed.

Together they hung a large picture. "Watson, what you classify as hideous, I have framed on my wall as an astute study. Facial characteristics are essential aspects of the skill of observation."

"How a florid face combines with shallow breath, sweating, and chest pain, to alert me to my patient's weak heart." They hung a similar-sized landscape photograph next to the first.

"Exactly, Watson! How the slight yellow cast of your thumb and first two fingers informed me of your preference for cigars. And that when preoccupied with a sense of chivalry or danger your limp disappears, and you run like a gazelle."

"Before my war service, I did play rugby. Holmes, your observational skill is astounding. How did you observe my chivalry?"

"Yesterday, from Bart's Laboratory window, the day we met, Doctor. I watched you as you ran for a cab on Giltspur Street. I knew it was a time when you would meet with competition as Bart's nurses were leaving and arriving. When you realized your opponent was a young lady, you doffed your hat and helped her into the cab you had flagged. Your leg performed perfectly all the while."

The Doctor was incredulous. "You were checking up on me?"

"Not at all. I was agitating a test tube for thirty-seconds time. This commonplace activity brought me to the window, and there you were. Serendipitous!" He leaned the ladder against the bookcase and climbed. "Hand me up those black-letter editions, will you, Watson?"

Like Doctor Watson, there were many things I found extraordinary about Mr. Holmes. His were the individual choices of a uniquely intelligent man. From what I have seen of our Scotland Yard inspectors, Mr. Holmes was unprecedented in the detection of crime. Yet, he was still forming his new art and retained some of the collegiate about him.

This young gentleman kept his tobacco in no less than the toe of a Persian slipper. When refilling the coal-scuttle, I discovered a box of Havanas tucked inside. His pipe collection also reflected his University tastes. His choice of tobacco was the least expensive and the strongest. When thinking over something, he smoked non-stop. That would give me a headache. These were small considerations when taken with the knowledge that justice and honour constantly occupied the thoughts of Mr. Sherlock Holmes. He solved problems that would otherwise be the ruin of the goodhearted Londoners he served.

The detective and the doctor filled the sitting-room with my old rattan, placed their desks at the street-front windows, and Mr. Holmes' chemical laboratory near to his bedroom. They used every cupboard, bookcase, bureau, and storage piece I had. In one day, they turned the old sitting-room into a miniature of the Reading Room in the British Museum. I will add some new pillows for the rattan. It was fitting I thought that much of James' old furniture now adorned the rooms where these two lively gentlemen resided.

Doctor Watson and Mr. Holmes entered his bedroom to place a table near the window. I was measuring the pillows in the sitting-room.

"Doctor, there is something wrong here. Did you wind my clock in the sitting-room?"

"No. It must be your decorations," he laughed.

"Shh, can you hear it?" He put his hand up for silence.

"Hear what?"

Mr. Holmes waved the Doctor away, put his finger to his lips, and listened.

Ticking!

"Mrs. Hudson, go downstairs immediately!" I did as he ordered and next, I knew they came thundering after me.

"Get out!" He threw the Doctor out the door with tremendous force and slammed it shut. "Now!" And he pushed Doctor Watson down the stairs.

They reached the ground floor almost on top of me when the explosion detonated!

Mr. Holmes looked at his watch, leapt back up, three stairs at a time.

When the Doctor and I followed him, the door to the hallway was lying flat on the carpet. The inner door was off its hinges. His bedroom was now a fog of gunpowder and goose down. Immediately, Mr. Holmes ran down to my bedroom, and we trailed after him.

"Mrs. Hudson, I must now inspect your bedroom." How could I deny him? He had just saved my life. I opened the door, he entered, and listened, then called in the same masterful tone, "Watson, the ladder!"

He searched every inch of my room, even climbed up to run his hands across the ceiling, checked every lamp, and took my bed apart.

"Forgive me, Mrs. Hudson," he said. "But this is no time for propriety, I must examine your armoire." When he finished his exacting investigation, he said, "Nothing suspicious, thankfully, no bomb apparatus, here."

"Who would do this?" the Doctor said.

Mr. Holmes took his hand and ran him upstairs. He motioned for Doctor Watson to remain on the second-floor landing.

"Watson, if I call out--Run!"

The Doctor related to me that Mr. Holmes cautiously opened the door to Doctor Watson's room and listened like a hare emerging from the safety of its lair. He entered and continued to listen. Then he repeated the same meticulous inspection. Ultimately proving the Doctor's bedroom was clear.

When the feather storm had subsided, Mr. Holmes, Doctor Watson, and I inspected the damage to the first-floor. It was considerable. The bed and mattress needed replacement. The wallpaper would also need to be restored. Was the structure sound? He examined his room for surprises, for surety, and for stability. Was the chimney sound? The window glass was shattered. The mirror on the heavy armoire was smashed, yet the piece seemed intact, and like the floors, ceiling and walls it needed repair. His dreadful portraits had crashed to the floor. There was nothing else. One bomb was enough.

I was rattled by the mess, but that was nothing to my fury over the imperilment of these fine gentlemen in my home. After ensuring they were all right, I moved into action. First, I sent three telegrams: one to my brother, Conall; one to my Guild furniture maker; and, finally, one to my featherbed maker. Second, I gathered Mr. Holmes' photos, swept up the glass, and sent them to the framer with the maid. When Conall arrived, he would ensure that the fireplace and the room were in good order. Then we would clean up the feathers and address each issue one at a time.

Mr. Holmes was underneath his bed, surveying the springs. He found traces of copper on some of them. Right, where his pillow was. He called us in.

"Mrs. Hudson, there was nothing significant to suggest the timing of this explosive. Yet I surmise it has been counting down not longer than twenty-four hours. Where were you then?"

"I was travelling back from my aunt's farm in Scotland. Do you mean someone came into my house and put this here while I was away?"

"Yes, and to curtail such criminal behaviour in future, Watson and I will promptly install a Chubb lock on your door. It would require new keys, yet ensure more security." He sucked on his finger to staunch the bleeding.

"Holmes, you are hurt."

"It is nothing, Doctor."

"That attitude has led to more dangerous infections than I care to relate. Excuse me, I will be right back with my bag."

"Mrs. Hudson, has anything like this happened before? Did anyone besides me have access to your house?"

"No, never! Thank you, a new lock is a good idea."

"Could you determine who might have done this?"

"Nihilists?"

He just looked at me and tapped his fingers against the mantle.

"Former tenants? But they are long gone, back to their home countries. I do not have any enemies. Do you, Mr. Holmes--"

There was a loud knocking at the door, and the maid let in Constable Broadleaf and Inspector Lestrade. Another constable stood outside our entrance in Baker Street. The constable and the inspector raced up our stairs.

The inspector tipped his hat. "Mrs. Hudson, what has happened? Constable Broadleaf here reported an explosion in your house. Luckily, I was in the neighbourhood. Er, Mr. Holmes? How is it you are here?"

"As of today, this is hearth and home, Lestrade."

"Would you mind telling me what happened!"

"The detonation occurred one hour ago in my bedroom. I have thoroughly inspected Mrs. Hudson's room and the other bedrooms. All but mine were exempt from explosives. And the discharge was confined to this room. I found evidence the timed device was fastened to my bedsprings with copper wire. I was in the process of furnishing my new rooms. No one was harmed. Mrs. Hudson states the damage is negligible and has called in her brother, Conall, a building construction engineer, to ensure there is no structural impairment. Your men are welcome to examine it." Constable Broadleaf looked into the bedroom.

"Constable, help me with these doors," Mr. Holmes said. "If we just lay them sideways against the wall that should keep them out of our way. Thank you."

"Inspector Lestrade, Mr. Holmes has this well in hand," I said, "He checked the ceilings, the carpets, every piece of furniture, and even crawled under the beds. And did this for every room in the house."

"Mr. Holmes, do you know why this happened?"

"Your question is premature." He lit a cigarette.

"Do you have any suspects?" said Inspector Lestrade.

"We were just talking about that and so far have no idea who did this," I said.

Inspector Lestrade took in the two disconnected doors, the odour, and the feathers. He walked into the bedroom. Mr. Holmes lifted the mangled bedsprings to show him and Constable Broadleaf the copper smudges where the bomb must have been secured.

"We surmise it had been introduced here when Mrs. Hudson was away for the holidays. Except for my occasional visits to transport my belongings, the house was empty for a fortnight. She returned yesterday. I arrived today. When I advanced into the room, I heard ticking. Doubtlessly it was a timed device set twenty-five hours ago at three p.m."

"Mr. Holmes, You cannot possibly know the time and date it was planted. Yet you do know that in our profession, we all have enemies. Change the door lock. That's my prescription."

"We agree with you, Inspector Lestrade," I said.

"This is a queer business. But there's not much more I can do except invite you to join the CID, Mr. Holmes."

"Generous of you, Lestrade. I prefer my freedom."

"Is freedom worth endangering your friends?"

I said, "Mr. Holmes saved my life today, Inspector."

Lestrade moved to the door. "Broadleaf! Mr. Holmes, come in and make a thorough report. Nice to meet you again, Mrs. Hudson." He nodded to her, put on his derby and left with the constable.

Mr. Holmes then unpacked his brandy from his chemical boxes and set it out on the sideboard.

Doctor Watson ran downstairs with his bag and a bottle of whisky, which he set beside the brandy. "Took me a while to find it," he said.

The Doctor cleaned Mr. Holmes' finger and applied a plaster. He worked the gasogene, filled three glasses and handed one to each of us. We sat around the table, and our day began to return to normal.

Mr. Holmes sipped his drink. "I will register that report. There is no need for you to visit the Yard, Mrs. Hudson."

"Thank you, Mr. Holmes. I will fix up the extra room. You and the Doctor will share a floor until repairs are complete." It was a good scotch.

"Thank you, Mrs. Hudson, I was worried I would get the couch."

I tasted it again. "I do not blame you for this. I am grateful for every day I have known you."

Mr. Holmes said, "I appreciate that."

"What report?"

"Watson, you missed Constable Broadleaf who stopped by to survey the damage. The possibility it was very likely a twenty-four-hour clock grants us some security. We may all sleep well tonight and without fear. Mrs Hudson, please send this off as soon as you can. It is a summons for the locksmith." He filled out a telegraph form and I pocketed it.

Doctor Watson was smiling. "Holmes you would never fit on the settee. I would come down in the morning to find you snoring on the floor."

"I do not snore, Doctor."

I said, "Whatever do you mean Doctor Watson? It is a fine couch."

Doctor Watson was keeping his laughter in check, "Holmes, your long legs would hang over the edge, one good turn and where would you be?"

"On the carpet!"

We laughed a little more than was necessary. I finished my drink and then went to make up the room. When I returned, I attended the fire. Mr. Holmes and Doctor Watson were persisting in their plans now with lighter hearts. Mr. Holmes did not wind the clock that night or for many nights to come.

"Watson, put down your glass and assist me. Let us reorganize the settee, someone more your size may need it. Good. Now this chair here. Yes, and the other, here. Capital!"

Mr. Holmes re-filled our glasses and handed them around.

"Have a cigar, Doctor?" He lit his pipe and sat in one of the basket chairs. "Watson, Mrs. Hudson, come join me by the fire."

After we settled into chairs, I raised my glass, "No. 221B and its brave and friendly inhabitants!"

Doctor Watson said, "Especially the blessed woman at its heart, Mrs. Hudson!"

"Hear, hear!" said Mr. Holmes.

"And to you Holmes!"

"And you, Watson!" Mr. Holmes added, "To friend Stamford, the reluctant bearer of good tidings!" They collapsed into more needed laughter at this man's expense.

I looked at these valiant gentlemen casually chiding each other in my home. Completely oblivious to what they had given me. For so many years these rooms had brought uncertainty and sometimes even misery into my life. Today it has all turned around. What will come of our friendship and Mr. Holmes' detective practice, I was sure would not just be good for us but for those who desperately sought him out.

Mr. Holmes was a young gentleman who would accomplish great things. Doctor Watson was a man of honour, and I was sure much more. I was looking ahead with hope, looking forward to 1881.

I raised my glass, "Happy New Year, 1881!"

Doctor Watson said, "Happy Neerday!"

"Hear, hear!" said Mr. Holmes, lighting his pipe.

And we three enjoyed the fire I had stoked for a good and welcome sense of home.

Chapter 6
WATSON'S GOOD FORTUNE
The Reminiscences of John H. Watson MD

"In one place he gathered up very carefully a little pile of grey dust from the floor, and packed it away in an envelope." – *A Study in Scarlet.*

The house on Baker Street, located within an easy amble to Regent's Park, might have been called Chef's Corner, or Saint Nicholas' Hearth instead it was whimsically titled No. 221B. A typical four-level London Georgian. Ground floor faced with white Portland Stone, a fanlight above the door and an ample backyard. First, second, & attics floors built from respectable red brick, each with two large street-facing windows. Identical to every other home on the street and presenting a terraced face to all.

The area included a post office on the opposite corner, the Underground entrance near Marylebone Road, a book shop, a pub, and further down, Madame Tussaud's Exhibition of Waxworks and Napoleonic Relics. The shops of Oxford Street were but a brisk walk south. This fortunate dwelling was the largely residential, affluent West London thoroughfare in which I gratefully found myself.

On occasion, Sherlock Holmes would invite me to disappear to my second-floor bedroom and promised to bring me down again immediately after his client left. I have conceded to this strange request several times. Once a raven-haired, fashionable ingenue of the West End called and left dabbing her eyes with a lace-edged handkerchief. Wiggins, a filthy youth appeared, Holmes slapped him on the back like a brother. An elder woman with the indifference to correctness shown by some aged followed closely on his heels. A short, muscled African gentleman, with a bearing of great dignity, his long hair tied in the back, tipped his hat to Mrs. Hudson and leapt up the stairs. On another occasion, a distinguished and likely noble white-haired gentleman entered my companion's domain.

43

I paused a moment outside our door. Completely unaware of my presence, Holmes absentmindedly brushed off his neat city frock-coat, placed his still-smoking pipe on the mantle, and combed his fingers through his hair. At relaxed attention, his left fist behind his back, he stood to greet his next client. A railway porter in his velveteen uniform appeared on the landing, entered the sitting-room, and shook the welcoming outstretched hand of Sherlock Holmes. And I mounted the stairs to my room.

Holmes and I were sharing the second-floor while Conall, Mrs. Hudson's brother worked diligently to restore the first-floor bedroom. At once, he affirmed the structure was sound. Presently, he was correcting surface abnormalities, glazing, painting, varnishing, and wallpapering, while Mrs. Hudson arranged for new furniture. Holmes' care with securing our rooms after the explosion, and his upright stance had me wondering whether he had military or police experience. But then it could just be his way. Sherlock Holmes took meticulous pains with everything he did.

Whatever this practice of his, it was of inconvenience to me. Nevertheless, it brought me to the quiet of my writing desk. I uncorked my fresh bottle of ink, dipped the pen to begin on humble foolscap. I had no issue with the blank page. Indeed, I had an eagerness to fill it. Holmes always thanked me and apologised afterwards, but it is I who should be thanking him for giving me the time and place to write.

With the exception of these daily sessions, it was not difficult to live with Holmes. Once illness and boredom were my constant companions and the lack of any activity which gives a man a sense of self. Now, a feeling of quiet excitement greeted me when I awoke. It was the wonder of it all that was flowing back into my life.

Holmes and I were young men, loose in London without attachments, years past parental and University influence. That time in a man's life before marriage, children, security, or even the acquirement of a home. When all possibilities ruled the day, the future was open, and dreams were the topic of conversation. I have been a soldier and an army surgeon. Could the dream of published authorship now be possible for me?

Sherlock Holmes was a friendly and studious gentleman. His handshake could eschew any animosity and always welcomed one in as an equal. Yet, Holmes was not understanding of those lazy or slow, and he shook me up when he thought I was not trying. I was always running to catch up with him. In the pitch of action, my war wounds became non-existent to him. He expected me to keep up, yet he was always so far ahead. To admit flaws in his thinking was rare. Thankfully, his natural humility was not. Holmes was a gentleman who cared intensely about mankind. He carried within him a mind profoundly focused on matters far beyond my reach.

How did friend Stamford put it? "It is not easy to express the inexpressible."

Holmes did like a good ramble. On a perfect, warm winter day, my flatmate and I jogged down to my tobacconist in Oxford Street. He never ambled when he could stretch his long legs into a stride.

Bradley's was much like a small gentlemen's club: leather chairs, wood panelling interspersed with well-lit bookcases, tabled with pedestal ashtrays and gentled by the music of a solo harp.

"Holmes, the smoking-room of Bradley's is unique in its comfort. An environment where gentlemen can taste a variety of flavours."

To my astonishment, he bought every conceivable cigarette type and brand the shop had available and placed others on order.

"Bradley's will still be here in a week when you need to refill your supply, Holmes," I said with a laugh.

"Science, Watson, science! These cigarettes will change the future of crime." He hailed a cab.

Crime? I thought, *Another clue? It seems my police theory is filling out.* "I would be glad to be of help in this, Holmes," I said as we travelled back to Baker Street.

"By all means, Watson. We launch this trial on our return."

He invited me into his experiment. We were to smoke each one with the prospect of collecting the complete cigarette ash for as many types as possible. I was not allowed to drop it in an ashtray or stop halfway. It had to be smoked through, and the ash deposited on a sheet of paper on his chemical table as complete as possible. Holmes and I shared a humorous view of the world, and we spent the afternoon gleefully competing for the longest ash produced.

"Forgive me, my friend, at my Montague Street digs I collected cigar and tobacco ash and presented it as a monograph. But have since found cigarette smoking becoming increasingly popular. I ordered through Bradley's an international assortment of cigarette types, as well as local mixtures rolled throughout England. Following our research, my second publishing shall include all these tobacco possibilities as a more complete, unabridged monograph."

"Holmes, if I may be permitted a comment, your zeal for this study is remarkable."

"Oh, Watson, you have collected more ash on your waistcoat than you have deposited on my table."

I tittered, "As have you, Holmes."

He grasped the brush and cleaned his vest. "Doctor, might I invite you and your waistcoat down to my photographer?" We guffawed, ruining the cigarette we each were presently smoking.

His scientist's mind had created the bizarre experiment, and he took prolific notes on each successful cigarette ash, drew accurate pictures, and brought each to be photographed. It was an ambitious proposition with cigarettes, and we tried again and again. Probably simpler with cigars.

"The addition of cigarette ash brings my study to completion. Did you know, even ladies partake? This expands my research into new and singular avenues," he said.

Our sitting-room was constantly filled with a fog of smoke mingled with flavours and scents during this time. Holmes methodically carried on until he had what he wanted. And to me, it was one more mystery.

There was another outcome to his research. This shared occupation built our friendship. Working together on Holmes' project revealed how our talents combined. And how contagious was his scientific excitement.

"Holmes, what is the point of all this?"

"Scientific progress, Watson!"

"A very messy science," I said as I took the brush from his hand.

"Ah, what would you say to Pasteur's fearless science, my boy. 'With the glass tube held between his lips, he drew the deadly saliva from the mouth of a rabid dog.' Keep smoking, Doctor!"

Have you ever tried to smoke a cigarette down to the end without losing its ash? And Holmes hopping around our sitting-room, like a magpie with new treasures excitedly remarking, measuring, sketching, and running down to the photographer, and back again, to repeat the process. Laughter is a most necessary consequence. It was the hilarity with which we undertook this procedure that shook our landlady's head with bewilderment. Naturally, Mrs. Hudson wondered what was taking place in her first-floor flat, with smoke billowing out windows and under doors.

It was Mrs. Hudson's sturdy Scots courtesy that made Baker Street a most pleasant place to live. Her management of the daily necessities left Holmes and myself free to carry on whatever it was we were doing. Her strength was amazing. Even in mourning, she had the ability to make us feel at home. I felt as if I had finally landed on

47

friendly shores. It has been a long and tedious journey. But her soft Scots lilt created an immediate sense of home to my ears and my whole being relaxed. Likely our presence has also helped dispel some of her loneliness. She has given me structure. What a welcome surprise that was. But I have always done better with a lady in my life. And this happy arrangement was free of awkward entanglement and full of all the good sense of womankind. I was a lucky chap indeed.

On 5th January, I was still reconnoitring around No. 221B. I looked out my window to the planetree and observed Mrs. Hudson, planting what looked like eggshells. I decided to investigate.

The garden door was open. "Good morning, Mrs. Hudson, beautiful day."

"Oh yes, it is, Doctor. I hope you like your new accommodations. Those stairs do not vex your injuries, I hope. So many men return from war a shell of their former selves. But you, Doctor, seem to have taken your experience in stride. I suspect you returned a wiser man."

"Well, I would not go that far. Thank you, Mrs. Hudson. You seem to possess some yourself. It is refreshing."

"Thank you, Doctor Watson," she said with a twinkle. "My brother is finished repairing Mr. Holmes' room; it was mostly surface damage. He will be able to move back today."

"Did you hang his portraits?"

"I reframed them; he can put them where he likes." She looked up at me. "What do you think of my little garden?"

"It seems well-organized for January."

She laughed. "It is that. In a month or two, you will see more. A garden takes careful planning and the ability to think ahead of each stage."

"Forgive my ignorance." I laughed. "Do you actually think something will grow from eggshells?"

"Oh, Doctor Watson, everything will. Eggshells are part of the magic, as is good smelly old fish stock. Please forgive me, you will learn not to open your window during this time of the year. They feed the earth magnificently so it can produce what I expect from it."

I squatted down, "If I read these packets correctly, you have planned quite a few flowers, as much or more than the hearty vegetables. Yet, I see no flowers in your home."

"Never pick a flower from a garden! They are the barriers that insects cannot penetrate. I plant marigolds first, to be the most protection for my young plants. You will see they are a formidable defender. Doctor, if you please?" I offered her my hand, and she rose. She really was a little thing.

"Flowers, who would think they have a definite use beyond the gift of beauty."

"And for the bees, gardens need bees to get along."

I indicated the tree that from my window represented nature to me. "Is that a rock garden for underneath the tree? I would think its shade would be a problem."

She rinsed her tools and her hands at the rain barrel. "Shade plants cannot weather direct sun. Doctor, you are welcome to join me when I begin my tilling."

"Yes, thank you, Mrs. Hudson, I would like that."

I thought, *How strange that Mrs. Hudson was an open book and Mr. Holmes such a conundrum! Well, I was forewarned.*

I do not understand my flatmate or his profession. But here, I felt a part of something. I lived in the sweet suspense of an Edgar Allan Poe story. Without the lurid horror. Though probably pure hubris, I felt I might try my hand at authorship if a suitable subject could be found.

Chapter 7
TO WEATHER THE STORM
From the Journal of Mrs. Hudson

"Few men were capable of greater muscular effort, and he was undoubtedly one of the finest boxers of his weight that I have ever seen." – John H. Watson MD "The Adventure of the Yellow Face."

30 January, 1881

While cleaning the first-floor rooms, I dusted Mr. Holmes' bookcases. A science library from chemistry to toxicology. And of course, British Law and *Sir Robert Peele's Rulebook*. Decades of *Who's Who* and the *Police Gazette*. I was tempted to sample the *Illustrated Police News*. There were some very unusual tomes: *Traite Des Poisons, Specimens of Arsenical Wall Papers, Tomlinson's Cyclopaedia of Useful Arts,* and *The Memoirs of Detective Vidocq*. Maps rolled up and precariously leaned in a corner of the room.

Downstairs, the aroma of rising dough invited me into my warm kitchen. I wondered how artists moved from completion to the creation of a new work. But wouldn't one have to start with a clean canvas?

I moved to the art form I knew best and set my stove to the proper temperature. Opened a jar of last season's strawberry preserves and baked tarts. Then met James' Aunty Amelia at the door.

As the tea steeped, we looked out to the garden. "Look, it is starting to snow," she said. "The work and love you and James put into the garden are evident, and it is clear you are continuing."

"Amelia, I am carrying on." We moved to the comfortable sitting-room fire. I poured the tea and offered honey cake and tarts. Their nutmeg, cinnamon, and ginger perfumed the air.

Aunty Amelia was dark, tall, thin, with intelligent blue eyes that filled easily with humour. Like her brother, Rabbi Moshe, she also shared the trait of youthful mischief. She studied at Girton College,

Cambridge. And tested for her History Masters at the University of London, the only way a woman could achieve a degree in England. Her husband was liberal and readily celebrated her exceptional achievements.

Some humour filled her face now. "Oh, Marti, I am sorry to bother you with this. The ladies of the West London Synagogue have found their voices and it is everything."

"That sounds exciting, not a bother."

"Marti, we are angry at the way our contributions are ignored. So much has changed in our unique synagogue, but this stays the same."

"Angry?"

"Yes, and it is liberating to express what has been denied for so long. It is as if all the great women of the past are standing with our little group."

"This could be a wonderful development for the West London."

"That is exactly how we see it," Amelia said.

"Auntie, now, I have caught your excitement. Thank you for sharing it with me."

We talked as the snow rose higher on the window panes. My aunt reminded me that I am still part of the world.

Amelia wrapped up in her coat, I opened my Baker Street door, and she hurried to the omnibus. A snowsquall was raging. Snow came early this year to London. In October we had six inches, so who knows what this will bring. Visibility was as bad as a peasouper fog. I quickly moved inside and locked my door.

The hall clock chimed, I stood at the door to James' study. Even in my home where order and cleanliness had value, adding my footprints to this carpet was unthinkable. Dust, and light, and darkness belonged here now. Yet, Mr. Holmes was due back at teatime. I introduced the key and stepped across the threshold.

51

The room was a conglomeration of purposes: A music room, scientist's laboratory, and writer's cabin. His music stand at the window, French Horn in its case on top of the sheet music cupboard. His long desk, the walls filled with bookcases and scientific illustrations of tomato varieties. The comfortable settee by the fireplace. The corner where he kept his fishing tackle. His pens, ink, and blotter, the dust of old books, the slight perfume of dried flowers, their petals curled with fading colours greeted me.

It did not take me long to find James' music and notes, an 1880 calendar, and his pocketbook. His Garden Journal was missing. Opening each felt like peering through an overgrown garden labyrinth to where my husband's spirit was dreaming. I sat on the settee, with boxes and papers around me. Dust motes floating in the window light. His words cried through me.

What I found for Mr. Holmes needed to be deciphered. I gently tidied the calendar back to its original state. I had already jotted down the dates for Mr. Holmes' calendar year.

James' pocketbook had a Sunday, 26 September, fishing date with Mr. Rosa pencilled in. James had the wonderful knack of living every minute of every day. A casual and happy man, bored with society's rules. He was most comfortable in nature. He said he found his soul in the music of the wild woods. Once on a bright, fall day, he shared this favourite pastime with me.

Packing a picnic, James and I drove out to Hampstead Heath, tramped through the Barrow to find fast-moving Highgate Stream. Standing in the cold water, both clothed in cumbersome Wellington waders, he laughingly instructed me in the art of fly fishing.

James said, "In order to live in the city, I must escape it."

He smiled and showed me how to hold the fishing rod. From the start, James called me by my childhood name.

"Marti, keep your wrist straight, as an extension of the rod. That is right. The weight of the line carries the cast. Flick the rod back behind you, then cast it forward so the fly is dropped exactly where you want it to land. Watch me!"

I had no experience at all in such things. Boned and correctly poached was my only relationship to fish. But James was so enthusiastic.

"It is beautiful here, James. I see why you come."

"Remember, Marti, you are a fly landing gently on the top of the water. Not that rock, or the log, or the tree on the other side. And if you snag a badger, watch out!"

I laughed. "Like this?" And my line landed in a tangle upstream.

He sent his fishing line singing through the air, hitting his target perfectly. "When one is silent, only the ripple of the stream is heard, and our alluring staccato taps at the surface. After a week of sitting in the horn section and London's persistent street noise, this is heaven to my ears."

"It reminds me it is alive and that great things happen there. I hope to live in the city," I said.

"Are you not living with your relative in Baker Street?" He cast his line again.

"Just temporarily, she is wonderful to host me during my studies, but I yearn for my own little house in town."

"Yet, it must have a garden," he said with excitement.

My cast landed on a rock, and I sighed, "Do fly fishermen ever stop to picnic?"

Over beef-and-pickle sandwiches with bottled ale, we indulged a favourite topic, the innovative gardening of the new Arts and Crafts Movement. We had begun to envision a real garden that would someday be rooted in the earth. James took my hand and then kissed me. I did not object. I wanted to continue.

Instead, like a proper lady, I put the lunch things away. James packed his fishing tackle and we hiked back through the woods stopping to consider trees, flowers, and edible flora. It was dusk before we emerged and cabbed back to town. He kissed me in the carriage. That incredible feeling! It was difficult to leave him.

It still was.

Suddenly, something large hit my front door. I started and instantly I was back in 1881, alone in James' dusty study. This moving back and forth in time, living in my memories, began that day in the morgue. Sometimes it took a moment for me to see what was in front of me.

Again my door was hit. I looked out to a horrifying scene.

A man was attacking Mr. Holmes right outside my window! His hands were around his neck! Mr. Holmes dropped a box onto the man's boot. He shot his arms up through the garrotter's grip to dislodge it. His attacker threw Mr. Holmes' wet heavy coat over his head and then pushed him over his boxes!

I opened wide my door, "Mr. Holmes! What is this?"

"Thank you, Mrs. Hudson, your timing is just what I require," he said, leaping to his feet. He scrutinized Baker Street, but the villain had vanished into the street, the squall, and the holiday revelry.

"Mr. Holmes, please come in! What are those marks on your neck? Are you all right?" I said.

He was dusting off the snow and carrying his boxes inside.

"Did you see his mask, Mrs. Hudson? I only got a glimpse. Did you recognize him?" Mr. Holmes said.

"No, he is a shorter man, in theatre dress."

"Like many in Baker Street tonight." He carried his boxes upstairs, "Yet he is no ordinary fiend," he said.

I brought Mr. Holmes' coat to the hearth hook and placed his hat where it would properly dry. Then made tea, with sandwiches and tarts, and brought them upstairs.

I knocked on the door, "Mr. Holmes?"

He opened it immediately. "Splendid! Let me take that Mrs. Hudson." He moved the tray to the table and held a chair for me.

"Mr. Holmes, those marks on your neck?"

"Nothing, Mrs. Hudson. A boxer learns to take his punches. Do not count me out yet. It is always well to keep one's wits about oneself in an altercation. In my fall, I ripped a coin from my adversary's watch chain."

"How clever, Mr. Holmes."

"Before I could reach my feet, you bravely came to my rescue, and the wretched man disappeared unseen behind the curtain of blinding white snowflakes. Yet I held in my hand a token that could lead me to his identity."

"Did you figure it out?"

Mr. Holmes had warmed to his subject, and I was treated to his enthusiasm over his new scientific approach. He took a sip of his tea.

"I added coal to your fire and towelled off, placed my boxes there to dry." He then displayed the silver memento on his magnifying glass stand.

"Here it is!" He handed it to me.

"I used my own method and lifted a fingerprint from the surface and filed it away. It is a new practice begun by Sir William James Herschel, of Jungipoor, India, and Professor Paul-Jean Coulier, of Paris, that I believe will change the way crime is solved."

"It is certainly different. I do not think I have ever seen a coin like it."

"Nor have I. Yet, I trust that Professor Dewberry at the British Museum shall be able to offer further clarification." He secreted it into a pocket of his waistcoat.

Mr. Holmes moved a tart to his plate and tasted it. "These are excellent! Do you make a game pie?"

I said, "Of course, steak and kidney, also."

"Ah, Mrs. Hudson, another delightful realisation of my good fortune. Yet, I find that I require access to synagogue gossip. Someone who might know names and information that could lead me to another link in my chain?"

"My aunt, Amelia Dreyfus, knows many of the ladies in the synagogue."

"Your aunt is a matchless choice, please give her my card." He wrote his new address on the back.

Chapter 8
A SCARLET THREAD OF MURDER
From the Journal of Mrs. Hudson

"I knew well that Holmes loved his art so, that he was ever as
ready to bring his aid as his client could be to receive it." – John
H. Watson MD, "The Adventure of the Naval Treaty"

10 March, 1881

Last week both of my gentlemen boarders became involved with
some extremely dangerous work for Scotland Yard. Mr. Holmes was
summoned by Inspector Gregson's telegram to the Brixton Road. And
this time Doctor Watson accompanied him. They left in a hurry.

It must have been a horrible sight because Doctor Watson, who is
a soldier and a surgeon, was troubled by what he saw. He fell out on
the settee in pain, both physical and spiritual. Mr Holmes was in high
spirits as in the thick of it seemed to be his best place.

There certainly was excitement at the end of the adventure. Mr.
Holmes captured the murderer right here in my house! Even the street
urchins Mr. Holmes called his Baker Street Irregulars played a part.
He and Doctor Watson returned triumphant from the gaol, and the
Doctor was writing it up. Such surprises in that gentleman. It was in the
papers, too:

> "The man was apprehended, it appears, in
> the rooms of a certain Mr. Sherlock
> Holmes."

Oh, Mr. Holmes warned me to hide safely away. There was a ferocious
struggle in the first-floor sitting-room. Thumping and crashing above
my head, I thought my ceiling would fall in. And I was terrified with
worry for their safety. It sounded like the murderer crashed through
the window. And that it also took all four men, the Inspectors Gregson
and Lestrade, Mr. Holmes, and the Doctor to subdue the powerful
American.

Another surprise appeared the next day in the newspaper. His heart gave out, and he died in his cell. An affair of the heart right to the end!

Mr. Holmes was a genius, no doubt. He stood alone in the talent, ability, and knowledge he has mastered. How many people could create a new science? I believe that was one of the distinctions of genius. Yet, I think Doctor Watson's involvement may add something more to the practice.

15 March, 1881

Inspector Lestrade ran up to Mr, Holmes' rooms about the time we were all preparing for a good night's sleep. He was highly distressed and proceeded to yell in a high-pitched voice at Mr. Holmes.

"A Fenian bomb was planted at the Mansion House, Mr. Holmes! The Lord Mayor, his family and staff are being moved to safety. My constables are on their way."

Mr. Holmes waved the Doctor to remain seated, packed a small bag, grabbed his hat, coat, and revolver, and left with the Inspector. I do hope he will be all right. Doctor Watson and I sat commiserating over a wee dram.

"For a man with no military training, Holmes' response to danger is certainly commendable. But why did he not call me in?"

"Doctor, can you not see his friendship in this?" I wrung my hands. "I am worried for Mr. Holmes."

Doctor Watson patted my hand, "Although the Mansion House is a substantial site to inspect, Holmes will have help from the CID, Mrs. Hudson."

"My worry, Doctor, is that time may run out."

We sipped our drinks. Doctor Watson's eyes briefly stole to Mr. Holmes' empty chair. Then we returned to our discussion.

"Mrs. Hudson, these appalling dynamite threats, will not bring the ends they want. Violence is never a solution. It is an illness that wreaks havoc on our society and becomes pandemic in war."

"Well said, Doctor. Surely there are better ways than terror for terror's sake. Why the American suffragists are achieving their goals with intelligence and organisation."

Doctor Watson chuckled, "Mrs. Hudson, I had no idea."

"Oh, Doctor, Her Majesty aside, a lady would have to be an imbecile not to support women's suffrage. Still, I am worried for Mr. Holmes. He did expertly handle that horror in my little home, but the Mansion House is five times the size."

The Doctor and I continued, talking and sharing his good scotch. Mr. Holmes was out in the city facing the worst danger possible. One thing I was sure of was Mr. Sherlock Holmes was the man for the job.

In no time, Mr. Holmes ran up the stairs and we surprised him at the door--both so happy to see him alive and well.

"Watson, Mrs. Hudson, I thought you would be asleep by now." He moved to the mantle and lit his pipe.

The Doctor awarded him a glass of whisky and said, "Holmes, we have been waiting on pins and needles. Tell us what happened."

We three sat around the fire, and he related the story to us.

Mr. Holmes said, "The cause of the Fenian Brotherhood is a worthy one, yet once they adopt the way of the nihilists, they become the enemies of all who believe in justice. The clumsiness of their bombs is nevertheless sharpening the skills of the CID.

"Lestrade and I rushed inside the Mansion House. A force of twenty constables waited. I immediately instructed them on how to conduct their reconnaissance. Each was assigned an area, from the magistrate's court to the cellar. I now had a constable's name associated with each part of the house. They reported back to me what they found, and I studied each anomaly. I directed the search from the Egyptian Hall."

"A good strategy, Holmes."

"Yes, as each reported to me, I could close off that part of the house, and reassign the constable, Watson."

"Ingenious, do you have military training?"

"Sun Tzu's *Art of War*, Doctor."

With some exasperation, I said, "Mr. Holmes, please continue."

"I directed them, 'Gentlemen, use your lanterns, be thorough. If you find the bomb, do not touch it and call me in. It is three-quarters to midnight. These criminals like to set to a certain time and midnight is a rather dramatic hour. Report back to me five minutes before then.'

"Inspector Lestrade, take four of your men and scour the outer perimeter of the House. Make sure you use your eyes not your hands and search along the walls to the bottom. I have assigned you the most crucial area, as the anarchists may not have entered the building.' They marched out."

"I instructed the next group of men in bomb detection, sent them off, and a glance at my watch showed the half-hour."

"My constables and I began evaluating each of the halls twenty columns two stories high. We lowered the chandeliers, explored the windows, sculptural niches, floor, walls, every lamp, curtain, and balcony.

"My watch showed the final quarter, as a young Bobbie ran in."

"He called, 'Mr. Holmes! Come at once!'

"He led me out to the George Street alleyway where an even younger constable stood near one of the Egyptian Hall windows with a smoking brown paper package in his hands, he was holding it completely still. The clock in the hall began to chime the midnight hour."

"Constable--?

"Cowell, sir."

"Do not move, Constable Cowell. We will do this together. Now, I will just open this. Ah, it is as I thought.

"Inside the package was a steel-reinforced deal box packed with old newspaper and fifteen pounds of coarse blasting powder, and the fuse was lit. I immediately cut the fuse, ground it into the pavement with my boot heel, and took the box from Constable Cowell. He then collapsed onto a step."

I interrupted him and said, "Thank God you were there, Mr. Holmes! That poor young man."

"Mrs. Hudson, I carefully examined the box. I had cut the fuse only inches from the powder, its shortness had endangered us all. I pulled the end of it out of the blasting powder, made sure there were no other fuses or triggers. Then sent all Lestrade's men to check the outer perimeter of the building for additional explosives. Constable Cowell's proved the sole device."

"I then celebrated his achievement by clapping him on the shoulder, 'Young man you have shown intelligence and courage in the most treacherous of circumstances. Tonight you held all our lives in your hands. You represented the Crown and our British Government by your actions and are to be congratulated.' I shook his hand, and his friends slapped his back.

"At the chime of midnight, Lestrade appeared."

"Lestrade, the bomb was disabled as soon as I cut the fuse."

"I was beginning to think I would never see my girl again," he said.

"There is still blasting powder in this box that demands careful disposal, but as long as you do not set it off by lighting it, all is now safe. Inspector, I suggest the CID organise an additional unit to address this concern. Nihilists rarely review their methods and plunge ever onward with their dangerous devices. They won't stop until stopped. I highly recommend Constable Cowell as one of the new inspectors. And, of course, I will be available to share any knowledge you deem necessary."

"Thank you, Mr. Holmes," Lestrade gratefully shook my hand. "Without your help, this great building, myself, and all my men could be rubble. But the bomb?"

"I handed it to Lestrade and then leapt into a cab and travelled back to where you were nervously waiting in Baker Street. Watson, it was worth it to watch Lestrade's face as I delivered the defused device into his timorous hands!"

A smile had come to Doctor Watson's face. "Lestrade seems a little rat-faced character. Do you see it?" It hit us in our funny bones.

"His moustache looks more like whiskers," I said and mimed a cat cleaning her ruff--more laughter.

"And his nose, very rat-like, do you see it?" said Doctor Watson. Our laughter filled the house.

"Beady eyes! His hair, his whole demeanour, and that squeak, most definitely rodent. I think you have him, Doctor," said Sherlock Holmes.

When our laughter died down, I said, "Do you think he has a tail?" We guffawed over this. Mr. Holmes laughed so hard he fell back limp into his chair. Our laughter was the curative we needed to free us from our hellish scare.

We finished our drinks, and all went to their beds. The Doctor and I were absolutely in agreement that London was safer with Mr. Holmes in town and that Constable Cowell was a brave young gentleman.

31 March, 1881

The moon was new, and my gardening began in earnest. Jack was helping me turn the soil. He was, I think ten or eleven, one of Mr. Holmes' dozen dirty and ragged little street urchins whom he called his unofficial police force. Jack was as sharp as the rest of them and had a wicked sense of humour, another most helpful ingredient in gardening. Why anyone would abandon him to the streets reflected the deplorable state of our East End.

Doctor Watson put his key into the lock, slammed the Baker Street door behind him, and ran through to the garden. Very uncharacteristic of him. He was hatless, out of breath, and looked highly distraught.

"Mrs. Hudson, an out-of-control carriage drawn by a pair bore down on me in Marylebone Road." He was catching his breath.

"Doctor Watson, please sit down. Jack, get the Doctor a glass of brandy.

"Water, if you please."

"Jack, you know where that is, also. Now, what is the trouble?" I sat next to him in a garden chair.

"I was crossing the road when suddenly I was faced with an incident which threw me into the thick of battle."

"Thank Providence you are all right! Here, take this." I handed the glass to him. The Doctor drank the water down.

"Thank you, Mrs. Hudson. It was odd. Time slowed, I felt the horse's breath, the cabby's whip on my back. Assuredly, he was attempting to control his runaway horses in the busy city thoroughfare. I fled the street and flew onto the crowded pavement."

"Horrible! Where Baker Street crosses Marylebone Road? Doctor, why would anyone want to run you down?"

"Hired by some evildoer, no doubt!" said Jack.

"No, it was just a runaway," Doctor Watson said.

I sent him up to relax and await his lunch. While putting away the tools another little mystery presented itself. I found a second shovel out of place, left with dirt still clinging to it.

Three months ago, when my new lodgers moved in, this house on Baker Street became another path for me. The skills I learned from my aunt also had a purpose in Mr. Holmes' new endeavour.

He was a generous man and shared with me some of the art of disguise for those unprecedented moments. The widowed landlady was my primary costume. I dressed older. It came in handy with those who found difficulty in addressing such a free young woman property owner.

"Mrs. Hudson, I see no reason for you to make this change, your youthful being will be much more enlightening to closed minds. Yet it is a skill I happily confer. This is how I transform into an aged countenance. First, apply this as a base to work on and then this to accentuate lines. Thinly apply purple on the lips for contrast. Not too much, it must not confer the idea that you are wearing makeup."

"Like a child's dress-up game?"

"It is an art also, and you are the canvas. This grey wig you may borrow whenever needed."

I applied the craft to my face. "How is this, Mr. Holmes?"

His eyes twinkled with humour, and he smiled. "Possibly a bit less and a bit more dignity. Right now, you might be exceedingly welcome in Upper Swandam Lane." We both laughed.

I adopted the role in service to the detective agency.

Mr. Holmes' time was filled with the creation of his own science, which he called the Art of Deduction and Analysis. Being the first at something required attention, persistence, and passion, which he has in abundance. I wish him well.

Chapter 9
WHAT DREYFUS HAD TO TELL
The Reminiscences of John H. Watson, MD

"My friend's powers upon the violin were very remarkable.
That he could play pieces, and difficult pieces, I knew well,
because at my request he has played me some of
Mendelssohn's lieder, and other favourites." – *A Study in
Scarlet.*

A rain-filled day, dark, with a shivered chill to remind one that spring
was sometimes closer to winter than to summer. The weight of the
water and the insufferable wind tore at the new green leaves, spotting
the garden with our tree's distinguishing shape. Thankfully, I now
knew what Holmes' practice was. As incredible as it seems, Holmes
also deemed me his associate. His consulting detective practice was
unprecedented, and where I fit was another mystery to be solved.

It was clear to me that I was in an apprenticeship of sorts, and I
was most grateful for his willingness to tutor me in his new science.
Holmes' practice was destined to conquer the unsolvable crime in the
capital. Yet even with all he had experienced while studying in those
deep, dangerous alleyways, he retained an uncommon ability to value
the diversity and potential for good that exists in mankind.

A wet and dirty street urchin delivered this missive to me:

> Watson.
> Dreyfus' office.
> 42 Baker Street.
> Come armed.
> S.H.

I hurried down Baker Street with my useless umbrella to a street-
facing office near Portman Square to meet Holmes. When I arrived,
Dreyfus was with a client, and Holmes was assessing his
surroundings. A wood-panelled room with framed watercolours of the
city's parks and the river. He asked me to take notes and handed me

his pocketbook and pencil. Dreyfus greeted and welcomed us into his office.

"Mr. Dreyfus, this is my colleague, Doctor Watson."

"How may I help you, gentlemen?" He brought us to chairs around his fireplace and joined us, poured tea.

"We are investigating the death of James Hudson."

"I thought that was over and done. Horrible business! Forgive me, but you are a bit young for a CID inspector, Mr. Holmes."

"I represent Mrs. Hudson. And hope to go deeper than Scotland Yard."

"Bless you."

"Mr. Dreyfus, you were not here when the murder occurred?"

"It was the 2nd night of Sukkot. I was in shul."

"Who has the keys to your office?"

"I do. I keep them on a key ring, but my assistants have their own."

"Your assistants?"

"A nice young gentleman, Saul, does my books, and my wife, Amelia. She types my letters when not at Cambridge. They work only a few days of the week. But never on Friday, Saturday or a holiday."

"I would like to speak with Saul, if I may."

"Anything to help Marti. James was my splendid, perfect nephew. Also a member of the West London Synagogue."

"You live there, do you not? In Seymour Place?"

"Mr. Holmes, I know nothing of this murder. I wish I had something more to give you."

"It seems you know a great deal."

"There are going to be rumours when one of our community is murdered."

66

"This is a ground floor office, with windows facing the street. Were there any windows broken or doors forced open?"

"There is a rear entrance. I think that was how he got in."

"May we see it?"

Mr. Dreyfus led us back, and Holmes observed the lock. A wooden slat was covering a broken windowpane near the door latch. He opened the door and, with a tweezer, picked up infinitesimal slices of glass underneath.

"So, either Hudson or his murderer entered this way. Mr. Dreyfus, you found the window broken? Who found the body?"

"The constable contacted me. When I got here we found poor James. Carpet soaked with his blood, I had the floor cleaned, and the carpet replaced as soon as they finished. Old Milverton, the glazier, seems to have forgotten us."

"Would you show us how the body lay?"

"Poor James was lying there in the waiting room, face down, his head towards my office. It was unthinkable."

Holmes lay recumbent on the new carpet. "Like this?"

"Yes."

He leapt to his feet, "Since Mr. Hudson was my height, the bullet would have lodged in that wall."

Holmes pulled a glass from his pocket and systematically searched the wall, the floor, climbing, and overturning furniture to do so. "Watson, your assistance, please." We removed chairs and tables. It did not take him long.

"Ha! We are getting somewhere."

He found the bullet embedded deeply into the dark panelling. To me, it looked like a flaw in the wood. But Holmes immediately dug the bullet from the wall, handled it gingerly, and dropped it in an envelope, then into his pocket.

67

"Watson, if England would adopt my fingerprint system, this little piece of evidence could catch our murderer all by itself."

"Mr. Dreyfus, what was disarrayed in this room when you entered?"

"Nothing but the carpet and poor James."

"Nothing?" I said, "So, Holmes, the murderer just walked in and shot Mr. Hudson on sight. He must have known him. It was a holiday, and the office was closed. Mr. Dreyfus, is there a guard who regularly checks your office?"

"Yes, there is Doctor Watson, but he doesn't come inside. I'll find you his name, as well." Dreyfus said.

Sherlock Holmes was observing me with amusement mixed with pride. "Thank you. He has been interviewed by Lestrade already, Watson. But we will speak with him. The bullet would certainly fit a police pistol or service revolver. Mr. Dreyfus, may we examine your books, and would you convey to me a list of your clients?"

"My clients, Mr. Holmes? Scotland Yard has not even asked that."

"Exactly. We may find the murderer there, or at least someone who knows something of him."

"If it will help, I have nothing to hide. My clients are all trustworthy. You will find no heavy-handed tactics here. I run my business like a small building and loan society. You are welcome in my office, gentlemen." We looked through the books, and Holmes directed me to take notes of specific names and information. Dreyfus compiled the inventory Holmes had requested.

"Thank you, Mr. Dreyfus. Your generosity should assist my investigation considerably. Might we inspect the old carpet?"

"It is behind the building."

"Then I will move my perlustration outside. My card if you think of anything else."

"And here are the addresses of my assistant and the guard."

"Thank you." We shook hands. The rain had stopped. By the slanting light of the setting sun, we found the rug. It was heavy with rain.

"Watson, let us roll this out." We spread the carpet on the cobblestones, and Holmes studied it, "Blood consistent with Hudson's wounding nothing more." We rolled it up. "I will study the marks and footprints around the door."

He lit his pocket lantern and completed his investigation. Holmes said, "All I can ascertain are the blundering attentions of Scotland Yard."

We cabbed down Regent's Street to the river, crossed the Vauxhall Bridge into Upper Kennington Lane, and stopped in at the guard's home in Gye Street. Wetherby was home, had just arisen, and was enjoying his breakfast. He was a sturdily built man with a sense of humour. He invited us in and offered tea.

"Sergeant Wetherby, did you enter Mr. Dreyfus' office the night of Mr. Hudson's murder, September last?"

"How did you know I was a sergeant?"

"Your salad and stripes are plainly displayed in the photograph of you in uniform on the cabinet. The Royal Marines?"

He looked at this young man Holmes with a smile, slapped his thigh and chuckled. "Why, you are a magician, Mr. Holmes!" He shook his head, bemused. "I saw the door had been opened and called a Bobbie but did not enter. He brought in Scotland Yard, and I went to telegraph Mr. Dreyfus but heard someone in the office. I assumed it was he."

Holmes was all attention. "When did you notice a person in the office?"

"As soon as I got there."

"Did you hear any conversation, notice shadowy forms? In your work, do you carry a pistol?"

"No, nothing like that, just sounds of movement. I have only my old service revolver. I never take it with me. Though now I think I might."

"Did you see anything else out of the ordinary? Anyone running?"

"The Yard didn't ask me that. Well, yes, Mr. Dreyfus' young gentleman and Mrs. Dreyfus came out of the office much later than either of them usually did. They were in a hurry."

"In relation to the murder, what time was this?"

"Not long before."

"They left through the back door?"

"Yes."

"Thank you for the tea, Sergeant. By the way, did you call out to Mr. Dreyfus to make sure it was he?"

"Yes, funny thing, he didn't answer. I thought he couldn't hear me. So I rattled the door and banged on it."

He saluted and escorted us out his door, where he accepted Holmes' card and good-naturedly shook both our hands.

"Watson, we will have to follow up on the assistant another time. Sergeant Wetherby's day is just beginning while ours is at an end." He yawned and patted my back and we cabbed up to Baker Street.

He asked, "Well, Watson, what do you think?"

"My theory has come to nothing, Holmes. Yet, I think interviewing the assistant may prove enlightening. I would like to join you on that. What about the clients? Will we visit them?"

"Certainly, my friend. I would greatly appreciate your aid. But what do you think of Dreyfus?"

"He was eager to help us and supply you with all you need," I said.

"He was lying, Watson."

"Holmes, how do you know this?"

"I know deception when I hear it."

Stepping out into our end of the street, we climbed the stairs and shared a quiet supper. I could see he was going over the events of the day. After Mrs. Hudson's baked apple and Wensleydale, Holmes addressed me again.

"Watson, did you notice anything singular about Mr. Dreyfus' hand?"

"I spotted no deformity."

"The muscles of his right thumb and forefinger are strong in a uniquely particular way."

"I saw nothing unusual."

"Well, I will not asseverate. Possibly something to docket."

We moved to the fire and shared a last smoke.

"Will you confront him, Holmes?"

"If it proves necessary."

"Watson, I would be grateful if you would pass me your pouch of Virginia flake. I must admit you have a discerning taste for fine tobacco."

I handed him my tobacco pouch.

"Thank you, Doctor." He tamped down and lit his pipe. His smoke billowed to the ceiling and our day wound to a close.

Up in my room, I wondered at Mr. Dreyfus. To me, he seemed a man of honour, but Holmes had an uncanny ability to see through deception. *What does this mean to the rest of the information he gave us? What was true and what was false?"*

The next morning I began my day as usual by opening windows to air out his horrid first pipeful.

"Watson, look at this!" He threw the quarterly journal of the Savile Club at me. I turned it over.

"No, no, the back page, the audition advertisement, read it aloud."

> Audition – Violinist
> To be held on 5th April, at 9 a.m.
> The Imperial Theatre Orchestra
> James Smith, Conductor.
> To be hired for the rest of the season.
> Permanent employment offered upon
> proven performance ability.

"Holmes, you are auditioning for this orchestra? Today?"

"Is it not the consummate way to gain access to Mr. Hudson's acquaintances? The audition is within the hour," he said as he put down his coffee cup. Then he opened the case of his Stradivarius and rosined the bow. He traded his dressing-gown for white tie and pince-nez. The short, boxed beard he had been growing and trimming the past few days now had a purpose. His scarf flying, violin case in hand, he was down the stairs and into a cab straight away. I was glad to note he had left his pistol behind.

Holmes arrived back in Baker Street at the dinner hour. His eyes filled with excitement, his arms and shoulders tired.

"Watson, you presently share rooms with the second violin for the Imperial Theatre Orchestra." And he bowed.

"Congratulations, Holmes! But not first?"

He cleaned, replaced a string, and carefully put away his Stradivarius. "In the orchestra, my alias is Keevan Sigerson. It would not do to be in the spotlight." He chuckled. "Between audition and rehearsal, I am weary."

He looked it but a happier form of tired than I have witnessed in him. During the three days of the case that began our partnership, I noticed that he didn't rest, and his violin playing was erratic and dissonant. Here his face was untroubled, relaxed, and he seemed younger than his twenty-seven years.

He held out his hand. "Tsk, tsk, I am out of shape and have callosities on top of callosities. Fortunately, I have a few days to heal before Saturday's performance. It is exceedingly unprofessional to bleed during a concert, Doctor." He laughed and loaded his pipe with my recent purchase.

"Watson I met with Maestro Smith and readily passed the audition. I was introduced to the orchestra and rehearsal began."

"During brief breaks, I chanced to speak with orchestra members presenting myself as a gossip-loving newcomer. Afterwards, I was invited to the Blue Boar Public House, and in future will pursue this aspect. My first foray was to the horn section. I met a French Horn player, and chatted about life in the orchestra."

Holmes then gave me a thorough account of his first orchestra interview.

"I lit a cigarette and we walked outside, I said, 'Mr, Taylor, your horn is magnificent." I put my hand out to shake his. "I am Sigerson, the new violinist."

"Taylor shook my hand. 'Second Violin.'"

"Yes, I am grateful for this chance. Yet I must admit that when we play some of my favourite pieces, it is difficult to keep in my place.' We stretched our legs walking beside the immense building."

"Life in an orchestra!' Taylor said and laughed."

"In what conservatory did you study?' I said."

"Self-taught, guess you'd brand me a child prodigy. And you?"

"Exceptional! I learned the conventional way. How do you find the orchestra?"

"Fixin' to be better than it used to be'. Taylor smiled, and we were called back to rehearsal."

"I am happy for you, Holmes. It is marvellous. But what if a client or some emergency transpires while you are with the orchestra?"

He waved it away. "Oh, Watson, your ready involvement in the Brixton Road Murder demonstrates you are qualified to handle whoever walks in our door." He smiled at me with that twinkle in his eye. "Better if she is a lady."

"Holmes, I will do my best, but my expertise is medical in nature. I do not have your skill or knowledge."

"Watson, if my involvement proves indispensable, please reconfigure our practice as an evening event." He lit his pipe and watched me through the smoke.

"Holmes, I do need to brush off my skills. I was almost trampled by a runaway cab last week."

"So Mrs. Hudson informed me. How are you, old man? Do you think there was evil intent?"

"No, just a runaway. It is amazing with all the horses in London there are not more of them, but my response could have been better."

"My friend, assuredly, your keen reflexes saved your life." He patted my shoulder.

"But Holmes, it was not merely my reflexes that saved me. A small gentleman leapt onto one of the horse's backs. The carriage driver attempted to hit him with the whip, but he flicked it out of his hand and cleverly turned the tables on the driver!"

"Ah huh," he said engrossed in his smoke rings.

"He brought the horses under control, but I was already on the pavement at that point. How such a man could mount a large out of control draft horse that way. I say I have never seen anything like it."

"Did you meet him? Or have you formed a detailed description of this exceptional horseman?"

"No, it was impossible. By the time I witnessed his prowess with horses, he had steered them off Marylebone Road and too far west for me to observe anything more."

With a sigh, he said, "Then, my dear Watson, surely the important point is that you escaped unharmed."

"Thank you, Holmes."

We finished dinner, and Holmes did not join me for a smoke at the fire but went straight to bed. I hoped the orchestra would become a regular part of his life. It could prove to be a balance for those times of boredom which I have experienced as extremely trying for his vigorous mind.

He had six days to rehearse with the Imperial Theatre Orchestra. The first three days, he returned happily exhausted and slept well. His iron constitution surfaced on the fourth, and he was now happily sailing through it. He would lark away the pieces of music they were learning and tick off orchestral musicians from his list of suspects.

"I will dispense with dinner for as long as this investigation lasts and have advised Mrs. Hudson that I shall take supper instead. Have you noticed she is remarkably adaptable to change? A most fortuitous living arrangement for two young gentlemen who happen to be a doctor and a detective." He relinquished his pipe and moved towards his door.

"I feel we are very lucky," I said. Goodnight old chap."

The next morning arrived bright and clear, the planetree covered with spring green leaves dancing in a March breeze. The kind of day that made one feel all was right with the world. At breakfast, our conversation surprised and reminded me, yet again, to never underestimate Mr. Sherlock Holmes.

Humming Mendelssohn, he prepared for his day. While shaving, he chuckled and said, "Watson, I met Miss Lily Langtry last night. Briefly, just for a few minutes. Do you know, she is one of the most beautiful women? With a face, a man might die for."

"Many probably have!"

I knew Miss Langtry was a celebrated beauty. But how was Sherlock Holmes involved? According to the gossip columns, she was embarking on a stage career, studying with our finest actresses. Miss Lily was popular amongst the most eligible gentlemen of London and Paris. If I were to write a play for her it could mean instant acclaim—!

Holmes drew me from my reverie with one of his, "Come now, Watson!" looks.

"There is something disarmingly unforgettable about our 'Jersey Lily.' Her eyes are violet, you know. She has a vitality and a wonderful sense of humour that is impossible to ignore. With self-confidence as I have never experienced in a lady, very unlike most ladies. And yet she is still a lady. Even more so."

"Holmes?"

"She has recently returned from Paris. We lunch at the New Bohemian Club," he said as he swirled his scarf about him and reached for his violin. "A short walk to the club. I will savour that walk down Pall Mall." He laughed. "I have her auspicious attention for one hour and then back to my orchestral slavery. Watson, have I ever mentioned my wayward youth spent on the stage? No? I grew up in Shakespeare country." On that tantalizing note, he departed.

When Holmes returned that night, dinner was long past, the table was cleared. I spread out newspaper and was cleaning my service revolver. He referred to his lunch with Miss Langtry.

"Arriving at Miss Langtry's I was surprised to encounter a singular gentleman on his way out."

"Are we not friends, Sherlock? Friends do not bow to each other.' He shook my hand and left.

"I offered my arm, and Miss Langtry tucked hers into it. She was dressed in city gentleman's attire, black frock coat, striped trousers, her beautiful hair beneath the topper. We entered the club and doffed our hats.

"Watson, I must admit, I was momentarily enthralled as her light auburn hair cascaded to her shoulders. She took my arm and we ascended to the dining room."

"Holmes? You have never—?"

"Research, Watson, purely research, old boy. We approved the wine and I said, 'I did not expect to find the Prince of Wales in your dressing room."

"Oh, Bertie has his little foibles.' She said, 'When it is His Royal Highness' turn, he will be such a welcome change. Just imagine the parties! Until then, he has two loyal friends to steer him safe from harm's way."

"Once again, I was awestruck, this time by her deduction, Watson, and inquired, 'How did you know of my involvement?"

"Sherlock, sometimes, you are so transparent. That knight's armour you sport so well beneath your frock coat. Your secret is safe with me."

"Your interest is purely political?"

"He is a good friend, like you, Sherlock."

"I am glad for your sympathetic guardianship."

"She laughed and it was the sound of a perfectly tuned bell. 'Oh, do not make me a saint, she said."

"Many saints began as sinners, I said."

"And that was essentially that, Watson. Lunch ended. She returned to her rehearsals, and I went back to my orchestral slavery." Holmes laughed and filled his pipe at our fire.

"The Prince of Wales, Holmes?"

"It is a clandestine involvement. Promptly forget it. How Miss Langtry deciphered it is a mystery, but you know the insightful ways of women, Watson. Have I ever mentioned my own natural intuitive ability?"

"Holmes, surely you are joking, we are men of science."

"An endowment from my grandmother, perhaps. Not spiritual in the least. An additional, tangible sense that is as consistently available to me as my sight." He struck a match and lit his pipe.

"I imagine it comes in very handy in your work."

He puffed a series of bluish smoke rings above us and continued, "Tonight, along with my excitement at performing with this estimable orchestra, there was another, darker sensation underlying it. One I equate as an intuitional warning."

"Holmes, will you heed it and leave the orchestra?"

"You know danger is an attractant to some, Watson. Otherwise, you would have left once you ascertained the truth of my profession. No, I will take it as confirmation of my quest within the orchestra's complement."

"Holmes, you are not alone in this. I am here to be used and here for you."

"Thank you, old chap. It seems your participation in our 'study in scarlet' has made a substantial impression upon you, and I am grateful for your interest. I observe you still keep your service revolver cleaned. Might I inquire as to your aim?"

An abrupt request, nonetheless, I saw this as a commander reviewing his troops.

"Holmes, I am not ashamed to say I qualified as a sharpshooter in the Fifth Northumberland Fusiliers, and proved my worth in the Berkshires. Both rifle and officer's handgun. My aim has been described as 'dead centre on the run.'"

"Ha, Watson, a most welcome surprise! Familiarity with a pistol proceeds naturally from your service history, but this level of accuracy is the extraordinary aim of a surgeon, my boy. Bravo!"

A brandy and last smoke at our hearth brought us finally to our beds.

Mr. Hudson's Garden
The Herb Garden

An excerpt from Mr. Hudson's Garden monograph found on page 230

Summer 1880

Mrs. Hudson's herb garden is beneath our London planetree and along the outer edges of the garden. Blue periwinkles at the base of the tree mixed with lily of the valley. Further out where the shade is lighter, and along the sunny sides, we plant Chives, Thyme, Basil, Tarragon, Marjoram, Borage, Garlic, Garden Cress, Mustard, Horseradish, Chervil, Angelica, Lemon Balm, Mint, Parsley, Rosemary, and Strawberry.

If you do plant Lily of the Valley, teach your children they are deadly poisonous. And plant herbs at a safe distance and catnip elsewhere.

Be careful with mint and strawberry. They will take over the garden if not regularly pruned. Periwinkle will choke the Lily if not cut back. Its evergreen qualities are especially welcome after most of the garden is fallow, and the planetree's leaves have fallen into our compost pile.

Plant rosemary throughout the garden and at the walls for its lavender-grey blooms and sweet scent. As the garden's early spring welcoming downbeat, this evergreen blooms before the return of any other scented flower in early March.

Note: When I invited our lodger to join me in the garden, he denied ever watching me at the window.

Chapter 10
COMMUNITY
From the Journal of Mrs. Hudson

"If of thy mortal goods thou art bereft, and of thy meagre store two loaves alone to thee are left, sell one, and with the dole buy hyacinths to feed thy soul." – Saadi.

4 April, 1881

I travelled west to Upper Berkeley Street with a gift of roses for James' parents, Rifka and Rabbi Moshe. Rifka greeted me warmly, and I joined in our shared custom of preparing tea with two women I held in high regard.

Amelia was delighted with Mr. Holmes' query and pocketed his card.

Her face became animated as she spoke of something her husband had told her. "You know, my husband is a boxing aficionado. There is a new boxer in London. My husband said this man is beating all our homegrown variety. Mr. Holmes might find something in this."

Together we readied tea and cakes for the Rabbi and the synagogue's board members. We shared memories of James as we worked, and consoled each other with that closeness of women related.

The West London Synagogue was inspired by the liberal European and American Reform Movements. They created their own unique Anglo-Jewish culture, the first of its kind in England.

Abruptly raised voices from the board meeting filled the kitchen. Rivka looked up, sighed, and waved them away.

"This is an assault on all humanity!" rang loudly from the Council Room.

To our joy, Auntie Amelia shared the substance of the meeting with us afterwards, though Rivka and I could certainly hear the chorus of upraised voices.

We trayed the tea things and Amelia bravely entered. The Rabbi nodded acknowledging his sister with a smile while she set up the tea. The board members continued their discussion of what was on everyone's minds. What role would they play in the plight of those fleeing the Russian pogroms?

A young scholar began, "In 1656, Rabbi Menasseh ben Israel encouraged Oliver Cromwell to reopen England to our people. But *we* did not come empty-handed. We Sephardim built the Bevis Marks Synagogue and after 140 years of chanting our beautiful *Baraka*, we formed our West London Synagogue. Now 40 years later, our history is one of centuries of impeccably concerted effort to reclaim our traditions and hold to our unique identity while assimilating with Britain. And we have succeeded as none before us."

Rabbi said, "Well done, Reuvan. I am glad you have accepted a position in our Hebrew School." He spoke to the whole gathering, "This is a history we all know. But our new neighbours now have no history, except as Jews."

Amelia said, "Forgive me, Rabbi. Gentlemen, recently an immigrant family arrived at this door. Rivka invited them for lunch. The father was a bootmaker, and his tools were all he carried from Odessa. His arms were as thick as a blacksmith for his hefting of the iron forms. Rabbi Moshe gave him the means to purchase leather and ordered his first pair. Then he sent them to his old neighbour in Leadenhall Street. We speak different languages, but are we not all Jews?"

Voices rose, some fuelled by what they considered a woman's impertinence.

"You will never see those boots, Reb!" chided Isaac.

Nathan said, "Have you read about this horror? The torture and slaughter are worse every day."

"Whole communities have been destroyed," said Jonathan.

"Our synagogue is a sanctuary for our community!" said Jacob.

Rabbi Moshe said, "What of the Ukraine synagogues, the Moscow shuls? What sanctuary are they now?" Standing, he thundered, "Community is who we are!" Then looking around the room he shrugged and lowered his voice to its normal level, "You are my friends, my community, together we are this great synagogue. Their community was thrown to the wolves and dashed across the Continent. Did not Prime Minister Disraeli say, 'The greatest good you can do for another is not just to share your riches but to reveal to him his own.'"

Jacob said, "This is a board meeting, madam. Are you a member of the board?"

"I am a member of the synagogue," Amelia said.

Joseph spoke up, "Let Bevis Marks handle the problems of the East End!"

"Rabbi Moshe, be realistic, by the reports, there are thousands heading here! How can we help them all?" said the synagogue president.

"We are British subjects," said Samuel. "We must be as liberal as our country and welcome them in."

"Welcome in a devastation of locusts?" Claude said.

"Reb, they will begin in the East End as we did!" said Rocha.

The Rabbi stood, "Ah, finally something to build upon. At last, we have a starting point. What was it we wanted when we were in their place? Surely there is enough heart in this room to wisely resolve their dilemma and ours. Thank you, Amelia, please leave the tea." And the conversation continued more positively.

As the council meeting was coming to a close, Amelia answered the synagogue door and re-entered the library with a young man. He was a diamond cutter from the Hatton Garden area. His head was bandaged, his face was bruised. The council crowded around him.

"Reb, last night, I stayed late to clean up and was alone in the cutting and polishing room. A man wearing a mask forced his way in and threatened me with a gun. He demanded I cut the most beautiful jewels I have ever seen. I could not. They were perfect. So he beat me and ran out. But I know gems, and these were flawlessly fashioned. Cut stolen jewels? That was not what my years of apprenticeship were for!"

Amelia checked his wounds and changed his bandage. The council discussed what this violence meant to the community. It was time for my Baker Street tea, so I invited them to join us. Amelia and I took a cab and brought young Laban, the diamond cutter, to meet Mr. Sherlock Holmes.

Mr. Holmes arrived straight from his meeting with Inspector Lestrade, and Amelia introduced Laban. With her encouragement, he related the story of his encounter with the gunman to Mr. Holmes. Amelia made the tea and served some of the cakes we prepared in the synagogue.

"Thank you, Amelia," Mr. Holmes said. He put his hand on the boy's shoulder. "Laban, you are a brave man to hold to your honour while facing a pistol in the hands of such a villain."

"It is who I am, Mr. Holmes. I could not answer any other way." He accepted a cup from Amelia, "Thank you."

"You say he was masked? This is suggestive and to my knowledge exceedingly rare."

"Yes, it was grey and covered his head."

Mr. Holmes nodded, "Similar to what a knight might wear underneath his armour? Anything else you can remember about him?" He said offering his cigarette case and lighting one.

"Thank you, no, I do not smoke," said Laban, "but I am enjoying this cake, Madam Dreyfus." He continued, "The gunman was dressed more like a labourer than a knight. Strong hands, Brown boots. He wore gloves."

"Well done. His voice, was it high or low?"

"High."

"His height, was he thick or thin?"

"Medium and thin."

"The jewels what were they like?"

"I only got a quick glimpse of them, but they were spectacularly wrought. To do what he wanted, I would have to take them out of the setting. It would be to destroy a work of art. The gold setting and foundation were unlike any I have seen."

"You mean, from another time or another place?"

"Maybe that is it, unusual in my experience. I would not call them antique, but might have been from an earlier date," said Laban, "I am sorry I cannot be more precise, Mr. Holmes."

"Laban, you are giving me all I require. Your professionalism is not in question. What were the stones?"

"I only saw it for a moment, sir. But my impression was of large and unusual pearls, with diamonds and emeralds. He wanted me to cut the jewels, not just detach them."

"Anything else?"

"I am glad I did not give in to his threats."

Mr. Holmes smiled and patted the boy on his shoulder. "Thank you, Laban. By your bravery, you have saved the others in your establishment. I will do what I can." Mr. Holmes gave him his card. "If you recall anything else get a message to me. Mrs. Dreyfus, please let me know if there are any rumours of this masked gunman. Unless he moves on to another city, I doubt he will abandon his pursuit."

Following the tea, Amelia and Laban left; he to the Underground and her to the omnibus. It was clear to me that I was becoming more involved in Mr. Holmes' detective agency.

Doctor Watson ran up the stairs and joined us. While dinner was baking, we three shared a sherry at the fire at the setting of the sun. Mr. Holmes told of his meeting with Lestrade.

85

"I shot through to his Great Scotland Yard office and addressed him, 'Inspector, I am investigating the death of Mr. Hudson. Will you grant me access to your files?'

"There's nothing there, Mr. Holmes.' He said, 'don't waste your time. It's a dead-end. It would be better if you studied how the Yard pursues a case. Or better still, join the force. You would learn discipline, young man."

Mr. Holmes laughed.

"Nevertheless, it may help Mrs. Hudson,' was my answer.

"Lestrade continued, 'Mr. Holmes, what we found would not bring her peace. But don't take my request lightly. You would be a worthy assistant."

Mr. Holmes laughed again, and we joined him.

"An assistant to Lestrade! Can you imagine that? What I said to him was, 'Lestrade, I see myself as a free agent, an independent adjunct to the force."

"He countered with more of the same bottomless assumptions, 'It was a messy business, Mr. Holmes. He led a double life.'

"I find that difficult to believe. Where are your facts, Lestrade?"

"Did you know the man?"

"Only what Mrs. Hudson has communicated with me. They were a devoted couple. He was a gifted musician, a gentleman of honour, performed with the Imperial Theatre Orchestra."

"Thank you, Mr. Holmes," I said.

"You are welcome, Mrs. Hudson, though I doubt he heard me. Lestrade persisted with great expression, 'That den! Remember when one of their circus lions escaped and went for the audience? Luckily, Eugenia Ronder subdued and brought the beast safely away. She certainly deserves her title as "Queen of the Beasts."

"This man is one of Scotland Yard's finest. I lit a cigarette and chuckled. 'I did not know you were a circus aficionado, Lestrade."

"I have children, Mr. Holmes. But be that as it may, Hudson was mixed up in dark deeds, no doubt about it. He was a bodybuilder and exposed to the Jewish underworld and illegal acts in his boxing club. He could have been a heavy for any of the moneylenders. Why else would he be shot so cleanly through the heart? His killer knew what he was doing. Debt or intrigue it must be."

"I said, 'What intrigue? There is no debt. Go on Lestrade and relinquish the file to me.'"

"The only thing in the file is where we found the body. You won't see my deductions there. Interview the Jew and he'll tell you nothing. He had no money, watch, keys, or any papers on him. Yet, Dreyfus knew him. You know how clannish they are."

"Then he called, 'Sergeant Wilkins! Bring me this file.' He handed him a note, the Sergeant saluted and left."

"That such prejudice exists in our Scotland Yard is abominable!" I said. "How can they tell the victim from the villain?"

"Exactly, Mrs. Hudson. At this point, I was sure he was right and there was nothing for me in the file. Yet, I hoped that Wilkins had added some facts to it. What I said to him was, 'I was present in the morgue, if you remember, Lestrade. Did you find anything, footprints around or near the body, the position, any mud on his clothes, marks on his jacket, shirt cuffs, or trousers? Do you have the bullet, or can you identify the gun used? I should like to examine his clothes, if I may?'"

"Mr. Holmes, he fell the way anyone would fall after being shot while charging his assassin, on his face. If there was any powder on his clothes, his bleeding out rendered it worthless."

"Your hypothesis?"

"Young man, who the devil are you to ask me that? You are no official agent. Your queer lurking around murder sites makes you someone to be watched. You are on thin ice, Mr. Holmes."

"I smiled and made a placating gesture by patting Lestrade's shoulder. 'You know there is no competition between us, Inspector. You have nothing to lose. I will share with you what I uncover."

"See that you do! Where we found him proves he was in debt and was killed for it. Or he may have been paid to rough up Dreyfus' debtors and met his match. It happens all the time. Dreyfus was a diamond cutter, he had tools in his office. He denies it, but I say it all adds up."

"So, Mr. Hudson was a shady character because you discovered him dead in a money lender's office and a thug because he had an athletic build?"

"That's my theory, Mr. Holmes. I look forward to yours.' He stood."

"Sergeant Wilkins brought in the file, saluted, gave it to Lestrade, who handed it to me. The Inspector walked out and said, 'Leave it on my desk."

"I left at this point. Wilkins had added the date was a holiday, Sukkot."

I said, "Oh, Sukkot, takes place out-of-doors, under a shelter, a week of gatherings to celebrate freedom."

"So, not held in the synagogue then?"

"These backyard festivities take place out on the patio with family, friends, and neighbours."

"Thank you, Mrs. Hudson."

Today, Mr. Holmes' detective business was the cause of many of the strange happenings at No. 221B Baker Street. Yet to me this illustrious endeavour was becoming ever more important.

Chapter 11
THE INVISIBLE GENTLEMAN
The Reminiscences of John H. Watson, MD

"If you tell the truth, you have infinite power supporting you; but if not, you have infinite power against you." – Major-General Charles George Gordon.

"Watson, now that your mind has been comprehensively expanded by the truth, would you run an errand for me, old boy? If you would be so kind."

My usual trip to the chemists was enhanced considerably as Holmes amended my list with his essentials. The post office, P. Webley & Son, and Griffiths Laboratory Suppliers were now my requisite destinations.

A well-dressed African gentleman passed me in the chemists. He was no more than five and a quarter foot tall, a compact being radiating power and self-possession. He was leaving the shop as I entered. Africans are unusual in the West End. Nonetheless, there was something familiar about him. Weighted down with packages as I was, I nodded to him.

Then called, "Sir, I say sir!"

He had the effrontery to knock into me and send my packages hither and yon. By the time I bustled my way out the door, he had disappeared. Could this be the man we were after? Holmes thought he was a shorter man.

When I returned. Holmes leapt up from his chemical table and quickly put his pipe on the mantle. He spirited me away from the fireplace, dumped the carpet bags on the table at the opposite end of our sitting-room, and rummaged through them.

"Watson, you forgot the gunpowder!"

"Holmes, no matter how hard I tried, the explosive emporium would not believe that I was one of the Lewisham Bonfire Boys. They

89

kept repeating that the fifth of November was seven months away. Forgive me, you are the accomplished actor, not I."

"That is your trouble right there. You try too hard, Doctor. It is best in such circumstances to be bored with your task and chummy with your adversaries. Chatter about anything other than what you are after, their families, the weather, do you see? The costume change I recommended would have carried you through it. Oh, well, I expect my potassium nitrate, brimstone, and sulphur should be delivered soon. I will make do."

"I did acquire flash powder."

"An expensive but worthy alternative. We will need a lot of flash powder if this is to succeed, Watson."

"You will also be happy to note that P. Webley & Son will address our depleted ammunition coffers in a day or two."

"You remembered to secure our pistol licences?"

"Yes, and a good thing I did, our year was up." I dropped it on his desk. "Ten shillings at the post office is a small price to pay to remain independent. Holmes, there was an African gentleman at the chemist's, I thought I also saw him in your consulting rooms the other day. Before I could get a good look at him, he sent my packages skittering across the floor. Could this be the man with deadly aspirations towards us?"

"Hmmm. Diminutive, robust, long hair?"

I nodded.

"It is of no importance, he said."

Holmes was happily, busily isolating and safely storing the contents of the bags. His chemical lab needed restocking for immediate scientific use. Holmes quick fingers systematically moved through his many drawers and chemistry shelves. He surveyed the completion of this task with pride.

90

"Watson, with the exception of the gunpowder, you have done well."

Once he concluded, I separated out the medical supplies and walked upstairs to replenish my shelves and Gladstone bag. When I came back into our sitting-room, I had but an instant to realize he had rigged up his gun and was pointing it at me!

I yelled, "Holmes!"

He closed his eyes, aimed it to the ceiling and shot the flash powder bullet!

"Watson, are you all right? I confess I may have overdone it a bit."

The lightning blast blinded both of us.

"Holmes, what a fantastic idea! No evildoer would be able to survive it. They would be out of commission and available for questioning as long as we will be. Any criminal activity or crime scene could be frozen in time."

"Yes, cutting it by half should do." He groped for his matches and lit a cigarette.

This I knew owing to the sound of a vesta strike and the sulphur smell mixed with strong tobacco smoke. I felt my way along the wall and slid into my chair. Then counted the seconds until my sight returned.

"Two minutes, fifteen seconds, Holmes."

"Ah, Watson, much mischief might be accomplished in that time. It appears to take me fifteen seconds less. I must consider the consequences of distance from the flash and the difference between open and enclosed space. Also how to define the beam of light and devise protection for ourselves. If fired directly at this evildoer and at night much more might be accomplished. Our tormentor will be exposed, and his escape cut off. We shall test it again later," he said, slipping his revolver into his pocket.

He leapt up and drew a leather case out of his desk drawer. From this, he pulled a pair of spectacles fitted with red-tinted lenses.

"If you would be so kind as to turn down the lamps, Doctor. It is time for darkness."

I did as he asked and found my way back to my chair.

"Holmes, what are you doing? Are you wearing red spectacles?"

"Keep the light at its lowest! Watson, our ancestors, once possessed nocturnal vision. For some time, I have been training my eyes to see in the dark."

"You pounce like a cat. Why not see like one? Is this truly possible, Holmes?"

"Thirty minutes of this before I go into the dark streets assists me in the detection of motion." He held his watch to the window light. "Another ten minutes. Watson, it would do well for you to remember to always carry your service revolver when abroad with me."

"But Holmes, I cannot see in the dark."

"No matter. There is something I want to examine tonight. Will you join me, Doctor?"

My Army experience taught me to load my pistol in complete darkness and I stashed it in my jacket. He removed his glasses, and we ran down the stairs into Baker Street.

"What do you see, Holmes?"

"The same phenomenon you do, Watson." He called, "Cab!"

"Practice peripheral vision, my friend. Focus your gaze on the sides of objects. Do not stare at one thing. Move your eyes to scan the area." In moments he knocked on the roof of the cab. "Let us disembark, Watson. This darkened street offers the best stage for my purposes."

North of the Marble Arch Holmes assumed a lookout position in an area where I could see nothing. The next thing I knew, he threw out his arm in caution and spoke at a low level.

"Wait! Do you see it, someone is hiding behind that carriage?"

"What carriage? Where?"

"Watson, night vision is the ability to interpret differing shades of black. But it is one thing to see and quite another to observe. Wait! He is running towards us. Get back!"

Someone bumped into me, and I was knocked to the pavement. "Damn, damn, double damn!"

"That is triple damn, Watson," he whispered, "Stay down!"

Holmes threw his walking stick and tripped the man. He landed beside me on the ground. "Ooof! Ow!"

He grabbed him by the collar. "What is your purpose, sir?" said Holmes.

"Where did you come from? Who are you? Let me go!"

"Be more careful." Holmes dropped him and the terrified gentleman flew from the gloom and darkness.

Then he clasped my hand and brought me to my feet.

"Thank you, Holmes."

"Ha! Watson. It is incredible! It will be the making of me."

We heard a shuffling noise down the street. Holmes put his lips to my ear and whispered.

"Stay close to me." He slipped his gloved hand into mine. "Run!"

We ran to the far end of the street where all was in shadow.

"Look away, Watson!" Holmes yelled, "Halt, what are you doing there!"

93

I could see nothing, yet heard footsteps running. Holmes sprinted after and fired his gun, for an instant the street lit up as a man leapt into a cab and whipped up the horse.

My friend returned shortly, seemingly without any effects of the flash powder.

"A well-planned escape, Watson. I retained the cab number. I imagine you could have also. No? Do you need spectacles, Doctor? Let us see what he was doing?"

He opened his pocket lantern adjusted a fine beam and for a brief instant, he shined it on the building then dashed the light. In whitewash letters on the door of the West London Synagogue for British Jews were painted, "DIE JEW!"

"Just as I thought, Watson. This case is certainly one of the darkest I have ever investigated. I fear this abominable message is also for us."

"But Holmes how does anti-Semitic vandalism touch our case? I do not see it."

He took up the brush and adding more whitewash, painted out the message. "Nor do I, Watson, yet I know it." Holmes put his arm in mine and led me out of the repugnant pitch-black lane. We cabbed back to the flickering lights of Baker Street.

"Holmes, there are many things I do not understand. This is an established synagogue, its members are in Parliament, lauded as councillors, doctors, and are prominent members of British society. Attacks like this have happened in the past—but today?"

"Prejudice is the child of ignorance, Doctor."

Back in our comfortable Baker Street digs, he put his key in the door and with respect for our lateness, quietly opened.

Upstairs in our rooms, he reached for one of the newspapers hanging over the back of our settee and began to read aloud to me.

DAILY CHRONICLE

4 April 1881

As we know, through elaborate and entirely illegal preparations, Tsar Alexander was assassinated in Saint Petersburg by anarchists. Without his hand to stay them, in recent weeks there resulted numerous anti-Semitic attacks or deplorable pogroms on Russian Jews. Therefore, thousands of immigrants are fleeing to the Continent for safety.

"Three weeks ago, Doctor." He dropped the paper to the floor. "The murderers were unusually thorough. They tunnelled beneath the road and filled it with formidable amounts of dynamite. Plus they had concocted three other plans. Ultimately, an anarchist walked up to the Tsar and exploded his bomb and himself. Utter insanity! Violence ever defeats its own ends, Watson."

"But surely this community would embrace these unfortunates, and ease their way into London?"

"One may only hope, Doctor."

"Holmes, with the addition of disenfranchised Scots and Irish crofters, and displaced Italian farmers, our East End is expanding its borders. Now with the increase of these Russian arrivals, how will it all end?"

"Unfortunately, it will lead to the kind of enterprise my practice was designed to address."

"With me by your side, Holmes."

"Thank you, old chap."

"But your ability to see in the dark? You accomplished this in thirty minutes time?"

"Watson, I began these carefully cultivated experiments at university. Tonight the spectacles hastened the process."

"Holmes, how do you know all this?"

"*Studies of Vision* by Leonardo da Vinci, Watson. You will find it next to Darwin's *The Expression of the Emotions in Man and Animals* on the third shelf, above your head. Plus, some eye-opening conversations in my youth with our vicar who was also an astronomer. More recently, I met a broad-minded young ophthalmologist. Tonight, my dear friend, you witnessed the splendid culmination of a work that began as a boyhood hobby. And its present-day use in my practice."

He filled two glasses and lit his pipe. I took mine, sat facing him in my basket chair, and stared into the whisky's golden colour.

"Holmes, how did you survive the flash powder bullet? Surely with your night vision, you were even more susceptible to the light?"

"The combination of my violin's dark velvet cover and the arm of my black coat was sufficient. The balance of probability the coat alone might work in a pinch," he said.

"So, did you see him?"

"Indelibly, Doctor. From the back. An old black coat probably from a charity shop worn by a lively young man. Threadbare shirt cuffs, no sleeve links, a dusty derby worn unevenly on the right. Old gloves, brown shoes, and paint-spattered grey pants with a military stripe. Thin, shorter than medium height. No jewellery or handkerchief of any kind. Which points to impoverishment. Yet, this involved act is not that of a man without resources."

"Or they were paint-spattered old work clothes," I said.

He patted my back with enthusiasm.

"Holmes, you whitewashed over the cursed message, erasing that horror. But they need to know."

"Never fear, Watson, I will visit Rabbi Moshe in the morning and explain my judicious brushwork."

"As a soldier, I learned to wait until my eyes adjusted to the darkness before squeezing the trigger. Of course, many nights, I did not have that luxury. Your accomplishment is brilliant."

"Thank you, Watson. It is another weapon in my arsenal. Did you truly not see that carriage?"

"Just like the gentleman who bowled me over; I could see nothing. But, Holmes, I was close enough to view the look on that poor man's face when you grabbed his collar. He thought he had seen a ghost! Woe to those with evil intent, Sherlock Holmes, has become invisible." Our hearty laughter soon brought this long day to rest.

Chapter 12
ARSÈNE LUPIN IN LONDON
The Reminiscences of John H. Watson, MD

"By a man's fingernails, by his coat-sleeve, by his boot, by his trouser-knees, by the callosities of his forefinger and thumb, by his expression, by his shirt-cuffs—by each of these things a man's calling is plainly revealed." – *A Study in Scarlet.*

I was awakened by a pounding on our Baker Street door and reached for my watch on the bedside table. It was exactly 6 a.m. In my dressing gown and slippers, I shooed the maid back to her room and marched to the door.

Constable Barrett in his crisp blue uniform rudely pushed by me. There were two Metropolitan Policemen and a Black Maria van guarding our Baker Street domicile. I ran after Barrett who was now standing over Holmes' bed and roughly shaking him by the shoulder.

I said, "Constable, what is this?"

In a voice loud enough to be heard during the raid of a disreputable establishment, he said, "Mr. Sherlock Holmes, Inspector Lestrade orders you to the Yard for questioning!"

"About what?" said Holmes.

"Hammer and tongs, is it? The inspector will let you know soon enough." I moved towards him as the enormous constable grabbed Holmes by the shoulders and yanked him from his bed.

"Point your smeller to your sit-upons and come with me unless it's an anointing you're after!"

"Surely, all this violence is unnecessary, Constable. Do you know who this is? Mr. Holmes solves all Scotland Yard's cases for them." I said.

The constable turned his red face upon me and shouted, "Obstructing justice, is it? There's room for you in the van, too."

Holmes shook his head at me and grabbed his cigarette case then dressed. He just had time to whisper, "Rabbi Moshe" to me as he passed. The constable grasped his shoulder, steered him down and out, and pushed him into the van. Standing in the doorway, I never felt so helpless in my life.

"Do you have a match, Constable?" I heard Holmes say as the doors were locked against him. Afterwards, in his half-humorous, half-cynical manner, he related his experience to me.

"At Great Scotland Yard, the unwavering Constable Barrett slammed me into a CID interrogation room."

"Coffee would be most welcome, Constable,' I said.

"The door was locked against me. I searched my pockets. 'Damn matches!"

"Lestrade walked in with another large policeman."

"Oh this is freakish,' he chuckled. 'Mr. Holmes, you look like you slept in the Canning Town docks. That ragged moustache and beard, and your hair falling in your eyes. What have you been doing?"

"I answered, 'Lestrade, your martinet dragged me straight from my bed without coffee or matches. I have always had a heavy beard. Get on with it. And do you have a light?"

"I have something better. Did you know Arsène Lupin is in London?' the little inspector said with pride."

"Not until this moment. Why would Lupin materialize here, Inspector?

"Watson, I immediately surmised a possible connection between Lestrade's ramblings and the recent attack on a young diamond cutter. My only concern was the time between the two events."

"Lestrade said, 'To escape from the French police, of course. I thought you knew these things, Mr. Holmes!'

"Inspector, I will look into it. I have appointments, let me go!"

"So you have not seen him?"

"No."

"Do you know where he's staying?' he said with a cat-ate-the-canary smile."

"Of course not, Lestrade!"

"Then answer me this, why did he sign the register of the Northumberland Hotel as Herlock Sholmes and then disappear?' He said triumphantly."

"Watson, I couldn't help it, I burst into laughter and then said, 'Lupin has a talent for evading capture, Inspector.' I pulled a cigarette from my case."

"You know him so well,' Lestrade squeaked."

"Anyone who reads the Paris papers would know as much.' I tamped down my cigarette. 'A match, Lestrade?"

"The inspector lit it. I inhaled deeply. 'Am I free to go?' I looked at my watch. 'My day with the orchestra commences in one and a quarter hours."

"Lestrade looked at me with a smug smile."

"The murder case in which we are both engaged, Lestrade,' I reminded him."

"He smirked. 'Of course. Do not leave the city. Stay in touch, especially if you hear anything from Lupin."

"I leapt into the first cab and flew north to Baker Street."

Holmes vaulted up to our landing and related Lestrade's story over breakfast.

Moments later, a tall, thin Frenchman in impeccable white tie placed his cape, top hat, gloves and ivory-handled walking stick in the hall. He had a thin handlebar moustache and wore a monocle that augmented his handsome, dark features.

Holmes grasped his hand like an old friend.

"Lupin! How good to see you. Are you in London long?"

"Watson, meet Arsène Lupin. Lupin, this is Doctor Watson, my friend—and partner."

I smiled. He had never called me that before. I liked the way it sounded.

"*Monsieur* Holmes, I see you have taken my advice and found yourself a worthy comrade. Even though we both enjoy the *bohémien* life of the wolf, it is always best to have a good man at your back in tight places, no?"

I put out my hand and the Frenchman shook it.

Lupin joined us at the breakfast table, and I said, "Holmes, I met with Rabbi Moshe as you instructed. He is enraged and afraid for his community. They are rinsing off the whitewash."

"Thank you, Watson, for putting this in the Rabbi's hands where it belongs."

Mrs. Hudson brought up fresh coffee and additional breakfast.

Lupin said, "If the object of that unflattering boxed beard is as masquerade, it is effective. With the simple addition of the pince-nez I see in your coat pocket, *mon ami*, I know your ability with disguise is not overrated."

"Ha! Praise from the master of disguise!" Holmes called to Mrs. Hudson as she turned to go, "Please alert us immediately if Scotland Yard attempts to gain entry. Thank you."

"Mr. Holmes, they would not have barged in this morning if they arrived at a decent hour," she said.

"*Merci,* Madame." Lupin bowed to her, kissed her hand as she left.

"Escape from my bedroom window is best unless the rooftops are more to your liking. That requires a trip up Doctor Watson's stairs to the attics. Inspector Lestrade is responsible for my sojourn to

Scotland Yard this morning to ascertain why you are here in London."

"*Pardon, Monsieur* Holmes, *j'ai peur* I need your *aide*, there has been the theft of a royal jewel from the *Musée de Louvre*."

Holmes said, "Ah, of course."

Lupin continued, "Since the death of Vidocq, the *Sureté* has lost its key to the underworld."

"Something you might return to them," said Holmes.

"Arsène Lupin reform the *Sureté?*" He snorted. *"You jest, Monsieur."*

Holmes was deadly serious. "How may I help?"

"The thief is *Afrique occidentale française,* French West African, and we think he is hiding in your city. My *clandestin* friends say he has an ally here," said Lupin.

"Describe the thief and anything you know of the ally." Holmes speared the last of his ham and eggs and poured another cup of coffee.

"He wasn't the man who planned the robbery. That man was killed during the attempt, possibly by the brute who escaped with the jewel. Young, of short height, dark-skinned, dressed as a guard during the theft, but his boots were scuffed and old. If either you or I were there, we would have spotted him *immédiatement."*

I said, "Holmes this sounds like the man—"

He kicked me under the table! Never taking his attention from Lupin he made a gesture that included the three of us, "Watson, there are graver issues here. Now Lupin, what else can you tell me?"

"*Le Musée du Louvre* guards were chloroformed and restrained. They described him as I have," Lupin said over his coffee."

"When do you think he arrived here?"

"I do not know. The robbery was Sunday, the 1st of August, last year."

"Now, *Monsieur*, why has it taken you so long to involve me?"

"*La Sûreté* have plodded all this time. Finally, in despair, they brought me in, but only recently. I do not wait. I act! And here I am," said Lupin.

"What did the *Sûreté* find at the site? Fingerprints? Footprints? Anything strange or unusual?"

"No, nothing like that. It was well-planned but without finesse. The fool threatened at gunpoint, smashed the case, left glass everywhere. There is one young *Gendarme*, Bonet. He is intelligent and brings me in."

Holmes looked at his watch. "Where are you staying? We might join you at supper tonight?"

"Ten p.m. The Northumberland Hotel?"

"It is clear you did not spend the night at your hotel," Holmes laughed. "Scotland Yard awaits you there. Another hiding place is warranted. I recommend the New Bohemian Club. It is a smaller club, not as known as the Pall Mall, with an excellent cellar and kitchen. But, Lupin, an alternative alias, please. Your last caused me a rude awakening."

"Ah, you know me too well, *Monsieur*, forgive *la farce*."

Holmes shaved, dressed, and prepared for his day. "Lupin, we meet at ten p.m. in the dining room. I am travelling south towards Westminster Abbey. May I drop you at the club?"

Two tall, dashing, young gentlemen dressed in unimpeachable white-tie stepped into the cab and proceeded south. Holmes was dressed for his day with the Imperial Theatre Orchestra. And for Lupin, "It is always the night."

At ten, I waited in the club's first-floor smoking room. Windows overlooked the entrance and allowed me a view of arrivals to the subdued gaslit portico. Holmes had access to the strangest places. I was used to the atmosphere of my sporting club, where boisterous conversation pervaded. But this was a quieter, reserved club. Only in the dining room was normal discourse allowed. There was no sign of Holmes.

A carriage pulled up, the door opened, and Lupin passionately embraced a young woman, holding a most intimate caress for some time. He left buttoning his trousers. Nonetheless, he was dressed in the height of fashion, his *affaire de coeur* had not moved a hair of his perfectly coifed head. She went off in the carriage, and he moved towards the entrance with the air of a man on top of the world. I joined him, and together we found our way up the red-carpeted stair.

His behaviour enraged me, and as soon as we entered, I let him know, "Mr. Lupin, this is not Paris. You may have ruined that young lady's reputation. You are no gentleman! Gentlemen do not behave in this way!"

Lupin threatened, "Doctor Watson, you will want to retract that statement!"

In an instant, Holmes appeared in rumpled white tie and yelled, "Down, Watson—!"

But it was too late. *Monsieur* Lupin slapped his glove across my face.

Holmes said, "Surely, Lupin, you do not actually intend to fight a duel with Doctor Watson over this? Think man, is it worth it? Watson?"

"You will be his second, no doubt, *Monsieur* Holmes? Please arrange for everything." Lupin bowed and walked from the dining room.

"Watson, you are not taking this seriously?"

"My honour and the honour of that young lady is at stake!" I said.

"This is not honour, it is pig-headedness, and it could get you killed, old man."

"Will you be my second, Holmes?"

"Do you even know the lady? Be reasonable, Watson. As good as you are, he is your match. Therefore it is only logical that one of you will be dead or seriously wounded tomorrow. Duelling is illegal in London! How can you agree to this?"

"Will I need to dig up Stamford?" I said.

"I will second you, Watson, of course, I always will. But, my friend, you are not thinking logically!"

I left Holmes to his arrangements. He shared his involvement in this curious meeting with me once the duel was completed. Other than the borrowing of the pistols, I cannot say I made much of it.

Holmes handed his card to a waiter to deliver to the gentleman whose name he wrote on the back. I believe I mentioned he has access to unusual places; this also includes unusual gentlemen of influence in all levels of society.

"What am I to do? This is childish but deadly, and what I hate most about gentlemanly ways," Holmes said, taking a seat and accepting a glass of wine.

"Arsène Lupin?" the other gentleman said.

"Yes." Holmes held the wine up to the light. "This is some of the '58?"

"I was wondering when you would notice. Inform your charges they will meet in Primrose Hill. There is a safe area away from the public near Shakespeare Oak."

He called for a servant.

"Please clean and load my duelling pistols and deliver them this evening to No. 221B Baker Street. Alert Doctor Periwinkle he will be needed and give him this note." He wrote it out.

Periwinkle,
7 A.M. duel.
Shakespeare Oak,
Primrose Hill.
M.

"You are certain all is well?"

"I will take care of it."

"Thank you."

Holmes returned to our lodgings and ran up to the first-floor.

I had never seen Sherlock Holmes in such distress. It was evident he was holding himself back and also evident he did not agree with this duel. Fighting a duel was not something I engaged in, but this was different. After all, it was my honour, not his.

The duelling pistols arrived. The final message was sent to Lupin. Doctor Periwinkle, a good man, agreed to preside over our health.

Rules agreed upon by Arsène Lupin and John H. Watson, MD:

1. The duel was to be fought to first blood.

2. Each party would fire one shot. If neither man were hit and the challenger satisfied, the duel ended. If the challenger was not satisfied, it may continue for three separate exchanges of pistol fire and no more.

3. The offended party could stop the duel at any time.

Friday, the next morning at seven we stood on Primrose Hill north of Regent's Park. My vision sharp, I could see views of Hampstead and Highgate. My military training had taken hold of me, and I was relaxed. We were the only ones in the park, it was a good stretch and thankfully there was no fog. Holmes measured and marked the ground planting a sword at each endpoint. Lupin and I took our points, raised our pistols. Holmes raised his handkerchief.

And then a familiar voice bellowed from the Shakespeare Oak, "All right gentlemen, that's enough, lower your pistols!" Inspector Lestrade walked into the sunlight. His men swarmed in and handcuffed Lupin. Who spat and swore loudly in French.

"Arsène Lupin, I arrest you in the name of the Queen. You can stop cursing now, your honour is intact. My involvement nullifies whatever insult you think Doctor Watson threw at you." He ordered his men, "Take him!"

"Lestrade, I was never so happy to see you!" Holmes shook his hand heartily.

"Mr. Holmes, you have some explaining to do, but that can wait until I throw this murderous thief in my gaol. Tsk, tsk, Doctor Watson, I thought you knew better than to get caught up in a Frenchman's sinister plot. Consider yourself rescued from your foolish pride. Doctor Periwinkle, come, you may ride with me."

I said, "Holmes you did this! You couldn't allow me to have this duel. What kind of gentleman are you to undercut my honour like this!"

Holmes put his hand on my shoulder. "Watson, I am just happy you are not arrested as a murderer or breathing your last. But you are wrong, old man. I did not call Lestrade. I organized the duel according to the rules you and Lupin set out. Doctor, I have never done anything so heinous in my life. Yet, according to those rules, your honour is now proved."

"I know this was onerous for you, Holmes. And you agreed to be my second even though you did not approve. Thank you, my friend."

We cleared the space and walked through the parks down to Baker Street.

"Watson, it is my job now to deliver Lupin from the gaol. I am sure Lestrade will see the light once he is informed of the clandestine mission. I doubt I will be performing with the orchestra today and Maestro Smith must now be told who I am and why I accepted the second violinist position. Would you mind bringing my swords up, old man? I will continue on in a cab. Go have your celebratory breakfast, I am sure Mrs. Hudson has prepared one for you."

Holmes told me he would first visit the New Bohemian Club, return the pistols, and ask his confederate to encourage a telegram from *La Sûreté* to Scotland Yard, explaining Lupin's purpose here.

Hours later when Mrs. Hudson brought up our dinner, Arsène Lupin again arrived in Baker Street. He was no longer the perfectly attired gentleman I met on Primrose Hill this morning. It was incredible how dirty the gaols were. His luggage was lost, and his finances disappeared as well. Yet, he was smiling, and his shabbiness did not hide the debonair gentleman before us, it granted him a rakish honour that I am sure has always been part of him.

Holmes took his hand and firmly held it in his. "Lupin if you had harmed my friend, Watson, today, you would have had me to answer to. I hope that is clear, *Monsieur*."

I was taken aback by the fierceness of his statement. Lupin nodded.

He opened a bottle of claret for our dinner and continued as if he hadn't just threatened Lupin with his life, "How did Scotland Yard treat you, *Monsieur*?"

"Nothing I have not experienced before. French jails are worse. *Monsieur* Holmes, hurting Doctor Watson was never my intention. Forgive me, gentlemen. I have learned not to take your partner for granted, Sherlock. You should also know, Lestrade makes a lot of imbecilic noise, but you both have friends in Scotland Yard. And

Monsieur Holmes please thank your influential comrade. *Merci*, I am grateful for your hand in my release."

Mrs. Hudson brought in a telegram. Lupin opened it. "This *télégramme* recalls me to Paris. *Monsieur* Holmes, it is much less pleasurable to work on your side of the law. Cut-and-dried, as you say. I thought the *petit* Bohemian Club one of your little jokes. But *mon ami*, compared with Scotland Yard it is a palace." He laughed.

"Lupin, your return to Paris may prove beneficial. I will take your jewel theft case but know that I am presently involved in a murder investigation."

"I am at your disposal, *Monsieur* Holmes. My 8 Rue Crevaux and Étretat addresses, plus my Sureté and Louvre contacts." He pushed a card across the table.

"Lupin, you are a shark out of water in London, as I would be in Paris. Working from our home cities, we may yet perform miracles. Research and inform me of anything you find about this thief. Why did you not have the Sureté advise Scotland Yard you are working for them?"

"If I waited for them to act, I would still be in Paris. But maybe that would have been better?" He shrugged.

Holmes shook his head, "When do you leave?"

"*Immédiatement!*"

"Stay here until you must leave for Paris. Mrs. Hudson will draw you a bath and see to your clothes."

"*Monsieur* Holmes you are a true gentleman."

He stood and I stood, he shook my hand. "Your honour is intact, Doctor. You are a brave man. I fear you would have shot me today. And *Monsieur* Holmes is very lucky to have you by his side."

While Lupin attended to his toilet, I said, "Holmes, he is a wanted criminal. Is that not why he was arrested today? The CID rarely goes through the process of arresting blameless people."

I had moved him from his reverie, and he snapped at me, "Oh, Watson, do you truly not see, he may be the making of this case!" Holmes filled and lit his cherrywood pipe and thoughtfully sent ribbons to the ceiling. "No, of course, how could you? Forgive me, Watson, you were not here at the time. Laban, a young and honourable diamond cutter, came to me when you were at your club. He was surprised one night by a violent man in a mask demanding he cut some exceptional but stolen jewels. He refused and was beaten. The two events coming at the same time must be connected."

Following dinner, Lupin went off to Paris. Holmes was silent through dinner and said no more until we seated at our fire, sharing the last smoke of the night. Holmes chose my lightest blend for his pipe and declined a brandy.

I could not sit quietly and again confronted him, "How could this diamond cutter be connected with Lupin's stolen jewels? They happened on opposite sides of the Channel. Holmes, I do not know why you insist on this fraternity when it could destroy your reputation and put both of us in gaol! Where would your new science be then?"

Exhausted from his long day, he smiled and patted my shoulder.

"Forgive me, Doctor, I know your experience is dissimilar from mine, but Lupin is a force for good."

"But Holmes didn't he steal a queen's necklace, the black pearl, art treasures? The list is very long."

"I applaud your research. Yes, my friend, in his Paris, he operates on the wrong side of the law, yet his position allows him to defeat worse villains than himself. Here he is serving with the *Sureté*, an affiliation I encourage. This morning you were willing to shoot him point-blank. I do not imagine you could accept him as a friend. You may excuse yourself if this affinity offends you."

"No, my expertise is more needed now than it was in Brixton Road. But Holmes, what I do not understand is, you are a man of the law. How can you consort with him?"

"There you are wrong, Doctor. I am my own man. Do not confuse me with the Metropolitan Police. My only superior is the cause of true justice. There are no limits to the means I use in my investigations. Illicit methods and tools serve me in achieving my ends. Though my understanding of the law is as good as any solicitor, it is my knowledge of a century of crime that assists me in every case. Underworld friends school me in their ways, keep me informed, and are my eyes and ears in dangerous places. I operate independently on this side of the law, yet I appreciate the good people on the other. Arsène Lupin is one of these."

Chapter 13
THE DAWN RISES AS BEFORE
From the Journal of Mrs. Hudson
"Poetry is a dangerous gift." – Grace Aguilar.

7 April, 1801

It was my day for washing linens. As I ascended the stairs to the first-floor, I could clearly hear my tenants' discourse.

"Watson, where have you been hiding?"

"I haven't left, Holmes."

From the hallway, I watched as Mr. Holmes grabbed Doctor Watson's right hand.

"Tsk, tsk, the state of your fingernails does not befit your profession. You do your hands a disservice, Doctor. Your soiled trouser knees suggest the nearby environs of Baker Street. Yet its reason, if reason it be, is hidden from me at present. It is surely not a proposal and in Regent's Park? The tell-tale signs of love are absent, thank heavens. Where would we put her? No, your sweaty brow and grimy collar, dusty boots, dishevelled clothes, and that blister forming between your forefinger and thumb show signs of physical labour, not romance."

The disdain Mr. Holmes showed for both labour and romance were expressed with equal amounts of contempt. I knocked on their open door and announced my purpose for being there. Mr. Holmes was preparing for his day with the orchestra.

"Thank you, Mrs. Hudson. I would now return your husband's notebook and letters to you. They were helpful. I will retain his music a while longer if that is acceptable?" He gave them to me and wiped off the last of his shaving soap and I retrieved the towel.

"Yes, Mr. Holmes. Doctor, thank you, again. You may drop off your laundry with me. That includes clothing and linen. Replaced by the end of the week. Or the next week if you get it to me late."

"Ah, it is Mrs. Hudson's lumber-room, am I right, madam?" he said.

Then, for a moment, Mr. Holmes assessed my appearance. "Are you both tunnelling somewhere, to Mrs. Turner's perhaps?"

I smiled and waved him away as I stepped to the second-floor to collect the bedroom linen.

"Holmes, I see why you try never to guess. This is all very humorous." Doctor Watson said as he mounted the steps to his room.

I walked down and entered Mr. Holmes' bedroom.

The Doctor called downstairs, "I invite you to glance out your rearward window before daylight descends."

In reply, Mr. Holmes laughed, "Where is the fun in that, Doctor?"

"Did you not tell me it is a capital mistake to theorise before you have all the evidence?" called Doctor Watson as he closed his door.

Minutes later, in a tweed jacket, cleaned hands, and trousers, he ran down with his laundry bundle and handed it to me. When the Doctor returned to the sitting-room, Mr Holmes was rosining his bow.

He watched the Doctor enter, locked the bow inside his violin case and smiled. "Watson, you are involved in Mrs. Hudson's accursed garden!"

"There's nothing accursed about my garden!" I announced from the landing. "But the state of your bedroom is quite another matter, Mr. Holmes."

Doctor Watson moved to the table, poured himself a cup of coffee. "She is right, it is a satisfying endeavour, Holmes. And it produces those deliciously fresh victuals we enjoy so much."

"I had enough of that gruellingly boring arboriculture as a child to last a lifetime!" Holmes exchanged his dressing gown for his frock coat.

"What was your life like then?"

"Dull, tiresome, mediocrity, I scorn commonplace existence. Oh, Watson, it is fine for some. I dare say, life from a seed has enormous possibilities. For me, it is slow and dirty!"

"Ho, Ho, between Jack's parodies and our laughter, the work is easy, even enjoyable. The drudgery of tilling has been banished. Mrs. Hudson is a knowledgeable gardener, and it mostly takes care of itself."

I stepped into the sitting room and said, "Mr. Holmes, I have twice found the garden tools in disarray, could it be you?"

"Preposterous!" He cursorily glanced at his fingernails and again waved me away.

As I descended with arms full of linen. These were dropped into my clothes washer to soak, for Molly to wash. I had to admit my doubts about Mr. Holmes using the garden tools. For Mr. Holmes, my bees were his only interest. Once I caught him sitting on the bench intensely studying them. But then, who did leave the tools out?

The doorbell rang. It was the postman with a letter from my Auntie Amelia.

> Marti, please come to our 12th April meeting, and you will find out how exceptional are the women of the West London Synagogue. Amelia.
>
> PS: Please take care. I read about the explosion and Mr. Holmes' handling of it. Thank heaven you are safe.

I had not read the newspaper accounts yet could imagine the sensational story Aunty Amelia read. Especially if Inspector Lestrade had anything to do with it. Mr. Holmes' calm and knowledgeable handling of this crisis was to be lauded; he was the hero of the day. Could my former lodgers be involved? It is absurd to think they would return from America or Bohemia to do this. I wish them well and hope they are happier back in their home countries.

Mr. Holmes plans to distil the poisonous concoctions from my lily of the valley and extract its delicate perfume. Also to test the highly touted poisonous nature of the tomato leaf. I could almost hear James' protests, "Poisonous, bah! There is nothing poisonous about tomatoes! Marti, look at this exceptional plant. Who would think this beautiful tomato specimen was poisonous?"

Whenever I heard this excited and reverential tone, I would leave my seeding, watering, or weeding and move to James' side. His tomatoes were the pride of our garden. He fed them with the best additions and compost. He was careful with watering as tomatoes can flood. He planted the largest and sweetest varieties and battled the pests for everyone.

We shared my kitchen, too. James was a better cook than I as his tastes were wide-ranging. Spicy Spanish gazpacho and Italian tomato sauce grew from his tomatoes. Both were capable of surviving the canning process exceptionally well and became an abundant addition to our kitchen larder through the winter.

James would dig down deep, turning the soil by hand, hard work. He did not care about hard work. He was drawn by the goal before him--the perfect tomato. Like learning a musical piece, he would work up to it until he had mastered what the composer had written, and then he would add his own flair. He believed the garden knew him, responded to his voice, and his steps on the earth.

He was the chef in our kitchen. Like the Spaniards he was descended from, he liked his gazpacho hot, all the doors and windows had to be opened whenever he cooked, as the simmering spice could choke anyone in the house. His first batch sent me running out to Baker Street, coughing with eyes streaming. He opened the entire house and brought me back in with a kiss.

115

"My little Scots wife is not accustomed to such spice, but you will acclimate as you have to our London fogs."

Alas, I never did.

Our trip to Picardy included an extended visit to where France touched the Alps. For Londoners, it was pure joy to breathe such unsullied air. The green of the land, the severe black of the rock contrasted with the glittering white of snow-topped peaks and glaciers. To James, the beauty of the growing fields of France was but a steppingstone to the unparalleled grandeur of the Alps. Wandering the wilderness paths at the foot of Eiger, Davos, or Rigi, was his great joy.

We returned to Baker Street on 21st August. Mrs Turner informed us she spied our lodger entertaining a visitor. What bothered her was it was unusual for him to have visitors.

To appease my cousin, James discussed this with our lodger. I was in the kitchen with the door open. They sat in chairs in the garden.

"Fiant, thank you, for keeping the garden so well-tended while we were away. Your good care shows."

"Your flowers remind me of home."

"While we were away, Mrs. Hudson's cousin said you had a visitor. I just want you to know we encourage you to invite your friends."

"What? That gossiping old biddy?" he laughed.

"I suppose she felt she was watching over us while we were away. Again, I am grateful for your care of the garden. Though it is a shame that one bed of tomatoes died."

"I could do nothing about it. Bad seed? Bad soil? Who can say? I'd leave it lie fallow for a year if I were you." He stood. "Are you about done? Goodnight." He said as he walked past me and upstairs.

James played his muted horn in the garden that night rehearsing the difficult Haydn concerto. It was like the repetitious calling of a high mournful bird. And when he conquered it and finally soared on Haydn's notes, it was magnificent.

That was almost a year ago. I believed my life ended when he did. Yet, all around me, life went on. This morning at sunrise, there returned to the planetree the same insistent raucous bird that jarred our days awake. Could it be the same one? Parrots may live longer than their masters. Maybe this was like that? Otherwise, along with learning exactly where to fly, it must learn to sing with all its might, the call for a mate.

It took me three-quarters of a year to realise James was not flying back. Our marriage was exceptional. We spoke as equals. We learned how to look in each other's eyes and find the loving person even at the worst moments or after the worst moments. We found that love was action, not staying the same, not expecting the same, and we grew up together. The work of the soul he called it.

The way I saw it: Humans disagreed, had flaws, some of them interesting. Perfection was for roses, not us. We made mistakes and judged each other for them. Sometimes we even walked away. What we humans had as lovers was the desire to try again, to want to give, grow, become more of whom we saw in our lover's eyes. We were social beings and literally needed each other to feel right. Love was all about the dance of possibilities, joyful expectations, dreams, and frailties. The moves were sometimes together and sometimes apart and many times flying beyond where we could go alone. And trusting in it.

Surviving James' sudden and inexplicable murder, plunged me horribly into the valley of the shadow of death. It opened the deeply hidden secrets of our lives and flailed me with them. I now know the constant pain of it was because I was attempting to live where I could not and did not belong.

Realizing I could no longer be where James was, shook me awake. Many run from this, for me it was an opportunity and a gift to discover this new path (or chasm) that opened up before me. Actually, I had no

117

choice, and it took great courage to step onto the way of my soul. The path that also took me away from James. My choice was very clear: to live the life I was called to or die. That sounded dramatic, but was my truth, nonetheless. What I was most grateful for was the extraordinary people I met on this path and where we were going together.

12 April, 1801

Amelia called the meeting together.

"To many, this gathering of women would seem as strange as the tents of the harem. We meet in the same spirit as a mikvah, in the same privacy as the sacred bath. Apart from men we share our sorrows, our joys, and our power. How is it our expansive and liberal Anglo-Jewish Community could embrace so much and yet overlook our education, our freedom?" she said.

This began a lively intelligent discussion. Immediately established was the idea that this group would break through the taboos on writing novels and forming women's journals.

Emily said, "We can raise our Jewish women's voices on the subject of emancipation. That may bring us allies."

"I will show our culture as it is and our gentlemen as heroes," Marion said.

"That will wake them up!" her sister, Celia said.

"Wonderful ideas," Grace said. "We could put Fagin and Shylock to shame, and the negative images of Jewish men."

"Yes, and demonstrate our true Anglo-Jewish Culture. Bring it to light. We wear British clothes, speak English in our Shul, are part of British society, we are not hidden anymore." Emily said.

These ideas were enthusiastically adopted. The meeting moved to Celia's reading the first pages of the novel she was writing to hearty applause.

I cabbed home, considerably impressed by what these women were proposing. Publishing novels as a form of emancipation was certainly unprecedented, but the added benefit of portraying a positive image of the Anglo-Jewish people was inspired.

Amelia wanted to bring me into something she knew would awaken my spirit. And this meeting certainly had.

Chapter 14
THE SCIENCE OF DEFENCE
The Reminiscences of John H. Watson, MD

"A gentleman only uses his hands to defend himself, and not to attack; we call the pugilistic art, for that reason, the noble science of defence." – Bill Richmond.

Holmes flew in the front door and out to the garden in tattered shirt sleeves and top hat, looking very much like one of his Irregulars.

"Watson!" he called. I ran down to him. He discarded clothing as he spoke.

"An acid throwing fiend accosted me. I smelled the sulphuric acid the instant it reacted with the silk of my disintegrating umbrella. My coat and waistcoat are discarded over there," he said while he placed his hat and watch chain on a chair. Then threw the remainder of his clothes to the pile with astonishing rapidity.

"My Heaven's Holmes! How may I help you?"

"Hurry, Doctor! Please make a paste of water and baking soda. Mrs. Hudson keeps it in the kitchen, there. Quickly! Examine me for burns. I feel no pain, but Oil of Vitriol requires perseverance. Now, turn on the hose from the kitchen!" he said as he stepped onto each of his gloved hands with the toes of his boots and released in this way. He removed his shoes and stockings and threw them on the pile. He stood on the garden path. I aimed the hose; gave him the soap and he washed his face and hands well. Following my close examination for any blemish or burnt hair, he lathered up repeatedly and had me douse him with the hose again and again. I examined him one last time. He raced upstairs and changed into untainted tweed trousers and waistcoat.

Thank Heaven, I could find nothing wrong, and the paste went unused. I carried up his watch and placed his top hat next to mine in the hall.

"Did you get a look at the man? Was he the same man?"

"Rarely am I unable to do so, but acid requires immediate action. Yet by the angle of dispersion, I deduce he is a shorter man. Thank you, Watson," he said as I handed him the watch and chain.

"Why would anyone do this?"

"It is maddening! A fourth attempt and we have nought to go on. That doesn't say much for my new science of deduction and analysis. The sequel to your runaway carriage, the dynamite in my bedroom, and the attack on Baker Street. I am proud to say quick thinking on both our parts eliminated the threats." He tied his brown boots, attached his watch chain, and stood, brushing his hair back, once more my dapper friend.

"There must be some way to force a solution to these blasted attacks!"

"Not since hanging in chains was abolished in 1834, Watson." He smiled. "Do we open our private lives up to the scrutiny of Scotland Yard? The CID? No. With careful consideration, we shall ourselves solve this conundrum. And it seems we have an ally. I would nonetheless have arrived here in much worse condition if the same man who helped you on Marylebone Road hadn't assisted me."

"Thank Providence he was there! Do you have any idea who this gentleman might be?"

"I have some thoughts on the subject, but must verify them."

"But Holmes, how do we operate under this cannonade?"

"It is a dark business. The fact that our assailant remains hidden may mean he is known to one of us, which underlines your thoughts it may be a client. And the fact that Mrs. Hudson though threatened is yet unscathed is suggestive. Taken together, his use of horses, vitriol, and munition. None of the villains harassing my clients has such murderous tendencies. Keep your wits about you. And must I again remind you to carry your Army revolver, Doctor? We have rattled an

121

experienced villain who is yet free. Our job is to find and secure him."

Mrs. Hudson arrived with a gentleman's card.

"Wonderful timing, as usual, Mrs. Hudson. Please take care. The pile of costuming in your garden was destroyed by acid—do not touch them! Forgive me for charging in your garden and using the garden hose. It was a hateful emergency. We will bury the clothing in the driest area of your yard, as soon as is possible. Please take with you Doctor Watson's water and baking soda paste. If perchance you do transfer some of the acid to your skin or clothes, apply the baking soda paste where needed, and then rinse off outside. For at least fifteen minutes. Be careful not to run the water down drains, into the earth only."

"Acid, Mr. Holmes! Please take care! Thank you for your caution with its disposal." She placed our dinner on the table and presented him with the card.

He thanked her and passed the card to me. Holmes shrugged on his mouse-coloured dressing gown and took his position by the door to greet our client. I stood next to him in relaxed attention. He smiled and thumped my back, acknowledging my ready participation.

A gentleman ran up our stairs two at a time and entered. With an open expression, looking straight at Holmes, he smiled and offered his hand.

Holmes shook it. "McMurdo, how are you? This is my friend and colleague, Doctor Watson. Please join us in some dinner. There is an urgency in your face and hands. Have a seat and tell us about it?"

Holding his cap, he said, "Pleased to meet you, sir. Mr. Holmes, it's bad news! I'm afeared my life's over as there's no other way!"

"From the beginning, McMurdo."

"Forgive me. You know my fists usually do the speakin'."

I filled another glass and gave the brandy into his meaty hands.

122

"Thank you. Is that wild hare I smell?" he said.

"What has happened?"

"Murder, Mr. Holmes, murder. Oh, my short, sweet life's over!" He looked around. "There's no mutton shunter's here?"

"Our office is confidential. You have nothing to fear," I said. McMurdo drank the brandy, "You will feel better after you've eaten."

"Thank you." He filled a plate. Holmes was on the edge of his seat, licking his lips, which may have been the result of Mrs. Hudson's Jugged Hare. Yet, I could see he was greatly interested in what McMurdo had to say.

Holmes said, "You have returned from the country. By the mud on your shoes, I would say Enfield. Travelled directly here by train and closed cab, without stopping at the boxing club. Which for you was unusual." He continued as the gentleman wolfed down our meal. "Recount your story from its inception, McMurdo, so that we may determine how to help you."

The boxer patted his lips with my napkin. "I'll tell you what I know. Hudson and I, we was chaps, and walkin' home as usual from the gym."

"James Hudson? When was this?"

McMurdo nodded. "It was a Sunday, September last." He counted on his fingers and said, "Yes, the twenty-first, Mr. Holmes."

Holmes moved into a cross-legged position, put his hands in meditation pose, closed his eyes, and said, "Pray, continue and leave nothing out."

"My ole way was to drop him in Baker Street and move south. But it was warm, and I stopped for a pint, ya know the pub down the way? I came back out dodgy. There was lurkers outside and police inside. I got close to see in the window, and there was Hudson ready for the eternity box. Blood everywhere. Oh, I should've stayed with him! He was the last man I'd have thought—who would top him?"

123

McMurdo was short in stature, deep-chested, muscled; his gruff voice gave the little gentleman a comic aspect. His hair was brown, and his eyes, dark with a boxer's ears and face, filled now with intense puzzlement.

"Mr. Holmes, we sparred at the gym, me and Hudson, and minutes later, there he was stone dead." He used his napkin. "It takes years to build a body like Hudson's, and he wasn't no bad boxer neither, but a better pal."

I said, "Mr. McMurdo, Mr. Holmes has solved many such crimes. I am sure he can also bring you satisfaction."

Holmes opened his eyes and was half smiling at me as I sat at the table, next to our visitor, patted his back, and refilled his brandy.

"Mr. Holmes, you knows a deal more about these things. Please help me to clear my name and find the dickens what did this!"

"Clear your name?"

McMurdo continued, "That night the police tried to pinch me! But I run off to my sister's in Enfield. Anytime soon, they'll light on me. You got to save me."

"If you had come to me on the 21st, it would have been infinitely more practical. Why have you waited so long?"

"They chased me all over London thinkin' I was the one what killed him. But I outlasted 'em and lost 'em in the Underground. And was tail down and hiding but came back to crack my friend's murder. He'd do it for me. He would. Mr. Holmes, there was another boxer. He had it in for James. You heard about Russia?" Holmes nodded. "Well, this mauler was pro there. And here, he was the hope of Jewish boxers. They're kept out, you see. I don't see where a chap's church or temple has anything to do with his good left hook."

"A fine philosophy, McMurdo," Holmes said as he changed into a tweed jacket. "What say you, Watson? Shall we visit the St. James's?"

We three cabbed to the gym where the gentlemen of the boxing fraternity eyed me with suspicion. Holmes walked in, and it became a reunion. He shook many hands, greeted everyone. I could see he was no stranger to these men.

"Who here knew my friend, James Hudson?" he said.

Six boxers joined us. We sat huddled together, and Holmes' interviews commenced.

"Doctor Watson is my second. At my order, he is taking notes to see me through this decision. I am searching for the solution to James Hudson's murder." I shook the hands of all six men, and mine still smarts thinking of it.

"McMurdo related to us that one minute they were walking home together, and in the time it took him to down a pint, Hudson was lying dead on the floor of Dreyfus' establishment in Baker Street. You may recall this was September last," Holmes continued.

They elbowed McMurdo about the pint. But another Jewish boxer spoke up, "Mr. Dreyfus is a good man and shouldn't face charges in this."

Holmes said, "Ezra, I agree with you and believe the true killer left as the police arrived, which is why they went for McMurdo. I am no official agent. Hudson's family and now McMurdo are my clients. Is there anything else you might tell me?"

"James Hudson was an honest fighter and a big-hearted man. Boxing for him was a way to build up, not a reason to roughhouse his opponent. I fought him sometimes and win or lose; he would treat me to a pint. A pint with James was always filled with humour. It was as much a part of him as his beard. How he met his end, I would swear he did not provoke it," Ezra said. The other boxers agreed with him.

Holmes was invited into the ring by the men, most of whom he put off to another time. It is one thing to discern that Holmes had this ability and quite another to witness the honour in which he was held by the gentlemen of the fancy.

One man, he did not refuse. And again, I was to be amazed by the mastery of Mr. Sherlock Holmes, this time by his unparalleled ability in the gentlemanly arts.

Holmes faced a powerful hulking pugilist who had been at the edge of our discussion. Abe had closely followed the conversation but did not join in. Later, I learned he had once been the club's champion.

Both men stripped down to their trousers, removed their boots and stockings. Holmes shook Abe's hand. They agreed to three rounds. It was clear from the first that this man was forceful, and I worried for Holmes, who though taller, was in another league altogether.

Holmes, with hands up, moved around Abe, assessing him. They were toe-to-toe. The other fighters made bets and cheered them on. Abe threw a left jab to the head. Holmes discerned a left foot tell and ducked in time. But before he could aright, Abe threw the same punch with his right and grazed Holmes shoulder as he slipped his position. Nevertheless, he felt the power behind that misplaced jab and moved back beyond Abe's compelling reach. I began to see Holmes' advantage. As in all things, he was incredibly fast on his feet, while the much stockier ex-champion was not.

Holmes entered the ring, body relaxed and mind excited at the prospect of the game. The force of Abe's attack electrified him. Shifting his feet along with his combinations, he began to land each blow with the precision of an anatomist. Then gauged his opponent's response—a right jab to Abe's nose, a left jab to his ear, another right to the head. Abe was hands-up, protecting himself. He feinted a crouch underneath Holmes' onslaught, from which he rose into a brutal uppercut. Holmes felt the hard edge of those iron-like knuckles and moved again to safety.

Abe countered with a right to the chin, but Holmes bent back out of the way. He returned with a left to the head, which Abe deflected. Holmes landed two more lefts in quick succession at Abe's head. He moved in close with a jab to the abdomen. Abe threw a one-two punch. Holmes' backpedalled out of range, but Abe took advantage of his backward motion and pushed him to the edge of the ring at the ropes. Before Holmes could escape the clinch, Abe rammed his head into Holmes' diaphragm.

I worried for Holmes absorbing such blows and yelled, "Bad form!"

To the referee, I hollered, "As per London Prize Ring Rules that is disqualifying behaviour! Abe should be censored!"

I was booed!

The round ended and as Holmes' second, I handed him a towel and gave him water to drink. He was grateful for my involvement yet said, "Watson, it is not my first fight."

The referee must not have heard me over the cheers, jeers, and betting and the fight continued.

Back in centre ring, a quick left and an answering right. Both men were now bleeding. Abe bobbed and weaved. But Holmes had the man's cut. Keeping him at arms-length, stepping in only to land a punch, and then immediately moving out of reach, he planted a right and a left on Abe's chin. Abe threw a right uppercut. Holmes deflected with his elbow and landed a left jab and three precise inside jabs. Abe was no longer throwing punches but only protecting himself.

Holmes ended the fight there. They finished with a handshake, and I attended their abrasions. While towelling and dressing, Abe took Holmes aside to talk.

We left, again shaking every hand in the place. Holmes' exuberance rang out as he called "Cab!" and we headed through

Piccadilly towards Baker Street. He knocked on the roof and redirected the driver down to the Strand.

"McMurdo devoured our hare, Watson. A little something nutritious at Simpson's?"

"Spending your winnings, Holmes? They should also have something rare. He clipped you one too many times," I said.

I examined his hands for consequences and asked, "Holmes, what did he say to you?"

"Abe confirmed Mrs. Dreyfus' information and added that he is a new Russian emigree. Built like a bear, and as impenetrable as a brick wall. His left breaks bones with one swipe of his paw. Plus he has the stamina to dominate every opponent. He masters every fight. Yet, it seems that Russian rules are not London's, Doctor."

"So this is McMurdo's fighter?"

"Yes, Watson. What he held against James Hudson was the loss of the club's championship fight. For the Russian, it was an important win that would give him club champion status. He could then arrange fights with champions from other clubs. Much bigger stakes were involved. But Hudson, as the referee, realised the Russian was beating the other fighter to death and directed his seconds to take their man to his corner. He then examined the other fighter and discontinued the fight according to London Rules. Abe was the other fighter, and James Hudson saved his life."

"And made an enemy. So revenge is the motive. Is this boxer our chief suspect?" I said.

"Watson, our list of suspects presently includes the 400 complement of the Imperial Theatre Orchestra and the membership of the West London Synagogue. With one exception, the St. James's Boxing Club is now struck off. Hopefully, you may disqualify the Savile Club members for me. Fool Lestrade is shaking down moneylenders. Nevertheless, it is necessary that I speak with this boxer," Holmes said.

At Simpson's, Sherlock Holmes stepped out of the cab and stretched, "Nothing like a little exercise to stimulate the appetite," he said.

"Holmes, you are not considering facing this Russian in the ring? Look at what your body has suffered at Abe's hands. As a doctor, I strongly urge you against it. Especially if he is a dirty fighter!"

"Focus your attention on fact, Doctor. The experienced detective is led by truth, verifiable truth." He stretched his arms above his head. "Watson, Abe has confirmed it. Though the challenge is appealing, very little conversation happens in a boxing ring. No, I shall find another means of taming The Bear."

Chapter 15
SAVILE CLUB INTERVIEWS
The Reminiscences of John H. Watson, MD

"What a tissue of mysteries and improbabilities the whole thing was! And yet I had so much faith in Sherlock Holmes's insight that I could not lose hope." – "The Boscombe Valley Mystery."

EVENING STANDARD
THE PASSING OF THE EARL OF BEACONSFIELD.

20 April 1881, London. Lord Beaconsfield, our Prime Minister, died at his house in Curzon Street at 4:30 a.m. yesterday, after his long illness, calmly, as if in sleep.

"Life is too short to be little. Man is never so manly as when he feels deeply, acts boldly, and expresses himself with frankness and with fervour."

"All power is a trust; that we are accountable for its exercise; that from the people and for the people all springs and all must exist."

And so passes Benjamin Disraeli, a great statesman, a great friend to Her Majesty, and a great PM for Great Britain and her people.

"What a shame, Doctor. He was a good Prime Minister for so many." Mrs. Hudson handed me the Evening Standard at tea. "At least his suffering is over. The Jewish Community will miss him most."

"I think Her Majesty the Queen would disagree with you," I said.

"Yes, a great man. What a loss," she said.

"And a man of letters. He said, 'Nurture your minds with great thoughts. To believe in the heroic makes heroes.' Only a novelist could say that."

The concert was ten days away, and to Sherlock Holmes, his place in the Imperial Theatre Orchestra came second only to his reason for being there.

To abbreviate the massive amount of interviews ahead of him, Holmes divided the orchestra into sections and addressed the woodwinds, brass, and percussion at the Blue Boar Pub. Strings during short rehearsal breaks in the theatre. He separated out the musicians Mrs. Hudson had noted as her husband's companions. This shortened his list considerably.

During a break in rehearsal, he interviewed the first violinist.

"Mr. Dill, I understand you were friends with James Hudson?"

"Yes, he was a fine musician and a better man," Dill said.

He then offered information unasked to Holmes about other orchestra members.

That night, Mrs. Hudson delivered a note from Mrs. Dreyfus with our supper. Holmes opened it, "Ah, the able Amelia Dreyfus has confirmed 'The Russian Bear' once the pride of Odessa is now the hope of London's Anglo-Jewry. He is their formidable entry into the sport. So, the pugilist has new handlers, a smart move on his part. She also offers condolences for the loss of the great Benjamin Disraeli."

Afterwards, Holmes taught me the art of false bearding for my interviews with the gentlemen of the Savile Club.

"Watson, tomorrow we will conference after lunch. Mr. Dreyfus' list is uncommonly detailed. Along with dates, he included each person's occupation and the reason for their borrowing. So, we have two musicians, three race enthusiasts, ten from the Jewish quarter, seven entrepreneurs, five young men about to be married, and another five from the Savile Club. If we drop the unlikely and the highly unlikely, this leaves us with two musicians and five from the Savile Club."

Holmes scribbled down names and details in his concise hand and gave me the list. "Doctor, you interview the musicians from the Savile Club. I will continue to question the orchestra multitude." He held up a telegram. "Dreyfus has hired us to clear his name."

In the morning, Holmes, lounged in his dressing-gown instructing me, while I dressed in my Sunday best, morning coat, topper, gloves, and stick.

"Watson, when you arrive for early luncheon at the Saville Club the seven musicians will be there. We are free of orchestral duties on Sunday. Ask only pertinent questions. Be your most cordial self, do not frighten them. If someone refuses to answer a question, continue to the next without referring to it and bring that back to me, do not press them or react in any way. Bring your pistol well-hidden, but do not take chances. We are dealing with an experienced killer. Do not attempt to take him on yourself, my friend."

I left for the Saville Club. My revolver tucked into an inner pocket. My sideburns were now bushy muttonchop's ending at my moustache. Arriving at the Saville, the club steward ushered me into the bar. I interviewed him first about suspicious activity among club members. Then checked the state of my beard and spoke separately with two musicians, introducing myself as Doctor Liam Caraway.

I shook hands with Mr. Taylor, he was easy to spot with his broad-brimmed hat. He enjoyed squeezing my hand with strong fingers. Just possibly, he didn't know his own strength.

I began, "I am here to speak with those who knew James Hudson. To discover anything that might help with this difficult investigation." I sat at his table.

"I had no idea doctors went in for this?" said Mr. Taylor watching my descent into the chair.

"I am a police surgeon."

"Isn't this against the club's privacy policy?"

"Mr. Hudson was a member, there are many at the Savile who would like to see justice done. Are you one of them, Mr. Taylor? You are not required to answer these questions. I am gathering information, but your cooperation will be noted. Did you know him?" I offered my cigar-case.

He pushed it away. "Horn players do not smoke, Doctor Caraway. But, I did not know him, he was before my time."

"Oh, sorry, I'm mistaken.

"Others have told me he was talented," Taylor said.

"Do you know of any Savile Club member who may have had it in for Mr. Hudson?"

He suddenly became suspicious, and I docketed it for Holmes.

"Aren't you at this late in the game? His death was months ago, wasn't it? What can you hope to find now?"

To lower his suspicion, I smiled, put down my pencil, and said, "The case is still open. These are just routine questions. Who but his friends would know? It is not necessary that you answer, this is the Savile Club bar, not Pentonville Prison."

"Orchestra's are filled with gossip. I've heard Hudson met with a young lady, here. As you can see, this is a liberal club. Besides attendance at our concerts, ladies are also allowed in at luncheon." he said.

"When was this? Do you know who she was?"

"I was told it was a few days, a week at most, before his death. And that she was pretty in a Jewish way. The wife of that moneylender on Baker Street, I suppose." He drank his pint. "Of course, his Jewish connections would be kept hidden as so many of them do. And who speaks of such things?"

133

"Anti-Semitic." I wrote. Then I made a show of crossing off his name. Thanked him, smiled, and shook his hand heartily. Again, he made a show of strength. Then I moved to the table of the clarinettist.

"Mr. Marietti, I am Doctor Liam Caraway and enquiring into James Hudson's untimely death for Scotland Yard."

"Why talk to me?"

"Heavy accented Italian," I wrote. "We are interviewing orchestra members. Can you think of any reason why someone should murder Mr. Hudson?"

"There are many rumours, but I do not believe any of them. It is such a strange thing to happen to such a well-liked *signore*."

"Were you close friends?"

"The musical world is a small one. We all know each other. But I was not a close friend."

"Why is that?"

"Oh, just different crowds."

"September, last, at luncheon, did you happen to observe James Hudson dining here with a lady of the Anglo-Jewish persuasion?"

"I do not recall ever seeing him dine here, but I am not here every day. He attended concerts with his wife."

"Thank you."

I crossed him off the list and shook his hand. Then spoke casually with Mr. Dreyfus' clients, the five club members.

I asked, "Can you think of any reason why anyone would murder James Hudson?"

"None. It makes you wonder."

"Wonder?"

"Well if it could happen to him, it could happen to anyone."

On that expression of wisdom, I moved to the bar for a whisky. The bartender concurred that as far as he knew, James Hudson did not dine at the club. Well, it could have just been a meeting. I took my leave shortly afterwards. Feeling very proud of my day's accomplishments and with a full pocketbook walked to Baker Street. I was sure this would be helpful to Holmes in solving this convoluted case for Mrs. Hudson.

My lovely April afternoon walk was filled with parades of spring finery. A welcome change from the earlier activity of my day. As I travelled north the banal thrust and parry of deceitful gentlemen were fading like morning fog on this exquisitely sunny day.

When I tipped my hat to a vibrant redhead opening her parasol, I was reminded of a young lady I glimpsed during a recent stroll with Holmes through our favourite people-watching parts of London. His behaviour that day was unusual, even for him. I noticed that he spent much of his time looking down at the ground. Seemingly oblivious to the beauty of the changing season and the multitudinous variety of humanity within our midst. He was as sharply focused as if he were working on a chemical analysis. As was his way, he occasionally murmured or shouted exclamations over something that was entirely invisible to me.

Returning from my walk across town, I entered our rooms quite looking forward to afternoon tea. Holmes was mixing plaster of Paris on his deal table. His hands were as white as a ghost and his hair dusted grey.

"Ah, Watson, my good man, come! Accompany me to Regent's Park."

He ran out in a hurry with his pail and led me at a run across the street, and into the park.

"Ah, perfect, perfect!"

He squatted down by the path and spread his plaster over the mud. Then jumped up and moved further down the path, exclaiming with excitement as he crouched over other spots of mud to spread plaster upon. When his pail was empty, he sat on a nearby bench.

"Watson, yesterday's rain has granted me pristine footprints! Now, all we need do is wait. Sit down, my friend." He patted the bench.

He pulled a sandwich out of his pocket, carefully tore it in two, and offered half to me. Then he called over the vendor and bought us sherbet to drink.

"What do you think Watson, Lemon or Cherry? Yes, I agree, Lemon is best!"

It was a good sandwich once I disposed of the dusty fingerprints.

"Do you know that plaster of Paris is the best preserver of footstep impresses?" he said.

"Holmes, what is all this?"

"You will excuse a certain abstraction of mind, my dear Doctor, I am composing a monograph 'Upon the Tracing of Footsteps."

"Of course, the way you read the footprints, horses' hooves, and carriage wheels on Brixton Road," I said. "And Scotland Yard practically obliterated it."

"Exactly! Would you mind, old chap, to stay here and protect them from pets or children while they dry? I will return to Baker Street and bring boxes for safe transport."

In fifteen minutes he was as good as his word. He had brushed his hair, washed his hands, changed his jacket, and brought additional sandwiches and coffee, which he arranged and carried in one of the boxes. Also a large metal spatula-like implement. Immediately upon returning he crouched in the mud and tested the plaster for dryness.

"Another few minutes," he murmured.

Holmes joined me on the bench, poured me a coffee, one for himself, and unwrapped a sandwich. We leaned back enjoying our picnic as unhurriedly as if we were up in our rooms sipping Mrs.

Hudson's tea. He looked at his watch, downed his coffee, slapped my leg, and jumped up.

"Now, Watson, this is the delicate part. You must hold this box on its side and steady, as close to the plaster form as possible while I scoop up the highly breakable cast and place it in the box. Right? Go!"

"Like this, Holmes?"

"Watson, concentration, not conversation!"

Well, we got them back up to our rooms. Holmes placed them high up on his chemical shelves to dry. The grasses and other vegetation to be trimmed off once hardened.

"Doctor, the ability to decipher the message of footprints is of great practical interest to the scientific detective. Photographs of the plaster casts will adorn the cover of my monograph or one of them will. The rest will walk through the pages of my descriptive experience. I will need to work closely with Mr. Finch to define their three-dimensionality. He is an admirable photographer and just down Baker Street. Have you noticed, Watson, the perfection of this address? Close enough to the centre of town yet far enough to find such entrepreneurs?"

And I wondered about the variety of genius. Holmes is unique in every sense of the term. In the short time, I have lived with him, I have discovered there are no means nor callipers to measure the inexplicable.

Chapter 16
BURIED TREASURE
From the Journal of Mrs. Hudson
"Of course, when people bury Treasure nowadays they do it in the Post Office bank. But there are always some lunatics about. It would be a dull world without them." – John H. Watson MD. "The Adventure of the Three Gables"

23 April, 1881 St. George's Day

Digging deep into the garden, I found a keyring filled with twenty-nine keys, clumped together and caked with dirt. I took them inside to clean. Mr. Holmes had just come in, so with my grime-covered hands, I showed him my treasure. He took them from me, laid out a napkin on the table and placed them on it as gently as if they were a small, injured animal.

He smelled them and scraped off some of the soil. Each was a different key, none was a duplicate. To discern this he separated and held up each one.

Mr. Holmes said, "Even at this stage one may observe how the different metals react differently to implantation. But what have we here? This evil corrosion resulted from the hand of man, not nature's bounty."

He rubbed one clean and discovered it had been etched or eaten away. To my dismay, he drew a chemical symbol on his shirt cuff in pencil. It was sometimes difficult to watch him at his deductions and not make objections.

"Mrs. Hudson, you may clean them, but please guard these keys carefully for they may prove to be of further importance."

Mr. Holmes then singled out the keyring pocket knife. He dampened his handkerchief in the sink, cleaned and studied it.

"This is ivory. A spiral is carved into it. The distinctive bee-shaped spring of the *Forge de Laguiole*. Was he French? Mrs. Hudson,

138

whoever he was, this man was no brute. I would like to study this singular knife more closely." He put it in an envelope and thrust it into his pocket. "Now, would you guide me to where you unearthed the keys?"

We went out to the garden, and I happily showed him our work in progress, hoping this might bring him in.

"It is St. George's Day, Mr. Holmes, please cut yourself a rose for your lapel. The beds near there are where Doctor Watson is working. And have you seen the glasshouse built by Jack? He is such a useful lad."

He cut me off, "Mrs. Hudson, why are you digging here, in this spot?" He pointed down at it.

"To plant my tomato crop, Mr. Holmes. I take the same care with them that James did and dig deeply. I found the keys at the bottom of the trench."

"Mrs. Hudson, you must dig deeper."

"Mr. Holmes?"

"These keys may be from a neighbour, a tenant, or possibly a previous owner. Or they may be something else, and that is what we must determine. Is there a secured room in the attics? Would any of these keys fit a previous lock of yours? Possibly the seal that originally guarded No. 221B when you moved in?"

"That was seven years ago, and nothing was changed until you installed the new Chubb lock."

"It is laudable that you and your husband have treated your garden in such a way. To bring science to the uncertainty of nature is a most worthy endeavour."

He asked my permission to release himself from his jacket and waistcoat and rolled up his shirt sleeves.

"Thank you, do you have a shovel?"

"I do not understand it, Mr. Holmes. I put it back in the shed, and here it is dirty and outside where it could rust in the rain. I just do not understand it! Do I have fairies? Is James trying to contact me? It is upsetting. If it is not fairies or James, then who is it? I am the only one here."

"Quite possibly the street urchins, they help in your garden, do they not?"

"No, they would not come in when I am not here."

"Are you getting forgetful, Mrs. Hudson?"

"Mr. Holmes, I am 26. Who gets forgetful at 26? Are all women doddering fools to you?"

He briefly smiled, took the spade and began. I had already shovelled a foot or so down into the plot. Having been excavated before, the soil removed more easily. Three feet down, he found a bone. This he brushed off and held up to the light.

"The upper condyle of a human femur," he murmured to himself.

Despite his complaints, that 'it was not work for a lady', I helped him dig the rest.

I pitched out a shovelful, "Mr. Holmes, do you believe in resurrection?"

"I believe in science and fact, Mrs. Hudson," He unearthed another layer.

"Resurrection is taught in church and so many believe it."

"Mrs. Hudson it is your grief talking. Forgive me, but from all I have seen and experienced it is clear that death is final."

"Yes." I shovelled. "James did not deserve this."

"I would like to have known your husband. As musicians, we would have had much in common. From his music choices, I feel I already know him to some extent."

140

I raised my head and watched him as he threw another shovelful.

"Yes, I think you would," I said.

Four feet down he found a decomposing body.

"I thought as much!" Mr. Holmes said, "Mrs. Hudson it is time for you to vacate this grave."

But really, he need not have bothered. I climbed out immediately. I was dismayed, yet he was riveted by this find; every ounce of him was focused upon it. He treated it with great care.

The way Mr. Holmes worked brought to mind a lecture given by Oxford's Professor Bellingham on archaeology to the women of Newnham College. Mr. Holmes drew detailed sketches in his pocketbook, jotting notes around them: the position of the body, the hands and feet, the direction of the head. Then he carefully examined each part. Finally, without upsetting his discovery, he removed with tweezers a bullet that was lodged against the backbone, put it in an envelope and into his pocket.

"Straight through the heart," he muttered to himself. "This poor wretch was killed here and either fell or was pushed into this trench. Generally, it takes about a year for a body buried in this way to decompose to this condition, so this is a recent planting."

"During the time I lived here?"

"Without doubt," he said as if he were answering his own question.

With the grace and speed of a great cat, Mr. Holmes leapt out of the trench and helped me to a garden chair, pulled another up to it. He sat holding my hand, his penetrating grey eyes looking into mine, now filled with compassion.

He patted my hand. "But most likely when you were away. Did you leave the house for a time during the previous year or the one before that?"

"James and I travelled to *Picardy* in the summer of '80. We stayed in the Somme Valley and a week in Switzerland."

"Any other dates during that time: a weekend visit to your aunt, a musical tour?" He said.

"I did not always go on his tours. I wish I had." I dried my eyes.

Mr. Holmes took my other hand in his and spoke very softly, "Mrs. Hudson, one cannot change the past. It must be left where it belongs so its treasures might be found and built upon. You have a life to live. I did not choose this flat for its lovely sitting-room only."

I thought, *Sometimes this young man seems like an old sage. Is it the weight of genius or something else?*

"You are right, Mr. Holmes. You and Doctor Watson are godsends. We did not leave here again that year. James did take fishing trips. My holiday trip to Scotland was not enough time for this poor person to be in this state."

"Do you, yourself keep a calendar, a diary, or a journal?" he said.

I stood, brushing the soil from my dress and said, "Yes, I will look into that." I thought, *If I could only find James' Garden Journal.*

Mr. Holmes also stood, "One more question. Which crop was last cultivated over this burial site? And did it yield well?"

"Heirloom Brandywine Tomatoes and all the plants died."

"When did this happen?" he said.

"I will look into that. James made some garden notes at the time."

"Thank you, Mrs Hudson. I am afraid you must plant your *solanum lycopersicum* in another section of the garden. The pit we unearthed is now a murder site. Please alert me if the next garden bed you dig also brings up unexpected artefacts. I will be bringing Scotland Yard in today. Would you remain?"

"No, Mr. Holmes. Mrs. Turner and I are emptying our winter larder and baking pies today. You may reach me there."

Mr. Hudson's Garden
The Abundant Harvest

An excerpt from Mr. Hudson's Garden monograph found on page 230

1 August, 1880

Our ancestors did celebrate the harvest from the fall equinox to Michaelmas on the 29th of September.

In our London garden, harvesting is an ongoing event that follows nature's timing. Every reaping of every crop has its own welcome and its own duties. Some happily become the following week's meals, some are gifts, preserving appropriately, adding to breads, cakes, pies, or trading for the things we need. Mrs. Hudson is creative in her use of this abundance as our lodgers and garden helpers can attest. Our kitchen bespeaks the joys of the harvest all year long.

Note: We replanted Heirloom Brandywine Tomatoes in last year's bed. The rest of the garden survived our time away, but these plants failed utterly.

Chapter 17
WHAT I FOUND
The Reminiscences of John H. Watson, MD

"I want to teach people that liberty does not consist in having your house robbed by organized gangs of thieves, and in leaving the principal streets of London in the nightly possession of drunken women and vagabonds." – Sir Robert Peel.

Two hours later, Holmes and I arrived back at Mrs. Hudson's garden with Inspector Gregson. A constable stood outside the door. Policemen raised the body for inspection.

My friend watched their progress, nonchalantly smoking. "Doctor, will you examine this poor unfortunate?" He asked.

Following my inspection, I said, "Holmes, other than the fact the bone structure makes it a male, but smaller than the average Englishman, his teeth show him to be approximately twenty-five to thirty years of age and he was buried here about a year ago, I have little with which to work. Yet, agree with you that he was murdered here. Poor Mrs. Hudson, what a shock for her."

Gregson was busily writing it down and said, "Thank you, Doctor. Where is Mrs. Hudson? I should like to talk with her. She is the landowner, is she not? Or have you two rogues already wrangled her out of it?"

Holmes sniffed. Then he offered me his cigarette case and lit one for me and for himself. He said in a bland voice, "Gregson, I have carried out that investigation and she knows nothing about this. As you may observe, the garden is open to anyone who might walk down this alleyway. If something else surfaces, I shall be happy to give you any verification I find."

"Thank you, Mr. Holmes. I'll need that report immediately. We believe her husband was up to no good. Everything leads to his being the murderer of this man. He was a Jewish boxer, found dead in a moneylender's office. No, Hudson buried this cadaver in his garden. Who digs a four-foot-deep garden plot? A guilty man burying something he doesn't want found, that's who. We have a body, what clearer proof?"

"Inspector, are you saying Hudson murdered himself?"

"Mr. Holmes, this is an open and shut case as plain as a pikestaff."

Holmes flicked his cigarette end into the compost.

I was standing by the excavation, looking up at the windows in the neighbouring buildings, shaking my head. "How did they get in, and how did they unearth the grave without being seen?"

"Watson, our new lock was not installed then. A glass pane could have been broken around the lock for simple entry. That is hypothesis number one. But I do not think it likely in lively Baker Street. Number two is to drop into the yard by a back window. They are not even locked. Supposition number three is roof access from the adjacent building. The houses are connected and effortless to pass from one to the next. Number four they entered behind the post office through to Park Lane. The alley leads directly into the backyards. This seems the most straightforward yet with all the watching window eyes it is unlikely. And number five is they walked in through the front door with a key, which is the most probable."

I said, "The Hudsons' garden would look like an open invitation for this dastardly planting. This type of bed once dug would not be difficult to do so again."

"All postulations but four could have been carried out on a night when the residents were out or if they had left on holiday. Mrs. Hudson said all the plants in this bed died." To Gregson, he said, "Though Doctor Watson believes I am ignorant of gardening methods when the crops were transplanted here, they would have required daily care to survive it," Holmes said.

145

"Mr. Holmes, do you truly think anyone would go to such pains to do this? Aren't you making an elephant out of a fly?" The Inspector guffawed over his joke.

"Nevertheless, Gregson, it was the desire of those who buried this cadaver here. Who was he and what was their purpose in burying him here? And further, what does it have to do with James Hudson's assassination?"

Holmes lit a cigarette blowing the smoke, like everything he said, above the Inspector's head.

"Oh, Mr. Holmes, that's too fanciful. The only glue between the two is Hudson. He did it as sure as I'm standing here. You sound like a rookie inspector who just got his blues, throwing out theories to impress. Take my advice, young man, and stick to the facts. That is the surer way."

Holmes stood taller. "I have already examined the body. You may remove it, Gregson."

They wrapped and stretchered and brought it past the craning necks to their growler in Baker Street.

Holmes and I were left alone in the garden, both looking up at the windows. Holmes measured out distances using his hand to focus his vision. A blister had formed on his palm, which he surveyed.

"We are mere flesh and blood, and bone, Watson. Held together with parchment and purpose."

"Perhaps a plaster?"

He lay on his back with his hands behind his head, looking up at the buildings nearest this yard. Then he jumped to his feet and drew out each window's placement in his pocketbook, and returned it to his jacket.

Mrs. Hudson and Mrs. Turner walked across from Mrs. Turner's yard.

"Is it gone?" said Mrs. Hudson.

146

"Yes," I said. "And on its way to Scotland Yard. Inspector Gregson wanted to question you, Mrs. Hudson, but Holmes forestalled him, saying he had already done so."

She took his hand, "Thank you, Mr. Holmes. You are the best tenant in London." Then she gave him a cable.

"Mrs. Hudson, what is this?"

"With all the police at my door, the poor boy rang Mrs. Turner's door instead. The envelope is marked PARIS."

Holmes ripped it open.

> MONSIEUR HOLMES. FOUND THE BROTHER OF YOUR THIEF. IN HIS LAST LETTER 18TH AUGUST 1880 HE MENTIONED BAKER STREET AND HIS IMMINENT RETURN. LUPIN.

He slipped it into his pocket.

"Thank you, Mrs. Hudson, would you please list for me all who would have had access to these windows. Do you recall when any of the surrounding residents went on holiday?"

She laughed. "I might do better with Scotland Yard."

"They will not ask you such questions if that is what you mean," said Holmes with a brief smile.

She pointed to the appropriate window and between herself and Mrs. Turner they rattled off the names and addresses while Holmes scribbled them down on the crude sketch in his pocketbook. "Thank you Mrs. Turner. Mrs. Hudson, I would like you to leave the site as it is for now while I look into the matter." He lit a cigarette and we went our ways: the two women to the kitchen, I awaited the arrival of dinner in our sitting-room, while Holmes cleaned his hands and changed into tweeds.

When the sun dipped below the buildings, he called me from his bedroom, "Watson, look at this!"

He was leaning out his opened window. He grabbed my sleeve and pulled me next to him. "Do you see it? It would have been elementary for someone to carry this off from my rear window. Tenants from the other buildings would not have thought it unusual for a man to be digging in the garden, and during the hours of long shadows, that tree would completely conceal him."

Our planetree now shaded the whole of our garden area. Even though it was still daylight, anyone moving or working at this time would be cloaked in shadow and indistinguishable by anyone at the windows. We looked at each other and raced up my stairs to my second-floor view. Holmes put his hand on my shoulder.

"Watson, this is a distinct possibility. With a key to No. 221B, all he need do is anticipate the proper moment, carry the cadaver in through the front door, in a portmanteau or the like, and out through Mrs. Hudson's garden door. The theft of keys is a simple accomplishment by pickpockets. A wax impress is just as easy when you know the right locksmith. Hudson had nothing on him when his body was found. His watch, chain, ring, and billfold, were gone. Let us consider for a moment, Scotland Yard's battle cry, that the simplest solution is the best. Was Hudson only killed for his keys?"

"I dare say the thought of it progressing through her kitchen would not be an agreeable one, but as you say, the easiest answer."

"A former tenant would have complete access," he said.

"But Holmes the two previous tenants were not even in England at the time."

He patted my shoulder. "Nevertheless, our mission is to find this assassin." He dashed out and I followed down to the first-floor, where we met Mrs. Hudson setting out our dinner.

"Thank you, Mrs. Hudson. Have you always been so resilient? Most ladies would collapse in a chair or take to their beds over the kind of day you have had."

"Mr. Holmes, I am not most ladies, and you obviously know nothing of ladies if you can group us all into one like that!" She turned on a dime and left.

Evidently, the solar system was not the only deficient in Holmes' education. I chalked it up to this poor lady's grief and indeed her need for a comfortable chair. Though her steak and kidney pie was exceptional.

The next day, Sunday, Holmes in his dapper best frockcoat and I in grey tweeds enjoyed our first-morning pipe. I raised the window to allow his fumes to move somewhere other than my olfactory senses. I do not understand how someone with such an acute sense of smell can assault it this way. In the eighteen weeks we have shared rooms, Holmes has never once acknowledged the strangeness of this behaviour. And I have adapted to my flatmate's peculiar habit of saving the previous day's tobacco dottles and smoking them in the next day's first pipe. A remnant from his college days, perhaps.

Our breakfast arrived and Holmes poured our coffee.

He said, "Watson, I require your assistance today."

"Holmes, what is it?"

"Do not worry yourself, Doctor. It is a visit to an old friend, yet one I would like you to meet. Since Canning Town is our destination, please bring your revolver." With breakfast finished, we flew down into a cab.

Holmes and I travelled south and east to Canning Town through some of the city's most dangerous and disreputable neighbourhoods. The dockside community in East London, beyond Limehouse, and Canary Wharf, to the River Lea.

We passed rows of small houses with clay pipe draining behind each into open cesspools. This inadequate arrangement led to innumerable health problems. Its odour was mixed with that of commercial oil boilers, gut spinners, varnish makers, printers ink makers who were also banished far from the centre of town. Canning Town was inhabited by London's newest arrivals from West Africa and the Caribbean.

Above Turner's Market on Bidder Street, we climbed a narrow flight of stairs and entered into an empty room with nought, but an immaculately dusted and cleaned, bleached wood floor. Doors opened to a space lit by windows on two sides. Holmes instructed me to sit on a cushion against the wall and not to take any action.

He looked out a window and waited. With lightning speed, a short, muscled, gentleman emerged from the opposite door and with his cane knocked Holmes' stick from his hand. Holmes rallied and hit him in the face with his topper. The gentleman knocked in Holmes' knees, grabbed his coattails and unbalanced him. Holmes crashed to the floor and released himself from his coat. He leapt again to his feet in a baritsu stance and swept his long leg underneath the gentleman's bare feet. He hopped over it and crashed his stick across Holmes' back. Holmes arm flew out and knocked the stick from his adversary. Next, he pitched his gloves into the man's face, grabbed his lapel and threw him to the floor. The fighter slapped the floor with his arm and gained his feet instantly. Now they stood facing each other as equals. The little man began to laugh, and Holmes joined him. They bowed from the waist in greeting.

"*Bienvenue chez vous,* welcome home, *Monsieur* Sherlock."

Holmes returned, "Nothing escapes you, Sensei." And he shook his offered hand.

"It is good that it is so, Sherlock. The white villain who is determined to kill you by any means might achieve his ends."

"Danger is part of my trade."

"I would hope *Monsieur* Sherlock Holmes could tell the difference between danger and a vendetta."

Holmes gestured for me to join them. "Félix Calabar, may I introduce my friend and partner, Doctor John Watson." I shook the little gentleman's hand.

He laughed. "You are a doctor? A good choice for a detective."

"Thank you for intervening on my behalf. You have a proficiency with horses."

"And you Doctor Watson have much to learn."

Holmes said, "Sensei, can you describe the coachman?"

"He wore a grey mask that covered his head." Mr. Calabar laughed. "When he saw me, he thought a few flicks of his whip would have me crying. But it was he who leapt undignified from the carriage after I taught him how to wield a whip."

"Ah, how do you know he is white-skinned?" said Holmes.

"His wrists when he attempted to horsewhip me were pale like yours, Sherlock."

"It seems I am somewhat rusty. It would be pleasurable to spar with you more often, Sensei."

"I would enjoy that, and Doctor, you are welcome to learn how to defend yourself and fight alongside my most honoured student."

"Thank you, that is generous, sir," I said.

He laughed. "*Nous verrons, Monsieur,* we will see."

Holmes later informed me that Félix Calabar was a West African gentleman of honour whose long dark hair expressed his pirate origins. He had escaped from an Atlantic slave ship that was plundered and sunk by privateers. Proving his strength and fighting skills, he was inducted into their crew. He learned the art of baritsu from a Cuban pirate. Here, in London, he taught this jujitsu-like martial art. Holmes sought him out years ago and was a master of the craft.

Now he requested Calabar's assistance in searching the docks for knowledge of the cadaver found in Mrs. Hudson's garden and offered to cover his expenses. His teacher agreed to do so.

Holmes said, "He was described as a short, dark, shabbily dressed Frenchman, who may have killed for the jewels and escaped to London. Here he met a man, who murdered him for the gems. It would be simple for the Frenchman to hide in Canning Town. If there is someone who knew him I should like to speak with them. It is his murderer I am after."

"*Tout à fait,* of course, *Monsieur* Sherlock. *Les gemmes alure,* one who is lost to the gems' allure."

Calabar's baritsu class arrived silently, sat cross-legged on cushions around the room and waited for their Sensei to begin. He directed them to find a sparring partner and they began with bamboo sticks. Their clacking sound filled the air.

"*Je comprends,* Sherlock, it is good you now have a partner. But what defence does he have?"

Holmes put his hand on my shoulder, "Doctor Watson fought in the Second Afghan War; he is an expert sharpshooter with ample common sense. He played rugby so has his share of courage under fire. You, on the other hand, stand out wherever you go in West London."

"*C'est la vie!*" said, Calabar.

Holmes bowed to his Sensei and we left for a cab.

152

Chapter 18
BLUE BOAR PUBLIC HOUSE
The Reminiscences of John H. Watson MD

"I have hitherto confined my investigations to this world,' said he. 'In a modest way I have combated evil, but to take on the Father of Evil himself would, perhaps, be too ambitious a task." – *The Hound of the Baskervilles.*

DAILY NEWS
OUR BRITISH SOCIETY
by LANGDALE PIKE

My dear readers,
   Russia has brutally attacked its own people, and they are finding sanctuary here in our liberal England. We are indeed the Empire on which the sun never sets. As British subjects, it is our duty to decry this horror.
   And to laud the efforts of our resident Anglo-Jewish and East End communities in their assistance to these new arrivals. Lion-like valour firmly belying their British beliefs. Bravo Gentlemen!

I was seated at the breakfast table reading the *Daily News*. Mrs. Hudson ascended the stairs with our coffee and breakfast."

Holmes brought a cup of coffee to his desk, unlocked his drawer and held a large keyring of keys up to the window light. Concentrating on each one, jotting notes.

Mrs. Hudson answered the doorbell and Mr. Franke, the locksmith entered.

Holmes swivelled his desk chair around to face him. "Good Morning, Mr. Franke, come in and join us. Doctor Watson will pour you a cup of coffee if you would like."

153

He was standing at the door, wringing his hat in his hands. "No, no, thank you."

"A cigar, then. You do not smoke?"

Franke blurted out, "Mr. Holmes, I had nothing to do with the cabbie's key to Lauriston Gardens. I swear it!"

"Ah. Thank you for that tidbit. Now that is out of the way, let us get down to business. I called you in your professional capacity, to help me identify this large set of keys. Please take a seat Mr. Franke."

Holmes gave the key ring into his hand.

"Watson, please forgive my interrupting your breakfast, will you take notes? I must prepare. Thank you."

"Most are door keys, Mr. Holmes."

"Yes, one at a time and in order, please. It may seem trifling to you but to some, these trifles may mean the difference between Pentonville Prison and freedom." Holmes emphasised his last words as he dropped his dressing gown and held up a key.

"This key, for instance, is it for entry to a house or possibly a club?" He tied his white bowtie and donned his waistcoat.

"A club key. And the next also. This is French, and this a church," said Franke.

"Or synagogue?"

"Yes, of course!"

It went on like this, interminably, until Holmes had many of the keys identified and Mr. Franke could give up no more of their secrets.

"Thank you, sir, your generosity is noted."

I walked him out. He ran out the door and away down Baker Street as if a banshee were after him.

Holmes thanked me and finished dressing. He had quickly consolidated our notes. His concentration on such things was admirable. Where I should see nothing, he could fill volumes with such minutiae. And extract from it the answers he sought.

"Holmes, I think it was his own freedom the man was worried for," I said.

"No doubt. Yet, he gave me what I wanted. Each man's keys defines him and create a picture of their owner." He put them in his drawer and took a knife from it. "Watson, this distinctive French knife was found attached to the keys. What do you see in it?"

"Mr. Holmes, your cab is here."

"Thank you, Mrs. Hudson. Give me your thoughts tonight, Doctor."

He locked the keys in his drawer and then, he did something that alarmed me. Holmes rarely carried a weapon other than his walking stick. This morning I watched as he swiftly pulled the sword out of his swordstick, testing its ease of drawing. Then he flew down the stairs with it and into a rumbustious Baker Street morning. If he was carrying deadly weapons, he believed he might be facing a violent situation, and the case was becoming serious. Why in good Providence would he not involve me? I know he was working under an alias, but I could don a workman's apron or something. To my combat-experienced mind, his solitary stance was becoming perilous! When he returned I would put it to him.

But that night when he returned, he was late to supper and intoxicated. Holmes knew his limit; this was exceedingly irregular. Then he told me the story of his day with the orchestra.

"Every morning on my cab ride to the theatre, Watson, I put aside my life as Sherlock Holmes and don the guise of Mr. Keevan Sigerson, the affable, second violinist. In this way, I pursue my friendly investigation of the Imperial Theatre Orchestra. Every evening following rehearsal, I cross Tothill Street to the Blue Boar Public House on Chapel Street. It is the regular haunt of jocular members of the orchestra."

"Now, I understand tonight's queer jocularity," I said.

He laughed. "Yes, I shall need to water down my drinks for the rest of this case. My acquaintanceship with Mr. Ronald Taylor had progressed to the pub.

"Tonight, over many pints, Taylor began to tell his own story to his mildly drunken new friend. Watson, I paid the landlord to add a half shot of gin to each pint ensuring Taylor's pliant drunkenness. I think the man misunderstood and also augmented mine. Thus tonight's inebriation."

"He told me Taylor was a stage name. Most assumed he was related to Raynor Taylor an American theater composer. He said, 'Do you know how I studied my horn? It was my father's idea to keep me from mischief."

"It is laudable that he so recognized your talent," I said. "I was expected to squire our land, as he did. Cattle, sheep, horses, hiring the vicar. He had no appreciation for music nor I for his land."

"Y'all a squire? If that don't beat all. Here I am drinking with a real British squire."

"He was a squire. I am just a gentleman, like you."

"Big hat—no cattle? No, not like me. I'm a full-blooded Southern gentleman." I raised my pint to my lips, and he downed his.

"Have you seen war, Sigerson? It's what my father tried to keep me from. But it was no use, I fought for Southern independence when I was 'bout just a kid. Towards the end of the war, all of us was needed. We made a game of catching their Yankee grenades with our blankets and pitching them back. You ain't heard nothing until you heard fields of men dying in the night and the smell like the sewers of hell."

"Why you are a poet, Mr. Taylor!"

"Is that how you see it?' His smile widened, he whispered in my ear, 'Hell, you don't wanna live in Whitechapel with the Russian Jews! They don't even speak English and there's more every day. I'd just as soon live up here, but I have got a bus to catch. He threw down silver."

"Watson, there was nothing for it but to celebrate a round with the woodwinds. At their table, I humorously interviewed and crossed off seven from my list."

"Holmes, will you continue with Mr. Taylor?"

"With so many to sift through, my interviews must be brief."

When Holmes arrived even later the next night, he did have more to share about the horn player.

"It is a pleasure to speak with someone who was a part of American history, I said as I purchased the first round."

Taylor said, "There are heroes where I come from in Texas. The most powerful men in the state lead them. After the war, they fought it over again through the power of their superior minds."

"A much better approach than the carpetbaggers."

"Did I tell you 'bout them? They left us to the swindlers and cheats! All our crops and plantations gone. Everything we built; they would steal. Did you ever hear 'bout the Knights of the White Camellia?"

I broke into his narrative and said, "Holmes, is this a secret society?"

"I was the picture of innocence, Watson. 'Surely, an American musical society?'"

"Approaching half-drunkenness, Taylor studied me intensely for a second."

"The hell you say! Not until I give the loan of my horn to it. These were the saviours of the South. Our own brand of peacekeepers. They

157

stormed those who treated our Southland as the spoils of victory. My father took the Knights of the White Camellia to glory. They did the job the North never took on. Protected our towns and raided the communities of savage conspirators who defiled our beautiful land. Papa had me play my horn during these chastisements – you following me?"

"Very clearly," I said. "What a story, but surely you are pulling my leg. This would make a great penny dreadful, right next to Buffalo Bill, and Deadwood Dick." I slapped him on the back in a friendly way.

"Taylor snapped, grabbed me by the lapels, put his face in mine and shouted that it was all true."

"No one knows this history but them that was there. By my father's beard, I swear it!"

"I broke his hold, none too gently. Watson, maybe the ale was affecting me then, for he surprised me with a misplaced jab. I find in situations like this, that one to the gut and another to the chin does the trick. My one-two punch laid him out. Between the landlord and myself we carried the unconscious man to a cab. I gave the Whitechapel address and then the cabby and I carried Taylor up to his room, using his keys to get in. I then directed the cabman here." He stretched his arms above his head and yawned.

"Holmes, will you continue this dangerous line of inquiry?"

"Watson, I am weaving my web. Good night, my friend."

"Good night old fella," I said as I closed the sitting-room door and climbed my stairs wondering how this American was involved and where in Good Providence was this case leading us.

Chapter 19
A NEW ALLIANCE
The Reminiscences of John H. Watson MD

> "It is possible that I may have to ask your company and assistance upon a small expedition which will have to be undertaken to-night, if my chain of reasoning should prove to be correct." – "The Adventure of the Six Napoleons."

Mrs. Hudson, Holmes, and I have been residing most amicably in Baker Street for the past five months. It may be the dangers we have shared or how she and I have become tangentially involved in Sherlock Holmes' detective practice, but we look out for each other. Today, I discovered this resourceful lady has other protectors.

Mrs. Hudson walked out this morning to Baker Street and locked her front door. From my first-floor perch, I watched as she enjoyed the uproar that was her busy London Street. The view through her merry eyes gave me a fresh perspective. It was both singular and marvellous to share rooms with the protagonists of the story I was writing.

But as she reached the Underground Station, Mrs. Hudson started. I jumped to my feet for a better view. All of a sudden, walking beside her, was a smallish man, brown hair, light-coloured spring suit with his back to me. My worries evaporated as her face relaxed into a smile and they entered the tearoom. I returned to my writing.

In an hour Mrs. Hudson reappeared on the arm of Mr. Rosa the farrier. He left her at her door, and she immediately climbed to the first-floor to relate her story.

"Doctor Watson, it was strange. My former lodger proposed to me in the teahouse! Mr. Fiant was very forward. He even said he had affection for me when he was my lodger. When he lived here, I was married to James!"

159

"Mrs. Hudson, please take a seat." She related her story to me, point for point.

"I was startled when he just appeared there, Doctor Watson."

"Mr Fiant, please forgive my surprise,' I said. 'I thought you left London months ago."

"In a day or two as soon as my business is complete. But, Mrs. Hudson, here we are at Mrs. Lovage's Tea Room. Would you please join me for a cup?"

"For a few moments, certainly,' I said. And we took a back table in the quiet teahouse."

"How have you been, Mr. Fiant?"

"Mrs. Hudson, I am sorry for your loss."

"Thank you."

"When our tea was served, he said, 'I was glad to see you had no difficulty renting my rooms."

I moved next to her in the settee and patted her hand, "Mrs. Hudson, how in the world did he know this?"

"Doctor Watson, I asked him exactly that. He acted as if he didn't hear me and went on with the tea."

"Mr. Fiant said, 'Honey, milk?'"

"Honey, thank you."

"Doctor, as I reached to stir the cup, he took my hand and said, 'Mrs. Hudson, Marti, dear, I hope you don't see this as forward. We Americans are so much less formal than you English. I'm sure you were aware of my affection for you when we shared the same home? I ask – plead with you, for your hand. I am a rich man, now. We can make a new start.' He brought my hand to his lips."

"I pulled away. 'Mr. Fiant, this is entirely inappropriate.' I looked to the back door. It was open."

"With all, we have meant to each other?"

160

"I stood and swiftly strode through the door. Mr. Fiant threw down some coins and chased after me. But I knew these alleyways well and ducked through to Blandford Street. Before he could catch up, I crossed into the farriers near Camden House to Mr. Rosa. He was a friend I inherited from James. He watched over me with the fellowship he and my husband had built. As I entered the blacksmith shop, Mr. Fiant tipped his hat and moved on."

"Marti, how nice to see you,' Mr. Rosa said."

"You are my place of refuge, David. My former lodger just proposed to me at the teahouse! I ducked into your smithy to dissuade any further attentions."

"I am glad you felt you could rely on me,' he said."

"What arrogance!"

"That is the word, Marti. I wish I had been there. Is he still here?"

"David stepped out to the alleyway and searched up and down. Then he returned to the forge and finished shoeing the hind leg of an enormous, speckled Percheron, stabled him, and offered me his arm."

"Walk with me, Marti. We will get you safely home,' he said as we threaded our way down back alleys and arrived at my Baker Street door."

Again, I broke into her narrative, "Mrs. Hudson I thought your lodger was in America."

"As did I, Doctor Watson. He said he was a rich man, yet his clothes were the same as when he lived here. Oh, well, he did say he was leaving in a few days. Maybe that will be the end of it."

"If you need a safe escort in the meantime, please call upon me," I said.

"Thank you, Doctor Watson, that is very kind. Sometimes just telling a scary story aloud helps to take the sting out of it. Well, I have dinner to plan. Is there anything I can get you?"

"I am writing, Mrs. Hudson, all I require is silence."

Holmes returned at dinnertime after a frustrating day with the orchestra. That he had taken it upon himself to survey all of the musicians was an insurmountable task. Yet, with Holmes' diligence, the numbers were dwindling.

He walked in wearily while I was opening a recent delivery. Immediately alert he rushed over, put his arm out as if to save me from falling off a cliff.

"Watson, be careful with that box!"

"It is from my tobacconists, harmless." I laughed.

"Did you order this?"

"No, but they are reputable, probably an advertisement."

"My dear Watson, considering our dangerous incidents of late, a conscientious approach to anything out of the ordinary is essential."

Holmes took the box from me, checked its weight in his hand, smelled and listened to it, explored the bottom and every side without changing its position. Slowly set it on the table. Carefully he cut the string, which he rubbed vigorously and smelled again. "Doctor, your stethoscope!" He listened to the package for a long while. Then with a lengthy pipette, he stood away and opened the lid very gently, without upsetting the box in any way.

Nothing happened, no fuse. He selected a sample with his tweezers, divided it, and placed it into different test tubes. Some he set to distilling. He tried chemicals on the rest. Using the same pipette, he felt around inside the box with infinite patience for abnormalities, tacks, snares, triggers. He opened the window in his room, carefully closed the box lid, retied the string, carried the parcel with infinite care, and dropped it into the garden below. Still, nothing happened.

He excitedly muttered, "Good, that confirms it."

162

"Watson, would you retrieve the box? As long as you do not touch the tobacco or the inside of its enclosure, you will be safe."

I put on my gloves, recovered it, and gingerly placed the box on his chemical table, eagerly watching his progress.

Again using his tweezers, he held the tobacco beneath his nose like the connoisseur he was. "A slight odour of garlic," he murmured and pulled away from it as if stung. Then blew his nose vigorously on his handkerchief, meticulously washed his hands and face.

He tested it with litmus and found the basic tobacco had been dosed with acid. When he was satisfied with his conclusion, he finally turned round to me on his stool.

"Aha, Watson, it is laced with arsenic! One pipeful would kill you."

I fell into my chair. "Thank Heavens, I opened it in your presence, Holmes!"

"Yet you would not have smoked it, old boy."

"How do you know that?" I said.

"It is shag."

"However, did this man know you smoke shag?"

Holmes stood and took down from his chemical shelf, hydrochloric acid and hydrogen sulphide, and began neutralizing the poison.

"There is no evidence to prove that surmise, Watson. It may just be what he smokes. It may be because it is inexpensive."

"Or because he has smoked with you?"

"Watson, that fine supposition could be half of London, including Scotland Yard, the CID, with you yourself the most promising culprit. Finding ways to narrow it down would be more appropriate," he said as he cleaned the poisonous material from his

163

chemical apparatus. "Yet, it seems our mysterious friend is now going for two on one. And patently knows where we live."

"That could be deduced from the bomb under your bed," I said.

"If it is one man, he is a master of disguise. Neither one of us has caught a glimpse of him."

Following supper, Holmes moved to his desk to clean and load his pistol. It was at this point that he began to carry his revolver.

"Holmes, surely you can now bring me in."

He packed his new cherrywood pipe. "Thank you, Watson." He patted my shoulder on the way to his chair. "You have become devoted to my little practice in such a short time. I hoped you would, and I admit your talents do fill a void."

I said, "As a doctor, I also possess some degree of observation skill. And when you have your violin in your hands, you are introspective and incapable of vigilance. They are two different things!"

He smiled at me. "Remember that to my orchestra friends, you are Doctor Liam Caraway and a policeman. My own precautions will keep it from becoming treacherous, my friend. After all, what can happen in an orchestra pit?"

"If you need firearms, this is serious—I ought to be part of it!"

Holmes seemed surprised at my vehemence but quickly relapsed to his humorous view of life. "Watson, indeed, you are welcome to attend the concert this Saturday. Scrutinize the horn section. You will enjoy that we are performing Mendelsohn's Violin Concerto in E. It takes all my strength not to command the lead."

"I imagine many second violinists feel the same. Holmes, I will be there and shall invite Mrs. Hudson to join me, if it is not too soon. This man plays the French Horn like her husband?"

"Taylor will be well occupied playing solo on Haydn's Concerto for Horn. If she would join us, it may be of service to me. But you must not greet me afterwards. It is too soon to doff my incognito."

"That is clear, Holmes."

He looked up and listened like a deer suspecting a hunter, then smiled. "Mrs. Hudson, please come in. How much have you heard?"

"All of it, sir."

Holmes and I glanced at each other.

She sat on the settee, placed her hands in her lap. "Mr. Holmes, of course, I will attend your concert and play my part."

"It is not too soon for you to visit the orchestra?" I said.

"If it helps your investigation, Mr. Holmes, Doctor Watson, I am your woman."

"Splendid!" He shook her hand, filled another glass, gave it to her with a half bow, and we toasted our new alliance.

Holmes now stood at the fireplace, fixed us with flashing eyes, and rubbed his hands together.

"Now, our orchestra plans," he said. "I will assure your presence is known. You will have box seats facing Mr. Taylor's side of the orchestra. As he is positioned far behind me on stage, he will be able to watch me, yet I will be blind to him. All the more reason for your involvement. Maestro Smith will dedicate a piece to your husband. You will stand at this juncture. Watson, you will rise and offer your arm for strength. You are to project your innate gentlemanly ability of strong sheltering support.

"Observe our man closely throughout. Bear in mind, it is just observation, not involvement, do not confront him. Nor approach me. Maintain my alias at all costs. Most likely, what will happen is you will enjoy a lovely concert. Remember, there is little I can do once the music has begun. I must play it through to the end, but so must he. And I will join you both back in Baker Street directly."

165

Chapter 20
THE ORCHESTRA CONCERT
The Reminiscences of John H. Watson MD

"We were warm, as the children say, at that inn," said he. "I seem to grow colder every step that I take away from it." – "The Adventure of the Priory School."

The Imperial Theatre was on Tothill, the most ancient street in Westminster. It encompassed three acres from Princes Street to the corner of Dartmouth Street. Fronted with Eastern-style ornamental cupolas rising as twin towers above its solid classical frontage. The most distinguishing feature was the vast domed roof of glass and iron, similar to that of the Crystal Palace. Once inside, a large, lofty Winter Garden Conservatory greeted one with lush foliage. It housed the Royal Aquarium, Ronder Circus, two theatres, restaurants, art galleries, shops, a library, a skating rink, and as one might expect, was a very popular attraction.

Mrs. Hudson and I entered the festive lobby and ascended the red-carpeted double stairway to our comfortable box seats. Conductor Smith and his famous orchestra filled the stage. Holmes in pince-nez and beard was remarkable in the string section. In the midst of the pack, his violin precise and distinctive was plainly above them all. When Mr. Sigerson became Sherlock Holmes again, he would no doubt be missed in the Imperial Theatre.

The enormous ensemble was well-directed by the conductor. As Holmes predicted, I did enjoy the Mendelsohn piece. Haydn Horn Concerto No. 1 with Mr. Taylor's French Horn solo was the piece chosen by Maestro Smith as the musical dedication to James Hudson. We had a clear view of the horn section.

Mr. Taylor played the difficult piece well, a virtuoso performance. When his stirring call asserted itself above the orchestra it advanced and illuminated Haydn's melody.

166

The conductor introduced Mrs. Hudson, and we stood. She was regal in her bow. She remembered him in the instant that Taylor recognized her. I steadied her and witnessed the extreme reaction of the man.

"Doctor Watson, it is my former lodger!"

"Mr. Taylor, the French Horn?"

"Not Taylor! That is Mr. Fiant. What is he doing here? He said he was leaving the city."

"Mrs. Hudson, I think he suspects you of uncovering his alias. But why would he need an alias?"

"I do not know, but James distrusted him, not at first, but towards the end of his life. And James always found the good in everybody."

I thought, *This does not feel right. I have never seen a more appalling expression of hate. Holmes didn't see it. But he did see our reaction to it. We are in a poor defensive position, yet the crowd may offer some protection. Do I wait for him to confront us here, or do we brave it?*

"Mrs. Hudson, you will need to stay close to me as we move through the hall. Please, take my arm. If something happens, if we are separated, continue, and take a cab home, do not wait for me."

"But Doctor?"

"I can take care of myself, and I know you can do this, Mrs. Hudson."

We entered the large hall, every stair emptied into it through the gilded double staircase. In a matter of moments, a huge crowd surrounded us, and we were immobilised. Someone knocked my legs out from under me as in a rugby game. Mrs. Hudson continued completely unaware of our separation. Her lodger pursued, and knife in hand materialized before her from within the crowd.

She screamed! Sherlock Holmes appeared from nowhere and whipped the assassin's face with his violin bow. Thrust himself like a shield between them and received the knife's blow. Firearms were useless here, and the villain escaped in the crowd. Mrs. Hudson's scream brought chaos as the graceful slow-moving audience suddenly gained a hysterical momentum and pushed past the doors. She was swept along with them.

We raced out after her. Holmes hunted for Taylor. I searched through the chaos of theatre-goers and carriages, calling out to ladies similarly dressed. We failed to find her, all of Holmes' clues had been trampled by the crowd. Had a heaven-sent cab whisked her away to the safety of Baker Street? Back inside the now-empty hall, against Holmes' protestations, I opened my Gladstone bag and tended his wound. The shouts of the police and their furious rattles filled the air.

"My friend, I have made a terrible blunder."

"Stay still, Holmes. I must stop the bleeding."

"I should have brought you in sooner, possibly even Scotland Yard. My orchestra mates volunteered that Mr. Taylor regularly upbraided those of the Jewish faith. I closely scrutinized him. I knew what this solitary man was capable of, his silence, his loneliness, and how a boy raised to violence could kill again. He was the image of Faustian youth, and I pitied him. I pitied him, Watson."

"My heavens, Holmes, what you observe in a matter of minutes is more than a man can in a lifetime. Faustian youth! It is a wonder you do not take up your pen with such imagery." My battlefield experience behind me, I worked fast to apply a 10% iodine solution and sterilized silk sutures. It was clear to me that whether he asked for it or not, Sherlock Holmes needed my assistance. It was the humanness of our association that would keep *him* from that Faustian bargain.

"When he plays his horn, he is exultant, triumphant, a powerful, mesmerizing call. Watson, I contrived this little drama to uncover our

168

man. I am to blame for this fiasco. To have my case well-rounded and complete, I have put Mrs. Hudson in grave danger. All the while, I thought I was bleeding information out of Taylor; he was masked and manipulating me. I should have seen it! Your warning on the nature of introspection and vigilance was a wise one, Doctor. I have been as blind as a beetle!"

"Holmes, Taylor is an alias. His real name is Fiant, Mrs. Hudson's former lodger. She recognized him from our box seats. Tonight's concert was a carefully staged trap set by you to expose the blackguard. And you have succeeded." Again, I staunched Holmes' wound. My final stitch was complete, I cut the thread.

"But, at what cost? Watson, this man is an unprincipled villain! Capable of anything. Anything! It is essential that we leave before the guardians of the law arrive. We must be free to act. Let me go! Find Mrs. Hudson!" He called as he bounded into the night.

Mrs. Hudson conveyed her horrible experience to me during her period of convalescence.

At the overcrowded entrance, she had searched in vain for a cab. Then from behind her, Mr. Fiant hissed, "How nice to see you again, Marti." He held his knife at her back. "What an insane crowd! Did you lose your escort? As ya'll can see, it's impossible to get a cab. And here we are. Best for you to come with me right now, I'll take you home, for old time's sake."

"Why are you doing this, Mr. Fiant? Surely my steak and kidney pie was not so bad?"

The man laughed horribly and offered his arm, pushing her into his carriage. Once inside, he ordered its driver to the Royal Aquarium end of the building in Dartmouth Street. The cab rocked as she attempted to escape. Fiant fought like a cad and nicked her with the knife, blood trickled onto her gown, as she attacked her assailant. Mrs. Hudson, though small and dainty, had been strengthened by her seasons of proper gardening. She knocked Fiant's knife to the floor of

169

the carriage with her beaded bag and attempted to wrestle out the door. Knowing he was capable of murdering her, she fought like one determined to live!

He released his chloroformed handkerchief and clamped it over her mouth and nose. In moments she stopped struggling and sagged unconscious against her seat. Fiant tied her hands and feet and threw her over his shoulder. He carried her constrained and half-conscious inside the darkened aquarium and dropped her into a deep glass tank.

From the ladder, he yelled down at her helpless form, "I loathe your English steak and kidney pie!" Then he paid the cabby to whip up his horse and travel up to Baker Street. Inside our home, Fiant lay in wait like a spider within his deep web.

As the theatre emptied, I finally found a hansom. Rushing through the night my cab reached Baker Street. I opened the door, calling out for Mrs. Hudson. She was not in her ground-floor apartment. I jogged up to our sitting-room, hoping to find her there. From the second-floor stairs, Fiant leapt down onto me. With the force of his lunge, my head was slammed into the wall, and I was overpowered by the strength of the insane and the potency of chloroform.

Holmes arrived and Fiant threw my bound and semi-conscious form at him. In his attempt to save me from the result of crashing down our seventeen stairs, Holmes was compromised, chloroformed, and secured. We were left side by side on Mrs. Hudson's carpet, breathing the noxious drug.

Fortunately for all of us, Jack, our ever-resourceful street urchin, found the door ajar and dashed in. He threw out the chloroformed rags and cut through our bonds. We ran out and retched in the garden. Here we discovered a lantern still burning, and a shovel showed where Fiant had found his prize. My one thought, *This would not have happened if we had entered together!*

We sat in the garden chairs and recovered. Rinsing our mouths with water from the rain barrel, coughing out the drug and breathing in clean air. In between gasps, I said, "Thank you, Holmes."

"He left me no choice, Watson, which was his intention. He knew me as well as I did him."

"You could have—" I coughed out more of the drug.

He put his hand gently upon my shoulder, "Stop this, Watson! Do you think me so cold?" He stood and paced.

"Never again," I coughed.

We heard Jack storm down the stairs and out to us. "I can't find the Mrs. anywhere. Searched top to bottom, forgive me, Doctor, even your room."

"Thank you, Jack. How did you locate us?"

"The door was open, and this was pinned on it, sir."

> "You have one chance before she drowns, which will happen in exactly five hours. Good luck, Sherlock Holmes!"

"She must be at the Aquarium, Watson."

"What if she is in the Thames? Or the Serpentine, or the basin of the Trafalgar Square Fountain—!"

Holmes held up his hand. "Even now, you question my methods? Use the next five hours to thoroughly search each body of water in London, if you like. I am returning to the Imperial Theatre. Join me there when you have realized your folly." We walked upstairs. Holmes loaded his pistol and pulled his jack-knife out of the mantle.

"Bring a sharp knife! Ropes swell underwater—will yield no other way! Watson, engage Prospero!" he hollered as he flew down to a hansom.

"To the Imperial Theatre, cabby, as fast as you can!"

Chapter 21
A WATERY GRAVE
The Reminiscences of John H. Watson MD

"What savage creature was it which might steal upon us out of the darkness? Was it a fierce tiger of crime, which could only be taken fighting hard with flashing fang and claw, or would it prove to be some skulking jackal, dangerous only to the weak and unguarded?" – "The Adventure of Black Peter."

Regent's Park was across Park Road from our residence. Jack and I took it at a run. The enormity of what I was attempting began to dawn on me as we entered through Clarence Gate. Jack had no such thoughts and whistled for his friends. We surveyed the Royal Botanical Society's Pond, the Boating Lake, and Regent's Canal with their help.

I spoke to the boys, "Do not enter the canal! It is so dirty that a boy fell in and was poisoned July last. Call me in if you find anything there."

Jack said, "Yeah, it was Joey; we mourned him good and proper down at Five Bells. Spread-out, gents!"

What had seemed at first to be impossible became simplified as these sharp boys searched the waterways. I thanked them, and what was more important to them, I paid them. Next, we cabbed into Hyde Park.

"Where are we going, Doctor Watson? The Serpentine is over there!" Jack said, pointing behind us.

"Right here, cabby." I entered Rotten Row Stables, Jack following.

"Doctor Watson, why are we in a stable?"

I saddled Prospero. "Come, old boy, we have work to do."

"What's this, a horse?"

172

"Prospero is Holmes' racehorse." I reached a hand to the boy. "Hurry, come up with me and we will cover the park better on his four legs."

If we were not here to foil such dastardly purpose, I would have enjoyed this ride. Prospero was a fine steed. As an officer, I rode a warhorse into battle. Luckily my orderly, Murray also had access to the lowly pack-horse that carried my wounded body to the British lines. I patted Prospero. Now it was his turn to save Mrs. Hudson if he could. We thundered around the perimeter of the Serpentine including the Long Water and Kensington Gardens Round Pond. But no trace of Mrs. Hudson was found. Yet we left a happier, well-exercised Prospero back at the stables. His involvement granted us more time for what I knew might be an unconquerable obstacle.

At Westminster Bridge, Jack and I hired a River Thames boatman and his paddleboat steamer to take us to areas we thought someone could be secured and waiting for the tide to rise. The fog was growing from the deep green water, and I worried whether we would be able to find her, even if she were here. Our search began with bridges and docks.

Captain Manning was in his early forties, yet his daily weathering on the river brought premature creases and a tan to his face. He wore a sailor's cap, and warm river tunic, and brought us aboard his craft with the pride a workman has for his own endeavour.

"Welcome aboard, mates! Did you know, the river rises 22 feet on the spring tides and 18 feet on the neap tides? That's from London Bridge, that is."

From the Westminster steps to where the Bow Creek spills into the River Thames, the seaman plied us with a constant stream of information about the river and proposed search areas. With the fog advancing, I glanced at my watch and knew that we had met our match.

173

"Excuse me, Captain, but we are here to foil a dastardly purpose and time is running out. Would you know where a person might be secured and positioned to drown at high tide?"

"Hey, what do you take me for? I run a clean ship, no skilamalink. Are you accusing me? Get out of it!"

He poised to throw Jack into the Thames. I firmly grasped his arm and said, "No, we are not the jackals, but searching for a victim in danger for her very life! I am Doctor John Watson, and Jack is an extremely helpful young friend of mine."

"A victim?" He said and released Jack into the boat.

I looked at my watch. "Yes, our only clue is that she is to drown in three hours with the high tide. Can you help us in this fog?"

"Well, I'd best be taking you back to the north side. As anyone can see, in three hours the river will be at low tide, not high," Captain Manning informed us. And he pointed out the Thames mudlarks already waiting along the riverbanks to gather what treasures they could find at low tide. I made a note of their possible enlistment if I am ever faced with such a task again.

"Gentlemen, just one stop to make, you won't mind, a moment to pick up my Canning Town passenger," the Captain said.

He docked his paddleboat steamer. The fog kept us from seeing more than a few feet in front of us. Our Captain kept our attention occupied with his recitation of where we might find our damsel in distress. As if from nowhere, strong arms grabbed and bundled us into sacks. Both Jack and I yelled bloody murder, yet no one interfered as we were carried, and dropped into the first-floor of a nearby building.

"I doubt the boy will bring anything," a voice said in gutter French. He kicked me. "But this gentleman is sure to fetch a fine ransom. We will be paid well."

They left us there and locked the door behind them. With the jack-knife Holmes had insisted I carry, I worked at my heavy burlap confinement. "Are you all right, Jack?"

"Goddamnit, how'd I get snatched!"

"They snatched me also, but my knife will get us out. You will have a chance to repay them. And the River Patrol will ensure that Captain Manning gets his due. I may be new to London, but no one treats John Watson and his friends like that and gets away with it. Come with me."

Fortunate for us, the storeroom we had been dumped in held the makings of what Holmes would consider adequate costuming. Leaving my jacket behind, we both donned aprons and liberally applied flour. In a pinch, brooms and commercial cleaning supplies made fine weapons. Jack, I crowned with my hat. If we ever returned to Baker Street my derby would require a serious brushing. As Holmes had impressed upon me in the garden, these rear-facing windows were unlocked. Jack and I climbed down and entered the pub below as a Baker and his son on a break. He elbowed me as we found a table. Sure enough, the fools were spending my wound pension on pints and attempting to sell my revolver. I brandished my knife and rose to approach their table.

At this instant, Félix Calabar ran in, holding a solid-looking walking stick in his right hand. He jumped on top of the table and flew at the men. Kicked my gun from the kidnaper's hand, his fine aim landed it a few inches from me. I picked it up and checked that it was still loaded. He gestured to us to "stay back." Jack yelled out as the thief grabbed our rescuer by the hair. The little fighter lifted him from his chair and threw him into the other one with accompanying groans. In the short interval, it took them to regain their feet, he knocked both of them out with a fancy brandishing of his cane. He then tied them hand and foot. Laughing, he signalled to the landlord.

"Hand these bilge rats over to the constable and tell him I will write it up when I return."

"Yes, Sensei!"

Calabar returned my wallet and gestured us out the door with an air of authority. Outside he shook his police rattle in the air for a good thirty seconds, and said, "You are going about this all wrong! Where is Sherlock?"

"Who are you?" said Jack.

"No expression of gratitude? I am the man who has just saved your life! You are lucky those fools knew nothing of Canning Town. Boy, are you always so ungracious? Doctor Watson, you have left Sherlock alone!"

He hailed a cab from the cabstand and bowed to Jack.

"My name is Félix Calabar. I am the pirate who instructed Mr. Holmes in the art of baritsu."

"Though he is my best pupil, Doctor, the danger he faces requires your constant attention. But there is time now only for action. Where is Sherlock? Doctor Watson, do I make myself clear?"

"Yes! And what's more, I agree with you. He is in the Imperial Theatre."

Calabar said, "Get in and you can explain everything you know about the Imperial Theatre on the way. Robert, take the Thames Path, Narrow Street, and the like which should allow you to travel as fast as you can to the West End."

"Yes, Sensei!" He whipped up his horse.

"And who is this knave?"

Jack introduced his sorry self and Calabar patted his head.

Jack flicked him away, and Calabar grabbed his wrist in a way that completely put Jack at his mercy. "You are well-named, knave! I can teach you to fight and then you will be of much more use to Sherlock." He let him go.

Jack said, "Do you mean that? I can't pay you."

Calabar waved it away.

I told him what little I knew. When we arrived, we found the side entrance Holmes had jemmied open. Followed our noses as we tramped through the ring of the Rounder Circus, with its dangerous human cannonball and high-wire paraphernalia, the ropes and net were especially harrowing in the dark. Caged animals awakened and complained at our presence. It was an unreal world in the shadowy theatre. I imagined I saw shapes moving at the edges of my sight, but I had not Holmes' night sight. The sharp zoo smell with the basest animal noises contrasted in the afternoons with the most ethereal music played by our best musicians. We tripped over a grizzly trail of dead carnivores. Now, I knew what I had seen.

Above it all, we heard a sound that curdled our blood! The roar of a lion can be heard over five miles. This beast was not caged and ahead of us! It reverberated throughout the enormous building. Then another joined it. Calabar urged us to cut down the net and rushed at once towards the sound. We carried the heavy net to where Holmes was staring down two of the biggest lions I have ever seen.

"My knife just enrages them, and my pistol is empty, Doctor."

Calabar leapt to the top of a cage and began singing softly in French. I climbed up, Jack fed us the net, and together we surprised and trapped the lions.

"I am glad for your involvement, Sensei. Beware, the *Panthera* has been released. Some of the cats are docile, but not all. Jack stay close to me!" Holmes said, "Watson, your revolver! To the Royal Aquarium, gentlemen! Hurry!"

Holmes immediately raced to the west end of the building. Jack and Calabar were keeping pace, and in this three-acre building, I followed behind, my revolver drawn. There were lights ahead, and Holmes found an occupied office. Lily Langtry was in conversation with a gentleman. Holmes bowed to her distinguished visitor.

From the door, a commanding voice said, "How may I be of service, Sherlock?"

Holmes enlisted the beautiful Miss Langtry and her gentleman, the Prince of Wales. On hearing of the uncaged animals, His Royal Highness loaded rifles with the excitement of a big game hunter. They joined our motley band in the quest to find Mrs. Hudson.

"Lily, you would enable our search considerably if you could direct us to the aquarium lights. We have reason to believe someone is being held captive, their life endangered."

She scolded him, "Sherlock, I believe to truly gain your attention. I must be bound or bleeding. But, of course, I will join your campaign and I offer a prize to whoever finds the victim first."

Miss Langtry took Holmes' arm, while the Prince of Wales led our charge to rescue Mrs. Hudson. His Royal Highness informed us the aquarium's unique water system design had experienced operating difficulties from the first. When we arrived, there were thirteen large tanks in differing stages of untenanted emptiness. He ordered us to quickly search each of the glass tanks. The Prince of Wales was obviously familiar with this attraction and instantly found Mrs. Hudson. We were summoned to carry her out.

Our poor Mrs. Hudson was awake, weary, and cold. Water that was inadequately filling the tank had swirled her chloroformed rag away. A thin trickle of blood from a cut below her neck showed how cruelly the villain had used her. I would shortly ascertain the seriousness of her ill-treatment. Of first importance was staunching the blood and her restoration to a safe human temperature.

From out of the darkness, a silent panther leapt at Jack, Calabar, knocked him down and faced the big cat. In the next instant, our hunter showed his worth by shooting the terrifying animal. Calabar's jacket, waistcoat and blouse were stained with blood, slashed by the animal's claws.

From the ladder, I yelled, "Miss Lilly please find a clean blouse. Jack press it tightly to Calabar's wounds." Keep pressing until I can get to him.

Holmes and I scaled the slippery barrier via ladder, cut the ropes that bound Mrs. Hudson, and brought her out of her glass-enclosed gaol. My finger on her thready pulse where the life trickled thin and small. The incised wound was not injurious, and I could attend it in the carriage. The ever-resourceful Lily Langtry produced a blanket and wrapped it about our Mrs. Hudson.

I surveyed Calabar's wounds. The bleeding was stanching thanks to Jack. This meant the gouges were not as deep as I feared. But those claws held the danger of infection and he needed immediate treatment. Jack ran out the nearest exit and hailed a carriage. We brought Mrs. Hudson out and Holmes helped Calabar into it.

"Sensei, this is Doctor Watson's finest skill."

Holmes exchanged revolvers with me and sent us on our way. Jack and I escorted this precious lady and the little pirate home to Baker Street. The boy held and patted her hand the entire way.

Chapter 22
HEALING MRS. HUDSON
The Reminiscences of John H. Watson, MD

"Our simple life and peaceful, healthy routine were violently interrupted." – "The Adventure of the Devil's Foot."

In our Baker Street abode, I concluded a thorough examination and diagnosis of Mrs. Hudson's state of health. She swooned in the cab, and I carried her to our settee. My patient's eyelids began to shiver open with the sharp ammonia I intermittently passed beneath her nose. Soon she looked up at me with recognition. She attempted to rise under her own power, her pale face a mixture of gratitude and defiance. Realizing her weakness prevented this she nevertheless objected, saying that she was fine and tried to wave me away.

"Do not fuss, Doctor. I am quite restored. A good meal and a good night's sleep will cure me," she said while shivering in front of a blazing fire.

I shook down the thermometer and gently introduced it under her tongue. Then patted her hand.

"Mrs. Hudson, surely that is my decision." I knew well how such trauma can lead to severe complications and directed her into her warmest, most comfortable clothes and dressing gown. I drew out the thermometer and did not like what I saw. This was hypothermia.

Jack became my dresser and our maid, Molly, my nurse.

"Molly you are to oversee this process immediately and to rub the warming embrocation I am preparing on her extremities." Following my orders, she fetched woollen and flannel clothes, warm socks, a wool hat, gloves, and extra blankets.

"On no account is Mrs. Hudson to wear either a corset or bustle for the whole of her recovery." If I had the power to influence their condemnation altogether, I would.

180

Jack and I retired to Holmes' bedroom while Molly carried out my mandates. Calabar was lying in Holmes' bed. He was a small man, yet every muscle was defined, I would not like to take him on in a fight. I now began with Jack's assistance to clean, disinfect, and sew his wounds. He learned quickly and his rapt attention at this task suggested a possible future for him.

"Mr. Calabar, I use Doctor Lister's antiseptic approach, so you have nothing to worry about. But the healing of your wounds will require you to remain here for at least three days. I will disinfect your lacerations and sew where necessary. Then apply carbolic acid."

"Do your worst, Doctor!"

Jack handed him a second glass of brandy, which he downed. We prepped with carbolic soap. I soaked the silk thread in iodoform, cleaned my tools in undiluted carbolic acid. Cleaned and flushed with water, then painted the deep gashes with iodoform. I was glad for my restored supplies as the stitches used much of my thread. Calabar passed out I think during the 40th, but I was far from done. Finally, we soaked Mrs. Hudson's clean cotton towels in diluted carbolic acid and applied them to Calabar's back. I knew the edges of the wounds might show mild burning by the carbolic acid. But compared with death from infection, what was this?

Molly knocked on Holmes' bedroom door.

"Doctor, you may come in, now."

Jack and I secured the little pirate to the bed. Jack's gratitude for the man's sacrifice had made him extremely attentive and a very fine helper for me. I left him to clean up and entered my sitting-room.

Mrs. Hudson was now wrapped in warm clothes, blankets, massaged with warming liniment, and ensconced in front of Molly's blazing fire.

"Mrs. Hudson, absolute rest is my prescription. You are forbidden to cook, clean, or do work of any kind, nor climb stairs, or serve us for a period of at least a week, most likely two. You are not to set foot in your kitchen or your garden. I will check on you daily. Please inform me if you have trouble sleeping, and I will administer God's own medicine."

"Doctor John Watson!" she said with a weak attempt at authority.

I held her hand and patted it. *Still very cold.* "Presently, I am much more than your tenant. I am your attending physician." I sent Molly up for my extra blankets and wrapped them about her. Then mixed a Linus powder in water. "Take this first. It will stimulate you towards healing. My next medication is this half glass of brandy. My dear Mrs. Hudson, you are suffering from the Aquarium's dismal damp cold and the effects of the chloroform gas. You are a strong young woman, and recovery should be swift. Without my attention, you would require hospitalization. The shock you have received requires a long rest for a full recovery. I recommend bringing in a relative."

The poor lady was exhausted from her ordeal and fell asleep in our settee. She probably had not heard most of my instructions.

From Holmes' bedroom, Mr. Calabar was yelling, calling me things for which I had no knowledge. I braced myself to face him and opened the door.

"Doctor Watson! What is this! No one ties me up like a dog and lives! Least of all a man who cannot even fight! You bound me to Holmes' bed! I am not a practical joke to play on him! I am Calabar!"

"Mr. Calabar, today you are my patient. If you continue in that manner, you will destroy all my stitches. And I am out of thread. I will release you."

I moved closer and untied him. As soon as he was free, he somehow tripped me onto the carpet and before I knew it tied my hands behind me with gauze. I tried to free myself but was helpless.

182

"Ha, ha, Doctor! You will treat Calabar with respect, or I will use you as a practice dummy! My newest students would beat you! How will you fight when the villain takes your gun away? Just as weakly as you are now. And what of Sherlock with a partner who cannot fight? I saw the fear in your face in Marylebone Road!" And he laughed so hard I worried for his stitches.

He sat down hard on the bed, his pained eyes showing the extent of his injuries. I gained my feet and demanded he release me, which he did. I asked if he had any pain.

"What do you think, Doctor?"

I examined his stitches and staunched the blood that had seeped from his wounds. Then reapplied new carbolic acid towels. I told him I would give him morphia for the pain to allow him to sleep.

I called for Jack and instructed him on what to expect. Then administered morphia to Calabar. Molly, I asked to remain by Mrs. Hudson's side until I returned.

Calabar was right, Holmes was alone. I loaded his Webley revolver.

Chapter 23
WEST END TOUR DE FORCE
Sherlock Holmes Reports

Forgive me, dear reader for abandoning my post. I am a doctor first and with our wounded, my attentions must go there. Holmes assured me that he was more than capable of reciting this passage. In haste I confer this to you in Sherlock Holmes' own words. – John H. Watson MD.

The injured are in Watson's capable hands. As we are now deep in the horror of the thing, his other talents are sorely missed. And I am saddled with imbeciles!

His Royal Highness said, "My God, Lily, that was the very tank where the deceased whale was exhibited." He laughed! "Do you remember it? The stench! The Aquarium could never sustain fish. It was their most famous attraction."

Lily Langtry awarded a kiss to the Prince of Wales for rescuing Mrs. Hudson.

At my insistence that time was of the essence, His Royal Highness' invited us into his fast carriage drawn by a glossy matched pair. I urged the driver to travel northwest, past the Marble Arch to Brunswick Mews and Rocha, the diamond cutter.

Nonetheless, the theatrics were not quite over as, Miss Lily said, "If you leave me out of this, Sherlock, I will never speak to you again!"

Both of my charges were children and I treated them as such. "By rights, I should leave you in this carriage. Instead, I charge you both with the care of the other. But you must follow my directions to the letter and with the utmost consideration." I turned to the Prince of Wales. "Will you do this, sir?"

"I will, Sherlock!" he said.

Before the carriage came to a full stop, I dashed into Rocha's house. To my astonishment, this was to be my first view of the powerful Russian boxer. He was pulling Mr. Rocha up from the floor. I immediately went for him with a straight left to the jaw. The big man took it on the chin. No glass jaw here.

Rocha, laughing, grabbed my arm to stop me, "Relax, my friend. The Bear is here to assist me. He is my protégé. Yet, I see that this match would be welcomed by you. It could be arranged, Mr. Holmes."

While we spoke, Miss Lily cleansed and bandaged Mr. Rocha's wounds. My admiration for the lady grew.

Rocha had stood his ground against Fiant's demands and had been left knocked down and bleeding.

"This man is crazy to attack me in my home! But Mr. Holmes, I cannot destroy such an exquisite piece of history. Thank you, Miss Langtry. I approve of this gentle partnership, Sherlock. But go, the demon cannot be far—Bear, go with them! They will need your help."

"You are a brave man, Mr. Rocha," the Prince of Wales said.

"And you grace my humble home beyond measure, Your Royal Highness." And he nodded his head in a bow.

This social nicety was hampering our quest, and I was impatient to be on with it. "Mr. Rocha, where would you try next if you were desperate?"

"Dreyfus!"

"In Baker Street?"

"No, his home. Seymour Place the brick building across from our synagogue. You know where it is. Go now! Save them," Rocha said.

His neighbours arrived to offer aid and the four rescuers left Rocha in good hands.

We drove the short distance to Upper Berkeley Street. Outside Dreyfus' house, I stopped, put my finger on my lips. My trained senses immediately surveyed the surroundings. We were alone in the dark street. Lights were lit in the synagogue. No obstacles barred our way.

I motioned to Lily and the Prince to stand guard. "Bear, come with me, but you must not make a sound," I whispered.

Employing a Seymour Place ground floor window, I observed that the evening shades were up, and the drapes were still open to the day. I moved to the window, leaned my head against the glass and heard a man sobbing. Then watched with eyes trained to discern every shade of black night. Through the darkness, I could see that Mr. Dreyfus was alone. The signal was given, Lily and the Prince of Wales joined us.

I rapped my walking stick on the door and called to Dreyfus. He opened, wiping at his eyes, a derringer in his hand. Which he immediately pocketed.

"Please come in, you are most welcome."

Lily took his arm, "What is bothering you, Mr. Dreyfus?"

"Look! Look at this! Do you know what that message says?" He pointed to the synagogue double doors.

It was in Hebrew, I read it aloud: "Your wife is the sacrifice!"

"What am I to do?" Dreyfus said.

"Fiant is in the synagogue!" I said.

Dreyfus said, "Who else? He wants me to bring my tools to cut the emeralds. How can I refuse? My poor brilliant Amelia in the hands of James' murderer! And who knows what else?"

I addressed him, "Your Royal Highness it is your duty to drive immediately down to Whitehall. Lestrade, or the inspector in charge and his constables are now needed. Direct them to the synagogue. Tell them there are captives and that Dreyfus, Bear and I are inside."

186

"Yes, Sherlock," he said. "Lily, I look forward to your recounting of this adventure. Mr. Holmes, take good care of her!" The Prince of Wales directed his driver and moved south to Great Scotland Yard.

My foot soldiers now comprised two men of action, one man whose private concerns could be helpful or harmful to my plans, with Lily, a tenuous link. I turned back to Mr. Dreyfus, "Why did you not tell me you were a diamond cutter?"

Dreyfus packing his tools, said, "You didn't ask. And I no longer earn my living that way, as you see it carries appalling risks. Mr. Holmes, you are an avenging angel. And a good friend to have."

"You lied to me about Mr. Hudson's death. You were not here or in the synagogue that night. Am I right?" I said.

"Mr. Holmes, I did not know you then. The police would assume I killed my own nephew. You know their prejudice. Then, I did not know you were a man of honour."

"That is a story for another day. I would like Mrs. Hudson to be present when you divulge it. Mr. Dreyfus, your reticence for the truth has played no little part in our present predicament. The evidence you withheld would have led me to this villain and surely spared Mrs. Hudson's and Mrs. Dreyfus's endangerment."

Dreyfus put his head in his hands and wailed, "You think I do not know it, Mr. Holmes!" I watched as the man took out his handkerchief and wiped his face, stood to his height, showed his ready involvement by picking up his carpetbag filled with tools, and patted his pocket. "My human frailties will be forgiven by the Almighty. Mr. Holmes, my pistol is loaded, I am ready to face Mr. Fiant, alone, if need be."

I involved him in my assistance. He drew out a rough floor plan of the synagogue. With Bear's participation, we next formed a strategy to secure the safety of the prisoners.

"Mr. Fiant does not know he is surrounded by the families of the man he murdered. It is another advantage for us," I said.

We crossed the street and Dreyfus bravely entered the synagogue from the front. Bear, Lily, and I went around gaining access through the Rabbi's quarters.

Once inside the building, Dreyfus called out, "I am here, Fiant. Release my wife!"

"Come to the library!" shouted Fiant.

I directed him to enter, and Dreyfus knocked on the library door.

From within, Fiant yelled, "How do I know it's you, Dreyfus?"

"Who else would it be? These tools are heavy, help me!"

Fiant unlocked the door and roughly brought him in. Searching for but not seeing us in the shadows. Through the doorway, I noted the layout of Fiant's stage of operations. He had a back way out through the Rabbi's rooms. The Rabbi, and his wife, Rivka, and Mrs. Dreyfus were bound and gagged, each shackled to a library chair. To some extent, Fiant trusted Dreyfus, this may be of use. He slammed shut the door and we went into action.

Lily discovered the choir in hiding and they were added to the rescue. They positioned themselves in the centre of the synagogue. From the Bimah, the acoustics would broadcast the sound of their vocalizations throughout the building.

Instructing the choir with hand gestures and whispering in ears. Miss Lily coached them to approximate the noise of Scotland Yarders entering the synagogue. I advised Miss Lily to wait five minutes and then advance.

I silently applied a burglar's tool to force the simple lock at the back of the library, and the door opened.

Fiant turned his gun to the dark hallway and fired. I returned his shot and shattered the lamp. In the dark, Dreyfus handed the Rabbi a sharp knife. The Bear charged in just as Fiant held his revolver to the Rabbi's head and cocked it. The huge pugilist stopped in his tracks.

"Now you're with me, Bear! Or I shoot my captives one by one. Dreyfus light another lamp! Bring Mr. Holmes in and secure him, Bear. Give me his gun. Thank you."

"Squire Holmes, is it now? Not Sigerson? Where have all your pains taken you?" He laughed horribly. "One chance and you shoot the lamp? These others I may let go, but I'll enjoy killing you, sir. If there were time, I'd let Bear do it." He laughed again.

While seemingly obeying Fiant's orders, Bear and Rabbi Moshe surreptitiously carried out mine. They cut the prisoners free. All were now feigning bondage and awaiting my order.

"Dreyfus, your wife's life is in my hands! Hell, what is the matter with you gem cutters? They are jewels like any other! Cut the damn emeralds! Or live the rest of your life wishing you had!" He stood over Dreyfus as the unfortunate man set up his tools.

I now had five allies, four of whom were inexperienced. Dreyfus and the Rabbi I was sure would prove their merit in a fight. My wild card was exceedingly dangerous. Facing a man with a loaded pistol was not for amateurs. Instead Bear and I would work to keep them safe.

"Oh, bless your heart, Sherlock, you brought me the greatest boxer in London today. Bear, keep watch at the door," Fiant ordered.

The choir began their foot-stomping, door slamming, shouting masquerade of the Metropolitan Police.

"What's this then!"

"You and your men search those offices in the back. And you men take the other rooms. Now go!"

"Yes sir!"

Fiant's reaction had all my attention. The instant his eyes moved from his captives; Rabbi Moshe took off his gag and stood, "You

189

killed my son," he said, "If I have to strangle you with my bare hands, I will avenge him!" Fiant shot the Rabbi. He fell to the floor. Dreyfus and the women went to his aid.

Fiant screamed, "Your plans are useless, Holmes! I beat you every time!"

The choir continued: "That was a gunshot!"

"Inspectors, draw your guns and come with me. If they fire, have no compunction about shooting them down."

"Yes, sir!"

They stomped around the synagogue making as much noise as possible.

I said, "It is not looking good for you Mr. Fiant, give yourself up!"

Like a cornered animal, Fiant grabbed the necklace and bolted towards the door. In a split second, I leapt at the villain, using my chair to knock him into the wall. We struggled over the gun. He aimed a kick at me, but I blocked it and responded with a strong left jab. Amazingly, Fiant held onto his gun and trained it upon me.

"Get him, Bear!" he ordered.

Bear swiped a right at the villain, knocking him down. Fiant aimed and shot him in the foot.

"I repeat, get him!"

Bleeding across the floor, Bear apologized as he came at me. I threw my hat into his eyes and using his disadvantage against him, I tripped him, bringing the big man down.

Fiant opened the door and aimed. "Y'all are a nuisance, sir!"

In the same instant that he fired at me, from the dark hallway a Webley pistol blazed, and the villain dropped, shrieking like a boy in surprise and pain. Fiant's left patella had been surgically removed. Thankfully the bullet he meant for me was lodged in the wall above the Rabbi and his three attendants. I relieved the fiend of his gun, while Dreyfus and Bear secured him hand and foot.

It was then my partner stepped into the light of the open door.

"Watson?" I called out.

"Yes, Holmes."

"What about Mrs. Hudson?" I said.

"She is sleeping. I thought you might need some help."

I put my hand on his shoulder. "Thank you for that exceptional consideration, my friend."

Together we approached the brave Rabbi.

"Mr. Holmes, this villain has ruined one of Rifka's good pot lids." He showed us his makeshift armour. "Forgive me, I thought it might help if I cleared the playing field."

I took his hand and raised him from the floor. "Thank you, Rabbi Moshe. A wise and effective wild card."

Led by Miss Lily Langtry, the choir arrived, singing, "We should be ruled by the surrounding quiet calm that ascends without waking."

"Bravo, gentlemen! An accurate improvisation, you have hidden talents," Rabbi Moshe said.

"Watson, would you tend to Bear? He deserves some solicitude after my propitious baritsu knockdown." I then safeguarded the jewels. "So much over so little."

Mr. Dreyfus encircled his wife in his arms.

Miss Lily said, "My, aren't you Amelia Dreyfus of the National Union of Women's Suffrage Societies?"

Dreyfus said, "My wife is a Cambridge student." She smiled at her husband.

"And didn't you just publish a noteworthy novel?"

"Yes, Miss Langtry, and thank you."

"Call me Lily," she said.

I handed Fiant's pistol to Dreyfus and checked the American's binds were tight. "Hold it on him and watch him like a hawk," I said.

Fiant said, "Y'all just gonna' let me bleed!"

Watson fashioned a tourniquet and swiftly bandaged his knee. "Forgive us, Mr Fiant, my friend was preoccupied saving the lives of your victims. But you will be in the hands of Scotland Yard momentarily. This is your one chance to tell your story."

"My Knights of the White Camellia will avenge me!"

I laughed. "And how will they do that? In Pentonville Prison? On the gallows? Your charge is murder, and you will hang for the cold-blooded killing of two men. Did your knights forget to inform you the United States government disbanded them ten years ago and all their horrific brothers?"

I pocketed his mask. Watson stood next to me and kept an eye on Fiant. Bear happily joined us. "Just a flesh wound, Holmes, The Russian Bear will be back in the ring in a few days."

"And I look forward to that event. Dreyfus, I would advise you now to put your jamb-peg, and tools safely away in a cupboard, you can retrieve them another day. Do you know these jewels?" I held them up.

"The Empress Emeralds, they are exquisite, are they not?" Rivka brought him to a back kitchen cabinet where he secreted his tools.

"Behind every exquisite gem lie murders, tragedies, and monstrous deeds," I said. And I placed them in my pocket.

Fiant looked at his watch and rose painfully to his feet. He was laughing. "Just when y'all thought my story was at an end, Sherlock Holmes! There's one more hand to play."

"What is that!"

"Y'all are celebrating, but you have no idea. You see, I've rigged your synagogue with enough dynamite to bring it down!" He looked

192

at his watch. "It should go off in the next fifteen minutes. So, Sherlock, you have very little time to negotiate."

"What do you want, Fiant?"

"Surely you know there's only one bargain I can make, Mr. Holmes! Let me go and I will tell you where it is."

"I agree. Where is it!"

"Not so fast, Sherlock. First I'll take back my gun. And my jewels." Holmes handed them to him. "This little party will remain here in the library. Second, you and your Doctor will escort me. He can be the leg he shot out from under me. Leave your gun, Doctor. That's right. Now, if any of you follow us, I will shoot them both."

We closed the library door and walked through the sanctuary to the staircase near the main entranceway that ascended to the ladies section. This we took to the top. From here the whole of the synagogue was laid out immediately beneath us. Fiant directed me to the front of the loft and there underneath the first bench was the bomb.

"Now you know where it is." He held his gun to Doctor Watson's head and cocked it. "Now Doctor, my freedom!"

"But Holmes—!"

"No time, Watson! I will take care of this—Go!"

Chapter 24
RETURN TO BAKER STREET
The Reminiscences of John H. Watson MD

"Here they were safe and sound, their work well done, and the plaudits of their companions in their ears." – *The Valley of Fear.*

At Holmes' order, I accompanied Fiant out and hailed him a cab. From the shadows, an elegant carriage led by two sleek and matched beauties pulled up. I helped Fiant to climb in.

Quickly moving into the light, the Prince of Wales said, "I'll take that gun. Do not think for an instant that I will not use this. I just bagged two lions, a leopard, and that panther you loosed on us in the Royal Aquarium. They were much nobler beasts than you."

Then it happened. We heard the explosion!

I rushed toward the blast! "Holmes! Are you all right?"

The Prince of Wales joined me behind the synagogue where I was franticly yelling, "Holmes, where are you?"

"Sherlock!" The masterful voice of His Royal Highness called. Then he stopped and put his hand on my arm, "Doctor, listen!"

We heard groans and swiftly moved towards them. Sherlock Holmes was knocked out and lying on a patch of clover grass in a well-tended flower garden. The collapsed wooden spines of a Sukkot shelter lying on top of him. We moved them aside and I checked his vitals. Through the application of ammonia and brandy at frequent intervals, he awoke.

"This must not be heaven, Watson, you look like hell." Holmes gestured for me to put my ear to his lips, he said, "Keep Miss Lily out of this."

"Holmes, we will see you back at Baker Street, momentarily, do not worry."

194

Lestrade informed me later that Fiant used the diversion to attempt an escape. When the inspector came on the scene the royal coachmen had well-secured the villain and threw him in Scotland Yard's police van. Now, the Prince of Wales and his royal coachmen were bearing Holmes safely to No. 221B. And I had another patient.

The great synagogue was intact. Holmes had saved it and all the lives inside. The explosion obliterated the wooden portico which caught fire. The Metropolitan Fire Brigade arrived and pumped water on the smouldering, burning rubble.

Back in the library, I said, "Mr. Dreyfus, in the morning I recommend you file a report at Whitehall. This and your bravery tonight should clear your name with the Yard. Please leave Miss Langtry out of it."

To Mrs. Dreyfus, I said, "Madam, I invite you to call upon your niece, Mrs. Hudson. She is in convalescence from Fiant's ill-treatment."

"Oh, no, Doctor, how is Marti?"

"She is a brave and courageous lady and is resting, but she has a long road back to health."

I hastily wrote up as much of the event as I knew for Lestrade, and James Hudson's family witnessed it.

I wrote out a message on the back of my card. "If it seems they will detain you in this, Mr. Dreyfus, give my card to the officer in charge and call me in. Farewell!"

"Doctor Watson, sometimes the smallest things may become a disguise," Mr. Dreyfus said.

I shook his hand, donned the offered kippah, and helped Miss Langtry into my London black coat. The coat and my frock coat were identical to all who watched in Seymour Place. Mrs. Dreyfus wrapped a scarf around Miss Langtry's auburn hair, as she would her own.

And we left the synagogue through the back door. Out in the street, Miss Langtry and I approximated a moustached Jewish gentleman and an astonishingly beautiful Jewess as we melted into the synagogue crowd and escaped to a George Street cab.

We returned to Baker Street minutes later. I now had three resident patients who needed my care. Mrs. Hudson was relaxing in the settee surrounded by pillows and rugs before a scorching-hot fire. Only her face peeped out, and she was on her second half-glass of brandy. Mr. Calabar was resting comfortably in a morphine sleep.

Our versatile young friends, Jack and Molly, prepared a late supper. Thankfully, Miss Langtry arrived in time to season the meal. I then checked in on Holmes. But he was not where the royal coachmen had left him. I descended to our sitting-room.

"Holmes," I said, "You just survived an explosion and a fire. There are times when even you require doctoring."

"Oh, Watson, do not start, put your bag away. I am fine, a headache is all."

I mixed Salicin powder in water. "Take this after dinner, old boy."

"Uh-huh."

Holmes was in his dressing gown at his desk composing a telegram. He used his blotter, folded the form, placed it in an envelope, and nonchalantly lit a cigarette.

Miss Langtry brought up dinner and went to him, kissed his cheek. "At Dreyfus's apartment, Sherlock, you peered through a dark window, through which I could see nothing. You ascertained with one glance his situation. Together you formed a plan of action on the spot, and you led us through it. At the synagogue, you broke in as quiet as a cat. You put your life at great risk to protect the captives and thwart this villain. And with Doctor Watson's fortuitous appearance, you conquered him."

196

Holmes stood and said, "And Miss Lily, you approached three desperate and dangerous situations tonight with a calm head and the desire to alleviate the victim's suffering. Thank you for your most gracious assistance." He bowed.

The look that passed between them might have put the fire to shame.

After dinner, we lit pipes and I said, "Holmes, it was this man Fiant who went after us? He attacked us like a wild man, in our own rooms. It was providential we survived."

Holmes blowing ribbons of smoke above our heads, said, "His mind was closed, Watson. He chose to concentrate blame on others rather than seize the power to reform his own life. His rigid beliefs formed the very result he thought others were inflicting upon him."

"Watson, at the concert you met a desperate man, with no foundation. His eviction from Baker Street left his buried trophy beyond his reach. His repulsion by Mrs. Hudson. Doctor, we populated what he considered 'his rooms.' That runaway carriage you escaped was not a fluke. Nor any of his schemes. I should have seen it for what it was. Thankfully, Félix Calabar did."

"Fiant very nearly did us in," I said.

"Attempts, Watson. Therefore meaningless." Holmes thumped Jack's back. "Our salvation was closer to home. Young man, Doctor Watson and I owe our lives to your quick thinking."

"And mine," Mrs. Hudson said. "You are always a welcome guest in this house."

Jack said, "Aw come on, anybody'd do what I did. It weren't nothin." He pocketed his worthy pay and moved to leave after being refused a cigar and whisky by Holmes. I stood and shook his hand. Holmes did the same and then gave his telegraph message to Jack, with instructions. The boy ran down and out to the street.

Their fate now sealed; Holmes revealed the jewels. The Empress Emeralds were an exquisite necklace of three large emeralds inlaid in gold with smaller emeralds. Seven overlarge teardrop pearls hung from it—each blue-green brilliant was surrounded by diamonds. As a parure, it matched the jewels in the Empress's crown and earrings on display at the *Musée de Louvre*. Even the smaller gems were worth a king's ransom. I could see why none of our London diamond cutters would choose to cut down even the least emerald in these royal jewels. To Fiant it was only a means to an end, transform the jewels to unrecognizable form, sell them, and leave England a very rich man.

Miss Langtry stood looking in our mantelpiece mirror and held the emeralds against her.

"I am too scarlet for them. One must be beyond pale to wear it. Yet aren't they magnificent jewels? See how the light sets them aflame? Mrs. Hudson, I think your colouring is more appropriate. Sherlock, please bring your mirror to the settee for me?" He smiled and complied with her wishes placing it on a side table.

Mrs. Hudson parted the rugs and sat up. "Lily, you are so right! But please call me Marti."

Holmes and I enjoyed this rare bit of feminine primping in our bachelor sitting-room. Miss Lily's attention brought more colour to Mrs. Hudson's cheeks than any of my treatments. At the appropriate time, Holmes escorted this exquisite flower to her home.

After they left I attended to Mr. Calabar. With all the attention he had from my assistants, he was well-fed and healing. I changed his dressing and allowed another shot of morphia for sleep and the ease of his considerable pain.

When Holmes returned, Mrs. Hudson said, "Who would think Lily Langtry would be so unassuming? I like her. Thank you for introducing us, Mr. Holmes."

Holmes stepped to the mantel and lit his pipe. A smile on his lips, he nodded to Mrs. Hudson as he did. Molly and I helped her to the bedroom we had arranged in her new sitting-room on the ground floor. It was cheery and airy, closer to amenities, and stairs were out of the question. Molly fetched some necessities and tucked her in.

Mrs. Hudson drifted off to a Morpheus sleep. Molly patted her and stayed with her until she knew she was sleeping comfortably. I worried for her health was still very fragile, her present state uncertain. Her spirit was returning. Of course, it had never left. She was indomitable. My job now was to bring her health equal to it.

We whispered at the bedside, "Molly, have you ever considered nursing as a profession?"

"Oh no, Doctor Watson, all the blood, patients screaming in pain, not for me. Besides this job is the best for me. The Mrs. is kind and treats me right. And there's always something exciting going on with you and Mr. Holmes."

Thankfully, my reply was lost by a ring at the doorbell, which I hurriedly answered myself. I delivered the telegram along with my encouragement to Holmes for a much-needed rest.

The following morning, we were happily surprised when Amelia Dreyfus rang our doorbell. We were at breakfast, the only meal Molly could accomplish, that is, if she attended to the sands of the egg-timer.

Mrs. Hudson's beloved Auntie Amelia would indeed join our little hospital staff and offer her most favourable solution.

Mrs. Dreyfus began by cleaning the kitchen top-to-bottom with boiling water and Fuller's earth, plus the assistance of Molly and Jack. The youngsters uncovered an older set of dishes stored in the box room and she arranged all foodstuffs appropriately for her management. Medically this was far beyond the usual, but I understood it was necessary for a kosher kitchen. Most helpful for Mrs. Hudson's health.

These ideas have been applied over many centuries before Lister's application of the germ theory, which has caused such distress in the medical field. Ridiculous! Grown men acting like children while their patients die miserably from infection. If I were in charge of a hospital, I should bring in the wives of Jewish doctors to explain the necessity of cleanliness to these fools.

I am daily impressed with Mrs. Dreyfus' knowledge. If she weren't already an author and historian of some note, I would recommend she take up the medical profession as nursing comes easily to her. In between her responsibilities, she and Holmes shared a lively scholarly discussion of historical perspective.

She tutored us in how to manage a kosher home. Holmes loved all of it and graciously regarded her superb cooking. He immediately saw its scientific relevance, and it was just what Mrs. Hudson required. As a doctor, I could easily find the wisdom in this time-honoured approach to cuisine. I must say I found excellent conversation in her kitchen.

"Mrs. Dreyfus, your *Stories of Jewish History* is an exceptional novel. And doing well?" I said.

"All of our women's novels are well-received in London," she said drying her hands on a towel. "A phenomenon of sorts." She smiled.

I said, "I hope it brings you the freedom you seek."

She seemed to stand taller as she said, "You know, Doctor Watson, we are not waiting for the conference of freedom. By becoming journalists, novelists, and historians we find we have it already."

As a new writer, I had many questions and wished I had access to her knowledge before entrusting so completely *A Study in Scarlet* to the *Christmas Annual*. We live and learn.

Mrs. Hudson from her bedroom was a bivouacked general. Each morning against my wishes, she sent her young troops to carry out her orders. She elbowed Jack into the garden and hustled the maid to her duties. Our landlady enjoyed the planning of that day's meals with Mrs. Dreyfus, and I could see no harm in that. Altogether a perfect arrangement for the healing of our most valiant Mrs. Hudson.

This morning, on Tuesday, the 3rd of May, barely four days after Mrs. Hudson's ordeal at the Royal Aquarium, a novel type of excitement entered through our door. A royal liveried gentleman delivered an enormous spring flowers box and a case of the best whisky available in London.

Written on the card: "My dear Mrs. Hudson, with best wishes for your good health. Your faithful friend, Bertie."

Before apoplexy set in, Holmes calmly explained, "Mrs. Hudson our Prince of Wales was visiting Miss Lily at the Imperial Theatre. He joined our rescue and led the charge. It was he who discovered where you were languishing in the Aquarium."

Amelia arranged the flowers in vases around her convalescent bedroom. And Mrs. Hudson looked healthier than she had in days.

Holmes and I returned to our pipes. In Mrs. Hudson's new bedroom, she and Mrs. Dreyfus caught up on their lives. The laughter we heard filtering up the stairs was proof of this healing arrangement.

During my next medical examination, Mrs. Hudson imparted their latest conversation to me. And I was grateful to be afforded a glimpse into this unique panacea.

"Marti, one of the wonderful things about our Anglo-Jewish community is that multiple solutions and ideas coexist and even thrive side by side." Mrs. Dreyfus said, "We had no voice within our community, so we became the voice of our people to the world."

Mrs. Hudson said, "I am reading your fine and daring book."

"Thank you. For years we have successfully fostered schools for Jewish girls and our ladies at Girton College. Created charitable organizations and overseen the English schools in the East End. No one is stopping us. Our community's openness to divergent ideas grants us more understanding than the suffragists have with Britain."

"I think our English gentlemen, especially those in Parliament, could learn much from the example of their Jewish brothers," Mrs. Hudson said. They laughed!

"Now, Marti, you still need rest. It is why I am here. Please finish breakfast, and we will talk after your nap," Mrs. Dreyfus said.

DAILY NEWS *OUR BRITISH SOCIETY*
by LANGDALE PIKE

My dear readers,
There are times when one must shout to the rafters for joy at the ingenuity of women. We lucky Londoners are witness to a lovely phenomenon that is taking the city by storm. Marvellous women authors have emerged from the Anglo-Jewish Community, informing us of their lives and their dreams.
The novel, *Stories of Jewish History* by Amelia Dreyfus, grants us a true picture of Jewish life. And it is nothing like Mr. Dickens' version. Shame on you, sir!
There are new heroines among us, and they are conquering the inequality within their lives with literary justice. Some might say they broke taboos, others that through their intelligence and gifts they proved the pen is mightier than the sword. Still, others might say that it was time for mankind to take a look around and find a better way to handle our disputes. Perhaps even a Jewish one.
Brava, ladies! Brava!

Chapter 25
THE KEYS OF DEATH
The Reminiscences of John H. Watson, MD

"For murder, though it have no tongue, will speak. With most miraculous organ." – William Shakespeare, *Hamlet*.

This 4th of May morning, I opened our Baker Street door to the exuberant and fashionable figure of Arsène Lupin.

"You are expected, sir," I said stiffly.

"Doctor Watson, you must shake my hand. It is the acknowledgement of your *triomphe* over me. For are we not friends fighting on the same side?" He shook my hand heartily and I matched him.

"Forgive my precocity, Doctor, but my presence is requested." He bounded up the stairs to meet Holmes who greeted him in his dressing gown. I followed.

Holmes laughed. "Lupin, this is sorcery! How did you arrive after such insufficient summons?"

"Oh, *Monsieur* Holmes, need you inquire? Our methods are similar. I deduced I would be needed soon, so I am here to receive your call." He bowed.

"Ha! I congratulate you!"

He grasped Holmes' hand with friendliness. Lupin said with a bit of awe in his voice, "The jewels, may I see them?"

Holmes drew the necklace from its soft felt bag and presented it to Lupin.

"*Magnifique!*" He produced a jeweller's loupe and examined it under the light. "Perfect, flawless, like the love that inspired them. *Le Musée du Louvre* will be happy to see them again."

"Would you join us in some breakfast," I said. Holmes smiled at my change of heart.

203

"*Avec regret,* I have an early train to catch, gentlemen. As you know, I am not my own man in this. *Le Musée du Louvre* and *La Sûreté* have no patience."

We saw him down to Baker Street, shook his hand at the door. Holmes said, "*Merci,* until the next time!"

"*Monsieur* Holmes, take *exceptionnelle* care of *Mademoiselle* Langtry. She is a treasure far beyond words. These are trumpery pendants in comparison." He laughed as he walked out to his carriage which trotted fast away.

"Well, it seems another long day ahead of us," I said as we climbed to our rooms.

Holmes smiled and patted my back. "Old chap, I am most grateful for your care of Mrs. Hudson."

We entered the sitting-room as Molly carried in our breakfast.

"Doctor Watson, Mr. Holmes, your little gentleman has disappeared! What could have happened?"

Holmes laughed and then explained, "Calabar is his own man. He comes and goes as he pleases. I suspect he didn't enjoy the Doctor's coddling and left to return to his life. Watson, he is in no danger, am I correct?"

"He is well, though I would have liked him to rest a few days more."

"Is that our breakfast, Molly?" Holmes said.

"Yes, sir." She arranged the covers and plates on our table and left.

I poured the coffee, and he broke open an egg. I turned to him, "Holmes, is Miss Lily—?"

"Oh, Watson, her perfume still lingers around you, I see. Despite what Lupin insinuates, she is a most welcome friend. Our competition is far beyond any one of us."

"But you do not hold any honour for the nobility, Holmes."

"I hold all men equally accountable to the law, Watson, and the Prince of Wales even more so."

We were surprised to find Mrs. Hudson looking in on us from the doorway, and both stood to help her. It seemed this was a day for discarding my prescriptions. Against medical advice, Mrs. Hudson stepped into our sitting-room. Without delay, I sat her comfortably in the settee, took her temperature and pulse, and wrapped her in blankets.

"Mr. Holmes, I know you told me to bury everything, but I felt that Scotland Yard might need some proof as to the outrages you and Doctor Watson suffered at the hands of Mr. Fiant." She placed a scarred old black boot on the side table. "That day I neutralized the acid with bicarbonate of soda and once the bubbling stopped I cleaned it. The acid stains can now be seen."

He smiled. "Mrs. Hudson, please forgive me for ever doubting your intelligence or your persistence. And thank you. Lestrade does like to have something in his hands. I think my boot will do nicely."

"Mr. Holmes, there is a question I should like to clear up before the Inspector arrives."

Holmes sat next to her on the settee.

"I assumed you found out about the New Year's vacancy through my former lodger," she said.

Holmes patted her hand. "I did not meet Mr. Fiant before I joined the orchestra, and then to me, he was Taylor. Mrs. Turner hoped to assist you, Mrs. Hudson. She was gracious enough to address my questions."

We heard the doorbell. Mr. Dreyfus arrived and was brought in by the maid. He stopped for a few minutes on the ground floor and then ascended to our sitting-room with his wife on his arm.

205

"How are you today, Mr. Dreyfus? Your marvellous wife has been taking admirable care of our little household."

"I am very well, Mr. Holmes, and an exceedingly blessed man to share my life with Amelia." She patted his arm and moved to the chair I held for her. "Due to your involvement, the man who has harassed me for so many months is in gaol. Thank you." He went to Mrs. Hudson and patted her hand, sat across from her in Holmes' chair." Marti, I hope you are well."

"Doctor Watson assures me, I am improving, uncle."

"Watson, get down your journal, you will want to make a record of this." Holmes moved to his leather chair.

I sat at my desk considering the family tableau before me and took out my pencil.

"Now, Mr. Dreyfus, will you relate to us what truly happened in your office the day James Hudson was murdered."

Dreyfus began, "Mr. Holmes, you know I am not a fighter but a man of peace. This Golem, Fiant, crouched in my waiting room for his chance. He overwhelmed and secured me to my own chair. Then attempted to force me to cut the Empress Emeralds as he tried last night. He is a man obsessed with what he cannot have. Nor does he believe I am a man of my word. I refused that day also until he threatened James' life."

"How long have you been a diamond cutter, Mr. Dreyfus?"

"It might be better to talk about the fifteen years I have operated my small Building and Loan Society. My diamond-cutter years are as lost as my childhood. Soon, young man, you may also know how celebrity lingers." He turned toward Mrs. Hudson and placed a ring in her hand. "Marti, forgive me, I thought I was protecting him and us, by removing any identification. I have his other things for you, also, with the exception of his keys." And he placed a box beside her.

She closed her hand tightly over the ring and whispered, "Thank you, Uncle."

"Marti, your James, rushed into my office like a hero. A young man of such promise. He saved us all."

Holmes said, "Hudson came in through the back door, breaking the small pane of glass to open it?"

"Yes, he found my wife and Saul, my bookkeeper, bound together and gagged in the backroom."

Amelia said, "James freed us, then led us to safety out the back. I did not want to leave, but he promised he would save my husband." She put her hand on Dreyfus' shoulder; he reached up and clasped it.

"Mrs. Dreyfus, why did you not alert Scotland Yard at this point?"

"That would not be the first thought of our people. Though we are a well-established London community, some still marginalize us. The anti-Semitism in our police force is well-known among us. The Italians and Irish, and all who must live in the parishes of the East End, do not see them as saviours, either. Surely, you know this, Mr. Holmes?"

"Forgive me, it is merely my desire for the facts, Mrs. Dreyfus."

"James followed our voices into my office. He was a warrior like Judah Maccabee. Appearing out of nowhere, he threw his knife at once and hit this man's hand so that he would drop the gun. It fell into my waiting room, and with an iron grip, James grabbed this evil man by the collar," Dreyfus said.

"Being the gentleman of conscience he was, James gave the villain a chance to explain himself.

"He said, 'Leave this man alone. What is the matter with you? This will only wind you in gaol?'

"This evil man Fiant said, 'Get off me, Jew! You followed me from St. James's. You have been spying on me. You evicted me from your house into vermin-infested Whitechapel!'

"Again James gave him a chance and said, 'I warn you, there's a guard outside. I am not alone. Be smart and give yourself up!' This fiend leapt into the next room and dove for his terrible pistol.'

"At last, this vindicates me!' the wicked man said.

"Like a David, James hit him with a right jab to the solar plexus, doubled the villain over, and he dropped the gun. But he kicked James, who blocked his next kick. James landed another punch. The villain then grabbed a chair and slammed it behind James' knees, bringing him down. He grabbed the gun before James reached his feet again.

"Now, I'd just as soon shoot both of you! Dreyfus, you can watch your hero die, or you can cut the gems! Which is it?'

"Fiant pointed the gun at James. I told him I would do it and unpacked my old tools. He turned to watch me at my work. James knew I no longer had the skill to cut these emeralds, so he charged the fiend. But bullets are faster than fists, and Fiant shot him. Poor James kept coming and then fell bleeding on the carpet. Mr. Holmes, this horrible man, Fiant, was laughing like a madman when he realised he had killed our splendid James. Thankfully, Mr. Wetherby began pounding and rattling my back door, calling my name, if he had only come seconds before. This bad man snatched the emeralds, ran out my Baker Street door, and was lost in the storm."

Mrs. Hudson said, "Thank you, Uncle Dreyfus, James' determination to use all his powers to create something good is so palpable. His choice touches me beyond measure. This is why. One brilliant moment, one unselfish act to save his aunt and uncle." She brought her handkerchief to her face.

After their many attentions of sympathy to our stalwart Mrs. Hudson, Mr. and Mrs. Dreyfus excused themselves and went out.

208

Sherlock Holmes sat across from her in his basket chair, he lit his long-stemmed cherrywood pipe and thoughtfully blew smoke rings to the ceiling. He pulled an ivory-handled folding knife from his waistcoat pocket and passed it to Mrs. Hudson.

"Mrs. Hudson, before Lestrade arrives, I must know where you stand in this. Tell me the truth about this knife."

She said, "Mr. Holmes, I could not let you know they were James' keys. Like you, I was sure there was something more buried in that bed. He would have been blamed for the murder of the Frenchman in our garden. Allow my husband to be remembered in that way—Never!"

"After our installation of the Chubb lock, Fiant must have buried James' keys with the Frenchman." Holmes took out the keyring. "He used acid to disguise the key to the Baker Street door."

"My thoughts also."

"This knife?"

"A souvenir of our Picardy trip. James admired the *Forge de Laguiole,* I gave the knife to him on his birthday. Mr. Holmes, please understand my reasons for keeping silent had only to do with James' honour."

"Mrs. Hudson, this deception has cost me time. This is the key to 221B, and this to his French Horn case, the attics, the garden door, the study, my rooms, Doctor Watson's, Molly's, his club, boxing club, the synagogue, these two presumably for old apartments, Peterhouse music room, the Imperial Theatre entrance, and the rest. But there were twenty-nine keys when we dug them up. Now there are twenty-eight. Why did you unlock my desk drawer and take the twenty-ninth key, Mrs. Hudson? It seems more than your husband's honour is at stake."

"Mr. Holmes, I found it!"

"What is it?"

"I found James' Garden Journal! That key led me to my husband's safe deposit box at the Capital and County's Bank. His journal was in the box, Mr. Holmes."

Holmes looked at his watch. "Do you think this touches upon our case, Mrs. Hudson?"

She carefully parted the book. "James wrote additional notes in some of the pages."

"Mrs. Hudson, we have had this conversation before." Holmes was disinterested and drumming his fingers on the arm of his chair.

"There is more. I think this book holds clues, Mr. Holmes. I think it is a message from James and he is trying to tell us something."

"Thank you, Mrs. Hudson, I will look into it. May I hold his journal for a time?"

"No, Mr. Holmes. There is no time for that. You must read it now before Inspector Lestrade arrives."

She was right, as usual, the messages within this volume were important to the clearing up of the case.

"Thank you, Mrs. Hudson. Your husband has corroborated my evidence and vindicated himself. Now, I will lock the keys, the journal, and the knife in my desk drawer." He smiled. "And will not hand you over to Lestrade for concealing crucial evidence."

She said, "Thank you, Mr. Holmes, it seems we have both taken liberties. You are right to put the jewels in *Monsieur* Lupin's hands."

Holmes smiled, locked his drawer and said, "Justice is not served by fostering injustice, Mrs. Hudson."

Chapter 26
SHERLOCK HOLMES ELUCIDATES
The Reminiscences of John H. Watson, MD

"His quiet, self-confident manner convinced me that he had already formed a theory which explained all the facts, though what it was I could not for an instant conjecture." – *A Study in Scarlet.*

Inspector Lestrade banged on our front door hours too late to encounter Arsène Lupin or Mr. Dreyfus and was met by a curtsying maid. A moment later he appeared at our sitting-room door and was taken aback when Mrs. Hudson made no move to leave.

"Excuse me, I seem to have walked in on a private conversation. Forgive me, madam," said Lestrade as he hung his hat.

"You are welcome to join us, Lestrade. Yet you may want to get out your pencil," said Holmes, rising and replacing the chairs at our table.

"I will sit here," he said, pouring himself a cup of coffee and pulling out his official notebook.

"Doctor Watson's prompt report was bare bones. I have come for your explanation of how this American managed the murder of two men in London. If you would be so kind." He read from his book, "Plus the assault and attempted murder of Mr. and Mrs. Dreyfus, Mr. Rocha, Mrs. Hudson, Doctor Watson, and you. We have also charged the Russian boxer. It took six of my best men to subdue him. Mr. Holmes, is it true that you floored him?"

"Bear is in gaol?" Holmes laughed. "But he is one of the heroes! An integral part of my rescue operation. As you know such a situation with the lives of captives at stake is a precarious one, Lestrade. Bear proved to be a fine actor and was wounded for his pains. I hope your surgeon treated him well. Inspector, if you incarcerate all our new immigrants, Pentonville Prison will swell to the size of the East End."

"And where would we put them all, Mr. Holmes!" Lestrade shook his head at Holmes and began his shorthand account. "He will be released upon my return to the Yard."

"The other man presently in your gaol, Mr Taylor, the Imperial Theatre Orchestra horn player, once lodged in Mrs. Hudson's home. His true name is Ronald Quarles Fiant. This was why she recognized him at the concert." Holmes moved to the mantelpiece and packed his pipe.

"I made meals for the fiend who killed my husband!"

"Mrs. Hudson, maybe it would be better if I escorted you back to your bedroom? You are still so ill."

"No, Doctor Watson, it would not!"

"Then please allow me?" I wrapped a rug around her shoulders. "Whisky and soda, Lestrade?"

"Leave out the soda for me, Doctor." Mrs. Hudson said.

"Madam, you were a target because he assumed you and your husband knew of his shameful acts?" said Lestrade.

Sherlock Holmes waved him away. "Let us begin at the beginning. There are two threads which lead us to the same chain of events," he said, lighting his pipe, pulling the blue smoke through its stem. He faced us.

"One: The Empress Emeralds were stolen from the Paris *Musée du Louvre.*

"Two: The Reconstruction era following the American Civil War and how it moulded the mind of Ronald Quarles Fiant.

"The men involved originated in two different places, the city of Paris, and the State of Texas.

"Both men had similar beliefs: That they could take what they wanted and get away with it. Both would kill or cause harm to get it. And both found refuge in London at the same time.

"During the theft, the brains behind this *Musée du Louvre* robbery was killed. His gunman, a thug, knew nothing of the planning. He saw his chance and took the jewels. By the merest coincidence, he escaped the museum, Paris, and arrived in our fair city.

"Arsène Lupin has established the dead man's identity for *La Sûreté*. I have returned the emeralds to the Louvre by way of my friend." Holmes laughed. "For Napoleon, François Eugène Vidocq, originally recovered these jewels. He used deductive reasoning and his knowledge of the underworld, Inspector. He then created *La Sûreté* and influenced the formation of our own Metropolitan Police as well as others. Like Lupin, he was a thief. But more than that, Vidocq was an exceptional man who rose far beyond his humble beginnings. His eighteenth-century life has much to teach us in the nineteenth."

"Mr. Holmes, you gave the jewels to Lupin!"

"He is the one man who would not steal them, Lestrade. *Monsieur* Lupin is a gentleman of honour."

"I don't believe it! They are evidence in this investigation. Arsène Lupin is a thief and a murderer, absurd, Mr. Holmes."

"My connections with the underworld are of necessity more diverse and more satisfying, Lestrade. Lupin has helped me before in the pursuit of justice and will do so again. Your information is incorrect. He is an expert thief but is also a man of conscience. He is not a murderer and is my *entre* into the Parisian underworld."

"Mr. Holmes, when you join the CID, all this foolishness will stop. There are clear lines between the lawful and the lawless, son."

"To continue our chain of events. The man who escaped during the most recent purloining of this necklace somehow met up with Fiant, our Texas horn player in London. Hopefully, in time he will be kind enough to fill in those details for us. According to the notes I found in Mr. Hudson's journal, Fiant helped the jewel thief locate a

213

hiding place in Canning Town. He believed his chance to come into a great deal of money was about to be realized. Here we see the workings of the gems' allure. I surmise he enticed the thief to Baker Street with the lie that a gem cutter was on the premises.

"Mrs. Hudson, your former lodger murdered the French thief in your garden. Shot through the heart at close range, and he took the jewels.

"I have both bullets, Lestrade. The one you missed that killed James Hudson. I pried it from the wall in Dreyfus' office. And the one I found lodged against the spine of the French cadaver. They match. We found him, with Mrs. Hudson's inestimable assistance, in the plot dug by James Hudson for his heirloom tomatoes. Fiant saw the convenience of this deeply dug trench for his dastardly plans. He hid the jewels at the same time. Lestrade, I would look to *La Sûreté* for the identity of the thief who took a chance in Paris and paid the price in London."

The inspector sipped his whisky, looked up at my friend, "Mr. Holmes, you will have to share that diary with me, the bullets, and any incriminating notes. They are evidence! Like the jewels."

"Of course, Lestrade, Watson and I will tie it up in a neat package with ribbon." Holmes looked at me.

"None of your sarcasm, young man!"

"What that monster did to James!"

"Lestrade, Mrs. Hudson's former tenant, lived here in the first-floor rooms in which the Doctor and I now reside. As Mrs. Hudson's tenant, Mr. Fiant was best placed to observe the superior gardening in her courtyard. Come with me!" He rushed past his laboratory to the open door of his room, gestured to us with some impatience, "Come on!" I joined him, and we moved his dressing table from the window.

214

"Watson, this is your doing." The others appeared, and he theatrically presented his argument. He began with his back to the window and his hand on my shoulder.

"Early on, in this case, the Doctor alerted me to the fact that from my bedroom window, the whole of the garden is displayed." He turned round to face it and I urged our little audience towards the window. "You see where Mrs. Hudson has rather appropriately planted lilies? That is the burial site, Lestrade. James Hudson knew his lodger watched as he dug a 4-foot-deep plot for his tomatoes. From our vantage, Fiant realized it is the perfect place to dispose of a body. With the added benefit of possibly incriminating Hudson, his hated rival, into the bargain.

"Hudson's healthy mind saw Fiant's interest as curiosity for the garden that brought him joy. He could never foresee Fiant's perverted purpose. The grave was unearthed and ready all he need do was invite his landlords to leave the garden in his hands and then tenant the plot. He carried out this murder and burial in August 1880 while the Hudsons vacationed in France."

"Holmes, let us adjourn to the sitting-room. Your decorations are not conducive to civilized conversation." I offered my arm to Mrs. Hudson.

"What did you mean by 'hated rival?'" Lestrade said as we returned to our landscape photographs and comfortable seats.

"Fiant believed he competed with Mr. Hudson for Mrs. Hudson's attentions. Did you know he proposed to her only a week ago? He could not accept a gentleman of the Jewish faith on equal footing and did not honour their marriage. Every orchestra member I interviewed corroborated his anti-Semitism.

"Hudson's Jewish background enraged Fiant. He saw Hudson's position in life as an attack on his father, his beliefs, and his life's purpose. No lesser being could be his equal! It was impossible for him to accept. In Fiant, Hudson's very being enkindled an endless,

215

ceaseless itching that daily inflamed the deep hatred bred into him. In the unbalanced mind of a man like Fiant, it can twist his thoughts to a malignancy that becomes the motive for murder."

"Mr. Holmes, it's all very fine to theorize, but we need more than speculation to convict Mr. Fiant," said Lestrade.

Holmes repacked and lit his pipe. "Every day for a week, I met with him at the Blue Boar, a public house the orchestra frequents. His was a story of horror told by one of the perpetrators of the horror. Fiant was ten when he fought in the American Civil War. It is a most preposterous way of settling a dispute, as well we know. The chaos of the Reconstruction period following this war led to disaster and savagery in the conquered South. African, Jewish, and European immigrants were cast as inferior creations whose freedom was considered an act against nature by these men. In contrast, the Knights of the White Camellia were seen as the saviours of their Texas South.

"The rise of militarist bands of masked and robbed crusaders began a rampage of whippings, tar-and-featherings raids, lynchings, burning down their victim's towns, raping, and killing. Similar to what is presently being inflicted upon Russian Jews. Yet the Americans have one further horror on their Russian brothers, the use of acid to brand their name on the faces of their prey."

"My lodger was part of this? How dreadful!"

"In the middle of Texas, in the centre of this horror, stood a boy blowing his horn. Its call became a feared symbol of the monstrous Knights. Its wretched purpose created an inflated identity in this boy growing into a young man. He robbed a bank, and to escape imprisonment, travelled to London.

"I do not know what childish fantasy led him to London, but he did not find it. What he found were the realities of our present-day metropolis. Itself reeling from an influx of disenfranchised European,

Irish and Scots families who were looking for sanctuary and expanding the East End to bursting.

"He was welcomed in and into the Hudsons' home. But history did him in. When the Russian pogroms evicted people of Jewish faith from their homeland, they were welcomed into England. Hundreds emigrated to the city. His Knights on the other side of the Atlantic, the boy who played his horn at the burning of churches and synagogues was alone. On the 18th of September of last year, Fiant was evicted from No. 221B Baker Street by his landlord, James Hudson, for default of payment. He moved into the East End which also housed London's newest immigrants. I believe when he found that England was a most liberal country, this was his final unhinging."

Lestrade said, "When will people leave their quarrels at home and not bring them here? This history is important, but what proof do you have? We have to convince a jury, or he goes free."

"Watson and I have amassed over one hundred interviews corroborating this. We three, including Mrs. Hudson, survived his murderous assaults. My attack in Baker Street, December last. The New Year's Day explosion. He entered with his lodger's key. Our installation of the new lock did not stop him. Watson's phantom trampling by runaway horses in Marylebone Road. The vitriol throwing, plus the deadly gift of arsenic-laden tobacco. Watson's testimony of Mrs. Hudson's injuries alone will move a jury. And she can relate to you the meaning of this boot." He placed it next to Lestrade's pocketbook.

"Mrs. Hudson, February last, on Candlemas, I brought the token I ripped from my attacker's watch chain to a historian at the British Museum. He spent some time endeavouring to unravel this little piece of history. As months elapsed, I had written off this thread. Yet, it was merely a matter of time before it came to fruition.

"Yesterday, Professor Dewberry confirmed that it is a currency used by Southern regiments during the American Civil War. He had

217

sent rubbings to Professor Hezekiah Howard the director of the Yale University Art Museum, in the State of Connecticut. Howard, who made a special study of these tokens, was able to confirm without doubt this one was of Texas origin."

"Watson, if you will please read it aloud?"

DEAR, MR. HOLMES. THE NAME G.W. KLARKSON LINKS THIS COIN WITH TEXAS. WITH THE COLLAPSE OF THE CONFEDERACY OLD CURRENCY WAS COUNTERSTAMPED WITH THE NAMES OF THOSE WHO PROVIDED FOR THE REGIMENTS. AT TIMES, THE ONLY MEDIUM OF EXCHANGE AVAILABLE TO REBEL SOLDIERS. IT WOULD BE AS VALUABLE AS ANY TOKEN WORN ON ONE'S WATCH CHAIN. DETAILED INFORMATION TO ARRIVE BY POST. A GREAT PLEASURE TO COLLABORATE WITH YOU. GOOD LUCK WITH YOUR INVESTIGATION. HOWARD.

"Thank you, Watson. You see, Lestrade, where the supreme qualities of an artistic mind prove useful for the detective."

"Do you expect me to prowl through their dirty garrets for clues, Mr. Holmes? It is hard enough to follow the facts!"

"Yes, I see that. Nevertheless, this studious act of generosity confirmed the December attack was conducted by Fiant. I had the final thread. Since none of these incursions affected us, they were hardly worth mentioning. It was here my suppositions became certainties. I now held in my hands all the threads that led indisputably to Mr. Fiant's execution of the Baker Street attacks and worst of all, Mrs. Hudson's Aquarium imprisonment."

He unrolled a piece of cloth. "You may want this, Inspector. It is the Knights of the White Camellia mask Fiant wore when he harassed London's honourable diamond cutters. The same mask that he used to terrorize his Texas victims. But to a British Judge, it just might be the linchpin."

"Thank you, Mr. Holmes."

"The emeralds and their French thief, Fiant saw as his only way to return to his Texas home or at any rate his Baker Street home. And to do that he had to rid Mrs. Hudson of the Doctor and myself. He killed the thief and buried him and the jewels in Hudson's garden. He believed this planting was a ticking bomb that would destroy Hudson's life. He harassed London's gem cutters searching for one who would reshape the French emeralds. The night he molested Dreyfus, he also murdered James Hudson.

"When he shot and killed Hudson, Fiant immediately auditioned for his spot in the orchestra, adopting the well-known musical name of Taylor."

I said, "His father is the organizer of these hellish Knights?"

"One of many politically powerful, secretive, and brutal organizations that rose from the Reconstruction Era, Watson."

"I cleaned his rooms and smiled on the man who killed my husband!"

"Another whisky, Mrs. Hudson?" as I filled her glass.

"But Holmes, where did he bury the emeralds?"

"That I did not solve, you may remember, until the very end, Doctor."

"My friends in Canning Town and a cable from Lupin corroborated the information that the thief mentioned Baker Street as the place his wishes would be finalized. Unfortunately for him, they were.

"In his youth, Dreyfus had the reputation as the best diamond cutter in London. He left this profession behind out of the danger it carried and set up his present successful business as a small Building and Loan Bank on Baker Street. He was known as an honest man, Lestrade. You will not find at his establishment the arm-twisting heavies that others employed. He has respect for his clients and was also known for his fairness. Surely, Sergeant Wetherby informed you of this when you spoke to him?

"On my request, Mrs. Hudson created a most fortuitous calendar of James Hudson's final year. In this way, I was able to track his movements. Did you and Mrs. Turner attend the theatre or some Saturday event that day? The date coincides with a fishing trip."

"Oh, yes, we were sweeping our front steps when my lodger ran down the stairs. He pressed upon us tickets to the South London Palace for that very evening. He said his girlfriend could not go and he thought we would enjoy it. I did not even know he had a girlfriend. I had never seen him so animated as when he described the Music Hall Show to us. Going on and on about Mr. Arthur Lloyd's abilities."

"Do you remember the date?"

She looked up with the realization of truth, "One Sunday in September, Mr. Holmes."

He searched through Mr. Hudson's notes. "That would be 12 September of 1880? He and Mr. Rosa were fishing that day. And if I recall, the South London Palace Orchestra performed a worthy selection from Verdi's *Traviata*, am I correct?"

"Mr. Spillane's band did do it justice. But we enjoyed Mr. Critchfield's comedy best. He had us laughing like children."

"I think we can confirm that date by searching through the theatre advertisements in the *Daily Chronicle*. Watson, would you mind? It should be in the 1880 September newspaper file underneath the gasogene stand, old man."

"Of course, Holmes. Yes, by George, here it is, 12 September 1880."

Holmes, with his long thin forefinger, checked off the dates upon the palm of his left hand: "8th – 22nd August 1880, the Hudsons visited Picardy and Switzerland. 19th August, Fiant killed his thief and buried him and the jewels in James Hudson's garden. 12th September 1880, Hudson was away fishing, and Mrs. Hudson was in South London attending the theatre. Fiant dug up the jewels and began harassing London's gem cutters. 21st September. Fiant killed James Hudson in Dreyfus' office."

"Since Fiant now lived in Whitechapel, he could never leave the emeralds behind. So, he buried them at least two more times in your garden, Mrs. Hudson. When we moved in, I believe he then acquired his own set of keys to No. 221B in order to retrieve his buried treasure. On the nights when Fiant visited diamond cutters, he dug up the jewels, walking in with a key when you were out, or the house was asleep. But each time, he left the shovel dirty, and that was noticed by our astute Mrs. Hudson.

"The final notation from James Hudson's journal:

"19 September. On my way home tonight, I spied Mr. Fiant in Baker Street intently watching the comings and goings from Uncle Dreyfus' office. What could he want here? I will keep an eye out."

"Two nights later, the night of 21st September, James Hudson walked home from the St. James's Athletic Club with boxer friend, McMurdo. Who then headed to the pub. On passing No. 42 Baker Street, Hudson observed something unusual at his uncle's window. As you know, Lestrade, Mr. Dreyfus' premises were fronted by large street-facing windows.

"On closer observation, he spied his Uncle Dreyfus imperilled and knew he had to help him. He may have thought it was an act of theft or anti-Semitism. Whatever the reason, James Hudson entered the office to rescue someone he knew was in danger. Hudson's unexpected appearance led to a courageous battle and the rescue of three innocent people. Dreyfus; his wife, Amelia; and his assistant, Saul. Mr. Dreyfus referred to Hudson as a hero."

"This was the way it really was, Mr. Holmes. James walked home from the St. James's. Piccadilly to Baker Street, walking the entirety. It was part of his routine."

"Thank you, Mrs. Hudson," I said. With my assistance, she returned to her bedroom, where I took her vitals. Her temperature was normal, I left Molly in charge and ran back up to Holmes.

Lestrade was speaking, "So, what you are saying is that when Hudson entered Dreyfus' office, it was a lucky break for Fiant. Did he believe that by threatening his nephew, Dreyfus could be forced into cutting the emeralds? Then why did he kill him?"

I said, "Lestrade, the jewels are priceless. Cutting just one of them into smaller and flawless emeralds could make him an extraordinarily rich man. Like Scotland Yard, Fiant thought that Hudson must know about the buried thief and the gems' hiding place. Yet, Hudson was completely innocent and was murdered during his act of bravery."

"Bravo, Doctor! In Fiant, intense hatred and rage fill where the being of a man should reside. To him, these people were lower than dogs; he spent his childhood witnessing the torturing, branding, and killing of such in Texas. Murder for him was an easy thing and deeply associated with familial and patriotic feelings for his Southland.

"Hudson's murder granted him four things: The end to a long-standing desire for revenge. A way to implicate him in the burial at No. 221B. Dreyfus' willing participation in cutting the emeralds. And, he thought, his reinstatement with Mrs. Hudson and her Baker Street home. To us, this last seems implausible, yet through his eyes, it was an essential part of his plan.

"Instead, Mr. and Mrs. Dreyfus have twice shown their lion-heartedness and are now willing witnesses for the Crown in his court case."

"Mr. Holmes, this is a fine piece of detective work. But you must admit some of it was merely by chance and could have gone another way. If you join us in the force, you will have professional support and learn the proven approach to crime-solving offered in the CID. Further, as my assistant, you will have the chance to move through the ranks quickly to detective level." He stood and put out his hand. "What do you say?"

Holmes gravely shook his hand. "I am touched by your kind words and your offer, Lestrade. I do thank you." His eyes twinkled as he smiled. "Scarlet, gold, purple, even dusty rose, but I am sorry, Inspector, BLUE is not my colour."

Lestrade shook his head. "Very funny, Mr. Holmes. But there might come a time when you're arrested at the scene of a crime. And where will you be then?" He shoved his book and pencil in his pocket and headed for the stairs.

From our window, we watched him slam the Baker Street door and climb into a cab. Holmes and I traded looks. Our laughter began as a titter and soon progressed into waves of guffaws. When it subsided, I wondered what Mrs. Hudson thought, but I knew she was preoccupied with other thoughts.

Chapter 27
MRS. HUDSON'S TOAST
The Reminiscences of John H. Watson MD

"His eyes fairly glittered as he spoke, and he put his hand over his heart and bowed as if to some applauding crowd conjured up by his imagination." – *A Study in Scarlet.*

After the conglomeration of friends had left our rooms, we refilled our pipes and returned to a gentlemanly comfort at our fire.

"Holmes, that was a superb sum-up of the facts. I doubt Lestrade has ever seen the like."

"Thank you, Watson." He smiled.

"Yet, I find myself agreeing with the Inspector on one point," I said.

He puffed on his pipe to get it going. "Hmmm?"

"My friend, it is clear to me you need more support. I know you are accustomed to bringing your cases to conclusion. But if we had entered this house together, Fiant would not have had a chance. If I have anything to say about it, your dangerous days as a lone wolf are over. There is enough danger for two. From now on, my service revolver and I will be by your side."

He smiled warmly, "Watson, no finer offer has ever been made. I accept." He shook my hand, sealing the bargain. Holmes again sat cross-legged in his chair, enjoying his smoke.

Mrs. Dreyfus and Mrs. Hudson knocked on our door and joined us with a bottle of princely scotch.

"Gentlemen, are we intruding?"

"Mrs. Hudson, you are supposed to be resting."

"Doctor, I am grateful for your expertise and am much healthier than I was when you carried me from that foul aquarium. Tonight I have something important to say. Mr. Holmes, will you fill two more

224

glasses with this marvellous whisky? Thank you." Mrs. Dreyfus sat in our little circle, accepted her glass, and looked up at her niece with pride.

"Tonight celebration is in order. Mr. Holmes, when you offered to take my husband's case, I hardly knew you and had little faith. Today, I do know what you are capable of, and I am proud you are here in my home. Thank you for granting me what I have been searching for since September—peace of mind. I began where most people believe is the correct place, in religious halls, and came up empty. In searching with you for James' killer, the gritty, dangerous, hateful truth is what has finally set me free. Thank you, Mr. Holmes, and thank you, Doctor Watson. Not only have you brought the killer to justice, but you did so in a way that rescued both Amelia and myself."

"Here, here!" I said.

Holmes toasted, "Mrs. Hudson, to your courage, strength, and friendship!"

"And your gallantry under fire!" toasted Amelia.

"May our glasses be ever full and may the roof over our heads be always strong," I said.

Mrs. Hudson continued, "I have been thinking we ought to have a plaque at the door, what do you think, Mr. Holmes?"

He put up a halting hand and said, "Private consulting detectives need not advertise where they live. No. 221B is a singular address in its own right. In all seriousness, I would rather retain my invisibility." Holmes and I guffawed. I explained the joke to our estimable ladies, who joined in.

"Can you actually turn invisible, Mr. Holmes?"

"Only at night and in the darkest alleys, Mrs. Hudson. Even so, it requires sustained and patient practice. I believe Lily gave a good account of its effects." We laughed and enjoyed another royal round.

I said, "Mrs. Hudson, I must admit you have been a model patient since your Aunt Amelia arrived And thank Providence, your health is improving. You had me worried."

"Doctor, you cannot keep a Scotswoman down."

"That doesn't mean you can go out dancing, yet. Stay the course, and Mrs. Dreyfus can return home in a week's time. We will sorely miss you around Baker Street, Mrs. Dreyfus, you have helped heal so much and opened our minds."

Holmes said, "Indeed, we will. I must now visit Seymour Place for such enlightening conversation."

"You know you are welcome, Mr. Holmes. A questioning mind like yours fits right in with our Jewish way of life," said Mrs. Dreyfus. Our laughter filled the room.

Molly ran up the stairs with a prestigious letter sporting a French Flag. "A footman delivered it; he didn't look English," she said.

Holmes opened it with a flourish, groaned, threw it to me and retired to his bedroom.

"Early day tomorrow, Watson. Molly, we will require coffee only, at 7:30, rest well, Mrs. Hudson, Mrs. Dreyfus." And he closed his door.

I read:

> Dear Mr. Holmes and Doctor Watson,
> You are cordially invited to breakfast tomorrow at the French Embassy. Your recovery of the Empress Emeralds deserves our most generous gratitude.
>
> *Albert Edward, Prince of Wales*
> *Louis Burnet, Curator Le Musée du Louvre*

Chapter 28
-EMBASSY HONOURS
The Reminiscences of John H. Watson MD

"Langdale Pike was his human book of reference upon all matters of social scandal. The receiving station, as well as the transmitter, for all the gossip of the Metropolis." – "The Adventure of the Three Gables."

Early next morning, while dressing, Holmes ran up to my room.

"Ah, of course, you wear your dress uniform, Watson. What do you think?"

He was dressed impeccably in a grey morning coat over a deep wine-red paisley waistcoat, a white blouse and dark navy-blue cravat. It was the tiepin he was questioning. I had never seen it before.

"A Tudor Rose, Holmes, is always in style. Are my stripes straight?"

"They are vertical. Your Aesculapius pouch is twisted, allow me, Doctor. The rose is my father's. He wore it on his watch chain. I had it reconstructed as a tiepin."

"It is silver on gold? Nicely done."

"He was proud of our Yorkshire heritage, prouder still of the brilliant unification this flower represents."

"Your father was a wise man . . . the Squire Holmes?"

"The sword belt suits you, dear Doctor. We must ready."

"My one claim to honour." I brushed off my bearskin cap.

"It will surely not be your last, my boy," he said as he adjusted his cuffs.

"Holmes?"

He glanced at his watch and quickly moved to the steps. "Come, Watson, we are late. Forget your hat!"

My dear Readers,

As you know, it is my great joy to report as truthfully and sweetly as possible the goings-on of our British Society. Today, I beg your pardon as I remove my critic's pince-nez to report on a genuinely honourable event. Be assured in my next column, that sharp focus will once again guide my pen.

Today, in London, a formal breakfast to honour Mr. Sherlock Holmes and Captain John H. Watson, M.D. was held at the French Embassy.

Among the guests were: His Royal Highness, The Prince of Wales. The delightful Miss Lily Langtry. *Monsieur* Burnet, Curator *Le Musée du Louvre* and Sir Edward Westerland, Principal Librarian of the British Museum. And indeed the Ambassadors of our countries and their lovely wives.

During the breakfast, *Messieurs* Holmes and Watson were lauded for their gallant recovery of the magnificent Empress Emeralds. Plus the gentlemen's fearless and unprecedented capture of the American thief. The jewels were returned to the *Louvre* where they were on display.

Our chivalrous gentlemen were appropriately rewarded with emerald sleeve links.

Seventy years ago, the Empress Emeralds were a gift from Emperor Napoleon Bonaparte to his Empress. Some said the gift was a request for forgiveness over some dalliance or other and that Josephine accepted the emeralds but was not moved to exoneration.

This morning we celebrated two triumphant British heroes whose combined knowledge and valour slashed through the peril they faced to retrieve the royal prize.

Our heroic Doctor Watson attired handsomely and smartly in his Fifth Northumberland Fusiliers dress uniform was wounded in action during the battle of Maiwand. May it be noted ladies: These gallant gentlemen were eligible bachelors.

Mr. Holmes, stylishly dressed and sporting a spectacular Tudor Rose tiepin, briefly stated:
"The recovery of the emeralds would not have been possible if not for our valiant friends within the Anglo-Jewish Community. It is to salute their gallantry that I accept this honour."

There is such promise in the pairing of these two adventurous young gentlemen. I shall happily inform you, dear readers, as to their delightful future endeavours.

The End

Mr. Hudson's Garden

"There is a logic of harmony deep-rooted in the dissonance of the world, like music, the growing garden can bring it to light." – James Hudson.

The twelve-page monograph presented here is filled with the timeless recommendations of a gentleman gardener. A life lived in pursuit of the perfect tomato.

The Garden Wall

You may be pleased to note that some roses are, in fact, evergreens. In these Isles, we celebrate roses in perfusion 'til December and beyond.

It is reasonable to dress our garden walls with whatever will make them look the best. For me, hardy varieties work well. We have trained Piccadilly and November Roses to climb as high as is possible and added clematis for early contrast.

Plant the November Roses at the wall. Train carefully. Bend only as each cane's direction permits and anchor them onto the wall. They will require pruning and redirecting. This process will take many seasons, yet its result is well worth the effort. Piccadilly and other varieties of climbing roses require less effort as it is in their nature.

Morning Glory and honeysuckle are other yet wilder choices. They will run up a wall of their own accord and will occur where they may. To be greeted by the brilliant, trumpeting Morning Glory is its own delight.

Early Spring Garden Preparation

1. A ball of twine. Two-foot-high Bamboo or wood stakes.

2. Decide upon the outer dimensions of your garden and the beds you want. With your paths, be generous. I recommend 3-foot-width beds with 3-foot-wide paths around for ease of working.

3. Measure out as many as your garden, and your helpers can support.

4. Stake out the corners of each bed and secure the twine stake to stake. These are your beds. At this point, you can reassess the layout, walk the paths and decide what changes are to be made.

5. The actual borders create with stone, log, board, or short fencing. Lay them out along the twined boundary. Wooden boards need to be lowered into the ground by fifty per cent.

6. The paths may be planted with ground cover yet will need to be scythed or mowed down occasionally and weeds pulled. They will lessen each year as the root takes them out.

7. Cover each bed with animal or fish manure. Best to do this late fall or winter as manure needs time to mature.

8. And be sure to have it finished by March. Although setting up in early spring, just before planting, is acceptable in a pinch.

Vegetables & Their Complements

Gardens do best when complemented by neighbourly vegetables and flowers. Marigolds, nasturtiums are especially good for keeping insects away. Plant liberally throughout the growing beds with the crops. Please find more ideas in the Companion Planting Guide at the end of these pages.

Do not worry about using space for growing vegetables. These flowers will pay their way by keeping your plants healthy and pest free.

Preparation for multiple plantings & the timing of the garden is essential. Lettuce comes up and grows fast. What will you next plant in that bed? Vegetables have their own best timing. For example, Spinach is an excellent bushy early crop. But as soon as the weather warms, it goes out like a candle — harvest as needed like lettuce. The choices of what to plant at this time of year are unlimited.

Winter gardening lengthens the growing season. Fresh food from the garden year-round is another joy of gardening in our British climate. We can still grow lettuces like kale, spinach, and chicory, cabbages, turnip, leek, Brussels sprout, and beetroot in much of winter. Plant late in the year and harvest throughout the cold months.

An example of these vegetables' immense benefits in our lives: For the last two hundred years, Cabbages and turnips have been cultivated as field crops for winter feeding of farm livestock. Because of this, we no longer need to create salt meat for the winter. Before this, scurvy and leprosy cases were frequent throughout the country, but thanks to cabbage and turnip, those terrible diseases are no longer with us.

Note: Our upstairs lodger shows an interest in the garden. He watches me from his bedroom window. I will invite him to join me next time I need a hand.

The English Cottage Vegetable Garden

Our seventy-foot square courtyard garden grows in Central London. The mature London planetree is centred on the north side. Growing beds on the south side, eight beds laid out as three-foot width-wise, each cut into three lengthwise rows—three-foot-wide paths in-between for working around. We do not have room for large rose bushes, yet our southern wall's trellised roses bloom throughout the summer and into the holidays.

British soil is rich and fertile. Our ideal weather is a blessing for growing things and requires only slight augmentation. London reflects the country, and my additions are few. There is no need for chemical fertilizer.

The varying condition of our air adds a distinct impediment. A good clean wet fog is enjoyed by the garden, but our dun-coloured yellow variety is not fit for flora or fauna.

What to use as garden amendment depends on what your town has available and what your soil requires. I find fertilizer from fish best and easily gained from the Worshipful Company of Fishmongers. Animal manure is best when composted in the sun for two years or more. Most farms will allow you to cart it away, but our city streets' ever-burgeoning state allows for simple acquisition. Mix it with rough milled alfalfa from animal feed. It forms a powerful combination to spring broadforking.

Recipe for Fish Fertilizer: Use a hand grinder. Grind up the fish waste: bones, intestines, liver, gall bladder, heart, fins, tail, scales, heads/gills, and skin. Liquify as much as possible and work it into the soil. The Natives of the Americas bury chunks of fish at the roots of their plants. It can also be added to your compost pile and then added to the garden this way.

Please be aware that the pungent odour of this potent fertilizer may draw interested animals to your garden. Well-mixed as compost and tilled into the soil may be the best approach for this. Plant it deeply or fence the garden appropriately.

Note: When I invited our lodger to join me in the garden, he denied ever watching me at the window.

The Rhythm of the Broadfork

In the early spring, nothing can convince me to break my back with a shovel or hoe to till my garden. How do I do so? The answer is the ease of working with a good broadfork in my planting rows. Mrs. Hudson likes best that one stands on it in a much more appropriate upright posture. And that one's back is not taxed in the digging.

Our blacksmith forged the iron blades, metal crossbar, and solid wooden handles. His design made assembly simple. The boy, Jack, placed carriage bolts into the slots and secured the ends of the Ash handles into the sockets welded to the end of the crossbar. A street urchin, there is nothing this boy cannot do with his quick and nimble hands. But there are some things I wish he wouldn't.

The powerful and highly efficient broadfork has been used for centuries. Gardeners use this tool to loosen clay, rocky, and dry soils and prepare it for the addition of amendments: harvesting potatoes, carrots, and other root vegetables. One stands on four broad pickaxes, using weight and gravity to till instead of bending one's back and blistering one's hands.

Brute strength is unnecessary in broadforking. The movement is rhythmic, almost balletic. There is a *giocoso* in it so that at the end, it seems to have gone by too fast. Try that with a shovel!

Tomato the Fruit of Life

MIKADO OR TURNER HYBRID TOMATO.

OLD FAVORITES MUST TAKE A BACK SEAT
MIKADO IS ONE OF THE EARLIEST AND OF THE LARGEST SIZE PERFECTLY SOLID AND OF UNSURPASSED QUALITY. THE EARLIEST TOMATOES ARE PRODUCED BY USING OUR NORTHERN GROWN SEED.

For centuries, the tomato had been patiently cultivated in the Americas before it arrived in Italy, Spain, and France. Gradually herded by careful selection and keen observation into the varieties we enjoy. Though in some countries, including ours, it had to prove itself worthy as it was once deemed poisonous.

It is vital to change sites each season. I dig 4-foot trenches for my tomato beds, fill them with compost, then topsoil for the last foot. It allows roots to grow deep. The plant equals it and grows tall. This gardening technique works well for all vegetables and transforms sandy soil into a rich garden. But it is unnecessary in good soil.

To me, the epitome of all this cultivation is the Heirloom Brandywine Tomato. They produce 16-oz. rosy-pink fruit, with a sweet flavour, and mature in 75 - 100 days. The amendment of fish shortens that somewhat. All tomatoes require full sun and are best in well-draining soil. Watering should be done depending on the weather. Water freely on dry days, and let it drain on wet.

Begin by cutting poles or bamboo to five- or six-foot height, enough for each plant. When the vines are tall enough, securely embed a pole for each, careful not to harm the roots. Thus, begins the process of tying up the tomatoes.

Tomato vines can happily crawl along the ground like squash, but this only affords the worms better access to the fruit. Instead, tie them up with long strips of soft cloth. It is a delicate process that requires some care as the vines break easily. Mrs. Hudson saves shirts of the lighter summer materials for each new season. You may tear long strips of at least one inch in width from the material. Wrap the cloth gently around the vine, crisscross the cloth loosely and tie the material to the pole, not the vine. Take care not to pinch the vine when tying.

Following average growth, it is necessary to untie gently and then retie the vine higher on the bamboo. One-pound fruit requires height and care to grow. The sweet scent of flowering and growing tomatoes and their anticipation makes tying the tomatoes my favourite part of gardening.

Note: We replanted Heirloom Brandywine Tomatoes in last year's bed. The rest of the garden survived our time away, but these plants failed utterly. Strange, they were thriving when we left.

The Glasshouse

Today Jack and his friends created a glasshouse in our garden out of old windows. Watching this handy young gentleman of the road oversee the building of a home for our growing seedlings was instructive in the utter uniqueness of the human spirit.

The size is six-foot-high by four-foot-wide. A wooden frame holds the windows. The roof is made of glass. The windows cascade from the top to prevent water leakage. Flagstones for flooring. And anchored to the wall. On a worktable, they are happily planting seedlings.

Mrs. Hudson and I are witnesses to the potential of these discarded and uneducated boys.

Herb Garden

Mrs. Hudson's herb garden is beneath our London planetree and along the outer edges of the garden. Blue periwinkles at the base of the tree mixed with lily of the valley. Further out where the shade is lighter, and along the sunny sides, we plant Chives, Thyme, Basil, Tarragon, Marjoram, Borage, Garlic, Garden Cress, Mustard, Horseradish, Chervil, Angelica, Lemon Balm, Mint, Parsley, Rosemary, and Strawberry.

If you do plant Lily of the Valley, teach your children they are deadly poisonous. And plant herbs at a safe distance and catnip elsewhere.

Be careful with mint and strawberry. They will take over the garden if not regularly pruned. Periwinkle will choke the Lily if not cut back. Its evergreen qualities are especially welcome after most of the garden is fallow, and the planetree's leaves have fallen into our compost pile.

Plant rosemary throughout the garden and at the edges for its lavender-grey blooms and sweet scent. As the garden's early spring welcoming downbeat, this evergreen blooms before the return of any other scented flower in early March.

Herb & Flower Pot-Pourri Recipe

Gather rose petals and sweet geranium. Dry and pack into jars with bay salt and kitchen salt. Sweet Verbena, Lavender, Bay, and Rosemary are prepared the same way. Cover Orange peel strips with Cloves. Combine in a large bowl adding equal amounts of Allspice, Clove, Mixed Spice, Mace, Gum Benzoin, Gum Storax or Styrax, and five times as much Atkinson's Violet powder. Petals, leaves, and orange are mixed well with spices and stored in glass jars for gifts.

> Note: 1st August. I followed our lodger tonight. This is hateful I know. But I fear for Marti. He met with a French gentleman in Canning Town. The man's extreme anxiety and Mr Fiant's expressions of anger left me with a feeling he is up to no good. I will give him notice tonight.

Practical Gardening

In the middle of June, when the garden is at its zenith, we might face a drought even in England. No rain for a month, the ground hard as iron. And from the east, the wind brings green-fly devastation.

Each day tending an English Cottage vegetable garden is new. I skilfully plan it out, and yet the garden takes me along on its wonderfully improvised journey. We rejoice in the fact our backyard garden is steps away from clear flowing water. It takes time, muscle, and commitment to keep it from parching in such drastic weather.

There are times in gardening when a drought, an early freeze, or an autumnal downpour, and not enough drainage or the beetles swarm in droves from above or below. The garden will not wait for our comprehension. The gardener must act in these unusual situations or face losing all.

"One just has to throw up one's hands for a moment, then pick up the pieces, and go on," said Mrs. Hudson.

This is the time to consult the friends we make in gardening clubs or our University Agricultural Colleges and Extensions. Proven scientific advice for farmers and gardeners is an invaluable resource in times of crisis. Never be afraid to ask for help or to learn something new. The English Arts & Crafts Movement has added much to our libraries, supporting a science of farming and gardening available to anyone.

Helpful Friends

1. University Extension Programs and Master Gardeners.
2. Local Horticultural and Garden Societies.
3. British Beekeepers Association: Stoneleigh, Coventry
4. Cambridge Department of Agriculture: Downing St., Cambridge.
5. The Royal Agricultural College: Cirencester, Gloucestershire.
6. The Bath and West of England Society and Southern Counties Association for the Encouragement of Agriculture, Arts, Manufactures, and Commerce: Bath.

The Abundant Harvest

Our ancestors did celebrate the harvest from the fall equinox to Michaelmas on the 29th of September. The large village festivals and feasts of old are stories of another time. Yet, we may still celebrate with a good goose supper and Mrs. Hudson's Michaelmas Bannock cake. Here and there, harvest fetes still exist. Even in London, you may find my favourite, the Harvest Festival of the Sea in Spitalfields.

Harvesting is an ongoing event that follows nature's timing. Every harvest of every crop has its own welcome and its own duties. Some happily become the following week's meals, some are gifts, preserving appropriately, adding to breads, cakes, pies, or trading for the things we need. Mrs. Hudson is creative in her use of this abundance and with lodgers also to feed and our street urchin helpers. Our kitchen bespeaks the joys of the harvest all year long.

Harvesting Seeds

As each crop reaches harvest, there is a further joy to be found in seed harvesting. Today's 19th-century gardener has access to a variety of seed catalogues. The seeds harvested from our own produce can become the basis for the coming year's abundance. Flowers are effortless to harvest. Within the divine beauty of each flower is its own perpetuation. Allow the seeds to dry on the stalks or vines and simply catch them before they fall. Crush the pods between your fingers or keep the dried flower intact and save it for the next planting.

Garner fruit or vegetable seeds from within the fruit before cooking. Clean off the pulp and air dry. Gather into labelled envelopes and keep them in a dry place, your earth or root cellar, near to where the herbs are hanging.

Strawberries, raspberries, and grapes are perennials and will continue to produce year in year out. It is their nature to proliferate and do require some thinning out.

Raspberry canes can be especially worrisome and require pruning or training into the shape you require. Yet, with good stout gloves, they prove a compelling challenge as you mould them. If you do not have the inclination to wrestle with this unruly fruit, I recommend keeping it out of your garden altogether.

Strawberries are prolific. Prune them to grow in the space allotted. These fruits require only sun and rain to produce a worthwhile crop. I have never grown wine grapes, so I have nothing to say on the subject.

Note: 19 September. On my way home tonight, I spied Mr Fiant in Baker Street intently watching the comings and goings from Uncle Dreyfus' office. What could he want here? I will keep an eye out.

Thoughts on Chemical Amendments

The recent turn towards chemical garden amendment in the gardening and farming community is one I staunchly find lacking, especially as the proven addition of fish manure to the garden or farm superbly enhanced its growth. Possibly some research into making this more accessible would prove worthy, but I can see no need for chemical enhancement.

I would invite you to take care when considering using any of these products. Some are primarily imported guano that has often been safely used as augmentation. There are now products that add to it substances created in a chemical laboratory. The promise of these chemicals is untested. What does the future hold for our good English soil, its helpful insects, and birds? Once it is infiltrated with chemicals, the price may be dear. It is yet to be determined and is entirely unnecessary.

From our island, we have access to the best fertilizer ever created, the fish of the rivers, lakes, and seas. This only adds to the soil that is natural to our diet. And adds only healthy material to our gardens.

As our world approaches the changes of the new century, we have as a people discovered the creation and sale of new products that later prove as false as Gripe Water. Or as harmful as cocaine. How many of us got involved with that manufactured evil because the medical profession touted it as the latest in chemical wonders? I believe this new approach to soil augmentation may hold similar disadvantages for the future of Britain.

Acknowledgements

"We are the music makers, and we are the dreamers of dreams."—Arthur O'Shaughnessy

First and foremost I thank Mattias Boström for his remarkable vision. *From Holmes to Sherlock,* his splendid history of the world of Sherlock Holmes. It connects us directly to Sir Arthur Conan Doyle and maps out the journey from *A Study in Scarlet* to Sherlock and beyond. To view this amazing and singular phenomenon as a whole and to know one's place in it is a tremendous gift.

Mattias' "Shake up Sherlock" has been with me throughout my growth as an author of Sherlock Holmes. His valiant statement has been the touchstone for the creation of my novels, daily cheering me onward. Thank you, sir!

To all my fellow Sherlock Holmes authors, portrayers, and scholars, beginning with Sir Arthur Conan Doyle, West End's Charles Brookfield, and Oxford's Monsignor Knox, I salute you. Today we are involved in an explosion and exploration of what Doyle began in November 1887. I celebrate this joyful Sherlockian and Holmesian community who continue to create the world of Sherlock Holmes. Bravo, Brava, and thank you.

MX Publishing, led by Steve Emecz, is always growing, always redefining the limits of this field, and always creating new ways of partnership, and building community. Modelling that the way through this pandemic is in reaching out to help others stay afloat. I am proud to be a part of this superb author collective, Sherlock Holmes Books, whose support and encouragement are rare treasures in the world of publishing today.

There are two timelines that I live by in writing my novels, one is the history of the day, time and place. The other is the history and timeline Doctor Watson created within Doyle's canon of Sherlock

Holmes stories. This very unique situation allows me to view the history of the world through the eyes of the characters created by Sir Arthur Conan Doyle. Reconciling these historical aspects is not always probable, and sometimes seemingly impossible. Yet a most singular way to write, and to survive our present pandemic.

I thank my fellow MX authors. Wendy Heyman-Marsaw, who I consider, the founder of the Mrs. Hudson books. Her research into her recipes and life in Baker Street, *Mrs. Hudson's Kitchen*, is a classic resource for the Sherlockian Community. Geri Schear, whose creation of Lady Beatrice as the consummate female companion to Sherlock Holmes is a splendid model of the art of characterization. Visiting Geri's lovely London Communities you feel your life has been enriched by the friends you've made in her books. Thank you both for granting me such astute assistance with this novel.

My tireless Beta Readers, from first to last offering positive comments and encouragement. Pamela Ann Russo. Robert Sturgeon. Douglas Altabef's knowledgeable coaching on Jewish life. Richard Clinchy for scholarly assistance on the American Civil War.

My editor, Richard T. Ryan, is a superb Sherlock Holmes author in his own right. He is also an expert at waking me like Doctor Watson complacently snoozing in front of the fire, to what is wrong and what is right with my MS.

My wonderful Scots narrator, J.T. McDaniel, whose marvellous voice acting is for me the embodiment of Doctor Watson. His experience as a Shakespearean actor affords me with a voice talent of wide-ranging proficiency and ability.

Thanks to my cheerleaders around the world: Mary Bruskewicz, Frank Bruskewicz, Gary and Jennifer Culp, Ann and Will Keech, Maureen Whittaker, Harry DeMaio, Craig Stephen Copland, Catherine Cooke and her researchers at the Westminster Research Library, Roger Johnson, Nicholas Meyer, Jayantika Ganguly, Nieves Fernandez, Christine Bush, Mark Sohn. Sherlock Holmes Books,

Mondadori Publishing, Mystery Magazine, Belanger Books, The Sherlock Holmes Journal, The Serpentine Muse, The Watsonian, and The Proceedings of the Pondicherry Lodge.

In these pages, the astute reader may discern homages to men or women who portrayed Sherlock Holmes on film, TV, Radio, theatre, disk, audiobook, and online. Or like Producer Michael Cox, who brought his dreams to life, behind the scenes. For me, they are all enlightening.

There is one exceptional gentleman actor, who leads them all, Mr. Jeremy Brett. His definitive portrayal of Sherlock Holmes in the Granada TV Series, and on stage. His striving for accuracy to Doyle's text, his research into the cracks in the marble of his character, and his determination to find the man inside the stone, and show him to us, inspire me to write my novels.

Epilogue

In the autumn of the year 2015, my beautiful and musically gifted husband, Michael, died suddenly 85 miles from home. He was a scientist involved with cutting-edge projects in New York's financial world. A peacemaker on Wall Street and a superb gardener. Why and how he died so young were still mysteries.

Surviving a beloved's unexpected and inexplicable death was a journey no one chose willingly. It was my hope that if I took on the mantle of Mrs. Hudson, together we could shine a lantern of possibility through the dark valley we have both walked. To show that from the horrible ashes of such grief, transformation beckons.

"But grief is a phoenix, Holmes. First, we burn with the searing pain of loss until we are reduced to grey ash. And then, surprisingly, there comes a time when life reasserts itself and new wings are born out of it. We are given a choice, to soar or to dive." – John H. Watson, MD, *Remarkable Power of Stimulus*.

Notes For Curious
Instead of footnotes

Glossary of Terms

Sitting Shiva – Mourning period, shared with family and friends, immediately following the death of a family member.

Mikvah, the sacred bath used for the purpose of ritual immersion.

Neerday – Scots call New Year's Day 'Ne'rday' or 'Neerday'.

The rod of Aesculapius – the universal symbol for Doctor of Medicine.

Box Room – A storage room, usually located in the attics and underneath the eaves.

Gaol – A British jail.

Sensei – Teacher.

19th Century Slang:

Hammer and tongs – Argument.

Smeller – The Nose.

Sit-upons – Trousers.

Anointing – To beat someone up.

Mutton Shunter – British Constable or Bobbie.

Eternity Box – Coffin.

Salad – is a light-hearted term denoting a large number of medals pinned on an officer's uniform.

Skilamalink – Secret, shady, doubtful.

Dodgy – Questionable, Suspicious.

Hogmagundy – The process by which the population is increased.

Boxing Parlance: *Floorer* – A blow sufficiently strong to knock a fighter down, usually the end of a fight.

Works Used Throughout (Chapter Notes Follow)

1. Doyle, Sir Arthur Conan. *The Complete Sherlock Holmes. Volume I and II.* New York: Doubleday.

2. Baring-Gold, William. *Sherlock Holmes of Baker Street: A Life of the World's First Consulting Detective.* British Columbia, Canada: Calabash Press, 1962.

3. Baring-Gold, William. *The Annotated Sherlock Holmes.* New York: Clarkson N. Potter, 1967.

4. Klinger, Leslie. *New Annotated Sherlock Holmes.* New York: W.W. Norton & Company, 2005.

5. Doyle, Sir Arthur Conan. *The Original Illustrated 'Strand' Sherlock Holmes.* Hertfordshire, UK: Wordsworth Editions, 1989.

6. *Bradshaw's Handbook 1861.* London: HarperCollins, 2014 (originally published as Bradshaw's Descriptive Railway Hand-Book of Great Britain and Ireland 1861).

7. *Bradshaw's Monthly Continental Railway, Steam Transit, and General Guide 1887* - Google Books.
   https://books.google.com/books?id=w3dKAAAAYAAJ&vq=calais&pg=PP1#v=onepage&q&f=false

8. Doyle, Sir Arthur Conan. *Memories and Adventures.* London: Hodder & Stoughton Ltd. 1924. The copyright for this publication is in the public domain.

9. Liebow, Ely M. *Doctor Joe Bell, Model for Sherlock Holmes.* Madison, Wisconsin: Popular Press, 2007.

10. BHO British History Online. IHR Institute of Historical Research, School of Advanced Study, University of London. https://www.british-history.ac.uk/

11. "The Arthur Conan Doyle Encyclopaedia." Maintained by Alexis Barquin: https://www.arthur-conan-doyle.com/index.php/Sherlock_Holmes/

12. National Library of Scotland, Georeferenced maps, London, 1893-6. I spend delightful days in research here.

https://maps.nls.uk/geo/find/#zoom=16&lat=51.50349&lon=-0.13541&layers=38&b=1&z=1&point=0,0

13. Altabef, Gretchen. *Sherlock Holmes These Scattered Houses.* MX Publishing, London. 2019.

14. Altabef, Gretchen. Sherlock Holmes *A Remarkable Power of Stimulus.* MX Publishing, London. 2020.

Note 1: Sir Arthur Conan Doyle wrote 60 Sherlock Holmes stories, 4 are novels. He was a prolific author of 1,874 works. He wrote more than 300 pieces of fiction (including 24 novels) of all genres: history, fantasy, drama, adventure, science-fiction, crime, war. Plus more than 1500 other works as essays, plays, poems, articles, letters to the press, pamphlets, and interviews on every subject such as politics, religion, war, crime, injustice, etc.

Note 2: The casting of Doctor Watson as the author of the Sherlock Holmes stories is based upon these beginning words of the first story, *A Study in Scarlet*: "Being a Reprint from the Reminiscences of John H. Watson, M.D. late of the Army Medical Department." They place Doctor Watson firmly in position as the author of the bulk of the Sherlock Holmes stories referred to as the canon. That Sir Arthur Conan Doyle must then be Watson's Literary Agent, also follows. This is what is referred to as The Game played by members of the worldwide Sherlock Holmes Literary Societies. They are known to adopt a half-humorous view of this, yet are also very serious about it.

Chapter 1

15. William Kent, progenitor of the naturalistic "English landscape." 1685-1748. Quote.

16. Peter M. Rhee, MD, MPH, Ernest E. Moore, MD, Bella Joseph, MD, Andrew Tang, MD, Viraj Pandit, MD, Gary Vercruysse, MD. *Trauma Acute Care Surgery Volume 80, Number 6.* "Gunshot wounds: A review of ballistics, bullets, weapons, and myths." The Division of Trauma, Critical Care, Burns and

Emergency Surgery, Department of Surgery, University of Arizona, Tucson, Arizona; and Department of Surgery, University of Colorado, Denver, Colorado.

Note 4: The Jewish people lived in England until 1290 when they were forced to leave. During the Inquisition, Sephardi families left Spain and Portugal after years of forced conversions. Some moved to England in 1497. Most to Amsterdam. Until Rabbi Menasseh ben Israel encouraged Oliver Cromwell to reopen England to the Jewish people in 1656. Many then moved to London and port cities. In 1701, Bevis Marks Synagogue was created in the East End. After 140 years Westminster families formed the West London Synagogue for British Jews. My story takes place 40 years later in 1881. The history of the Anglo-Jewish Community is unique in English and Jewish History.

Chapter 2

Note 5: "In England Jews did not gain political equality as a result of a sudden revolution or political change. It came as the crown of a process of integration into English society which had been proceeding for more than a century, delayed only because of the range of the problem and the innate conservatism of the English people." *Jewish disabilities in nineteenth-century England.* - Gene Ray Freitag.

17. Heyman-Marsaw, Wendy. *Memoirs from Mrs. Hudson's Kitchen.* London: MX Publishing, 2017.

Chapter 3

18. Saadi. Persian Sufi poet, *Gulistan* (The Rose Garden). 1258. Quote.

19. 1880-81: Early snowfall! 6 inches of snow fell in October in London! January, 3 feet of snow fell from East Devon to the Isle of Wight! 10-foot drifts in Evesham. Dartmoor recorded 4 feet. Very Snowy Winter. History of British Winters, Netweather. TV. So my 29 November squall is entirely possible.

20. The character of Amelia Dreyfus is patterned after the novelist and historian, Grace Aguilar. "Aguilar sought to give Jewish women a proud identity," Galchinsky wrote. "Her accounts of biblical and historical Jewish women in *The Women of Israel,* combined with her occasional lyrics and domestic fictions... argued for changes in what women and girls could learn and how they could learn it."

Chapter 4

21. Beeton, Mrs. Isabella. *The Book of Household Management.* Published Originally By S. O. Beeton in 24 Monthly Parts 1859-1861. First Published in a Bound Edition 1861. The Project Gutenberg eBook. An essential resource for the Victorian historical author.

Note 6: West London Synagogue for British Jews. History: On 15 April 1840, twenty-four gentlemen held a meeting. They aimed to found a new synagogue that would allow those Jews who had previously attended London's two principal synagogues, both on the edge of the City, to worship nearer their own homes in the West End. They were also anxious to provide in their religious services, a sermon in English, provision for the teaching of Hebrew and Judaism, and a coming together of both branches of English Jews, the Sephardim and Ashkenazim. Thus was born the first Reform Synagogue in England, unique in London. https://www.wls.org.uk/

22. Zara, Alfred A. "The Sephardim of England." Foundation for the Advancement of Sephardic Studies and Culture, 2002.

Kershen, Anne J. and Romain, Jonathan A. *Tradition and change: a history of Reform Judaism in Britain, 1840–1995.* London; Portland, Oregon: Valentine Mitchell, 1995.

23. Jewish Virtual Library, United Kingdom Virtual Jewish History Tour: https://www.jewishvirtuallibrary.org/united-kingdom-virtual-jewish-history-tour

Chapter 5

Note 7: Pritchard, Linda; Warner, Mary Ann. *On The Wings Of Paradise. The Jeremy Brett-Linda Pritchard Story.* Printed by the authors, 2011. Many of the statements about life and death expressed by Rabbi Moshe and Rifka are paraphrased or quoted from this book. And are attributed to Mr. Jeremy Brett.

24. Katye Anna Clark. A true modern-day medium. https://www.katyeanna.com/

Chapter 6

Note 8: *In dir ist freude* ("In you is joy"). A choral prelude written for organ by Johann Sebastian Bach. The Victorians had rediscovered Bach and were busily resurrecting his music.

25. Gillard, D (2018) "Education in England: a history" www.educationengland.org.uk/history
26. Fergusson, Robert. *The Draft Days.* 1772. Born in 1750 in Edinburgh, Scottish poet Robert Fergusson was one of the most influential writers of his time despite dying at the tender age of twenty-four. https://mypoeticside.com/poets/robert-fergusson-poems. Quote.

Chapter 7

Note 9: To be precise, to all British subjects, when the first-floor is mentioned it is the floor in a dwelling immediately above the ground floor or street level. In America, this is the second-floor. It proceeds from this that Watson's bedroom would be on the third-floor in America while remaining squarely on the second-floor in England.

Chapter 8

27. "I have been guilty of several monographs. They are all upon technical subjects. Here, for example, is one 'Upon the Distinction Between the Ashes of the Various Tobaccos.'" – Sherlock Holmes mentions this monograph in *The Sign of Four*.

Chapter 9

28. Doyle, Arthur Conan. *A Study in Scarlet.* Beeton's Christmas Annual, Ward, Lock & Co. London, 1887.

29. Hazlitt, William. *The Collected Works Of William Hazlitt.* London, J. M. Dent & CO. New York, McClure, Phillips & CO. 1903. Quotes: "Violence ever defeats its own ends." "Prejudice is the child of ignorance."

30. Porter, Bernard. *The Origins of the Vigilant State: The London Metropolitan Police Special Branch Before the First World War.* United Kingdom, Boydell Press, 1991.

31. Sir William George Granville Venables Vernon Harcourt KC (14 October 1827 – 1 October 1904.) About the Fenians, he wrote to the Queen's secretary: "The clumsiness of their contrivances and the stupidity of their proceedings are childish in the extreme." British lawyer, journalist, Liberal statesman, MP, Home Secretary, Chancellor of the Exchequer under William Ewart Gladstone before becoming Leader of the Opposition. As Home Secretary, he shepherded the Explosive Substances Act 1883 which passed in the shortest time on record.

32. Kenna, Shane. *War in The Shadows: The Irish-American Fenians Who Bombed Victorian Britain.* Ireland, Merrion Press, 2014.

Chapter 10

Note 10: Lily Langtry (1853–1929) The Jersey Lily, rose from an obscure life on the Isle of Jersey to become celebrated as the most beautiful woman of her era. She dated all the most eligible bachelors, including the Prince of Wales. As an actress, she managed the Imperial Theatre, from 1900 to 1903. Oscar Wilde said, "I would rather have discovered Mrs. Langtry than have discovered America." She is also thought to be Sir Arthur Conan Doyle's model for Irene Adler.

33. Brough, James. *The Prince and the Lily: The Story of Lillie Langtry—The Greatest International Beauty of Her Day.* NY: Coward, McCann & Geoghegan, 1975.

34. Cypser, Darlene A. *The Consulting Detective Trilogy Part II: On Stage.* Foolscap & Quill, Morrison, Colorado, USA. 2017. Holmes reference to his youth on the stage will be found within the pages of this marvellous book.

Chapter 11

35. Marchione, Dr. Victor. *Natural ways to improve night vision.* 2016.

36. Borgia, Michael. *Human Vision and The Night Sky: How to Improve Your Observing Skills.* Springer, New York, 2006.

Chapter 12

37. Leblanc, Maurice. *Arsène Lupin Versus Herlock Sholmes.* Chicago, M.A. Donahue & Co, 1910.

Note 11: Around this time, The New Bohemian Club underwent a change of management. The actual date is obscure, possibly a localized fire or flood rendered the records unreadable. Nevertheless, we believe it was transformed into the most secretive of establishments ever to be considered one of the Men's Clubs of London – the Diogenes Club.

Note 12: Joséphine de Beauharnais had many parures, or sets, of jewelry. There were several inventories made of her impressive collection, but since jewellery was often gifted to family members and passed down through lines of inheritance, and since some of Joséphine's jewellery was passed on to Napoléon I's new wife, Marie-Louise, it's unclear where a lot of it ended up.

Chapter 13

38. Galchinsky, Michael. *The Origin of The Modern Jewish Woman Writer. Romance and Reform in Victorian England.* Wayne State University Press, Detroit, Michigan, 1996.

39. The women of the Anglo-Jewish culture were precursors of the women's suffrage movement. They began writing their novels, poetry, and journals in 1840. The British women's suffrage movement began in 1866. Americans in 1848.

Chapter 14

40. Williams, Luke G. *Richmond Unchained: the biography of the world's first black sporting superstar*. Amberley, 2015. Quote.

Chapter 15

41. "Here is my monograph upon the tracing of footsteps, with some remarks upon the uses of plaster of Paris as a preserver of impresses." Holmes first mentioned it in *The Sign of Four*.

Chapter 16

42. Forensic Anthropology Center, University of Tennessee, USA. Established in 1980 by anthropologist William M. Bass as the first facility for the study of the decomposition of human remains. "The Body Farm is an ideal setting to scientifically document post-mortem change. The collection holds resources for students, researchers, and law enforcement agencies. includes skeletal collections, decomposition facilities, biometrics, remote sensing studies, etc." http://fac.utk.edu/collections-and-research/

Chapter 17

43. Sir Robert Peel (1778-1850), British home minister. Formed London's first organized police force with the implementation of the Metropolitan Police Act, passed by Parliament in 1829. Peel, with the help of Eugène-François Vidocq (founder of the French *Sûreté*), selected the original site on Whitehall Place for the new police headquarters. Quote.

44. Nix, Elizabeth. History Channel. British History. December 10, 2014 "Why are British police officers called 'Bobbies'?" After Sir Robert Peel. https://www.history.com/news/why-are-british-police-officers-called-bobbies

45. Dent B.B.; Forbes S.L.; Stuart B.H. "Review of human decomposition processes in soil." Environmental Geology. 45 (4): 576–585. 2004.

Note 13: Félix Calabar, Sherlock Holmes' Sensei. According to my research from beyond the Canon, the practice of *baritsu* was derived from the martial art, *Jujitsu,* that reportedly began to be taught in 1898 London. Yet Doctor Watson records Sherlock Holmes' statement of his mastery in the art in the spring of 1891. There must have been a way to master this martial art before the 4th of May 1891.

Chapter 18

46. "Ku Klux Klan A History of Racism and Violence." Compiled by the staff of the Klanwatch Project of the Southern Poverty Law Center, Montgomery, Alabama, 2011.
https://www.splcenter.org/sites/default/files/Ku-Klux-Klan-A-History-of-Racism.pdf

47. Griffith, D. W. *The Birth of a Nation.* Griffith Feature Films, 1912. This propaganda film offers a means to understand the feelings of those who lived through the Reconstruction Era in the South. It gave me access to my villain in a way all my research could not.

48. Cody, William F. *The Life of Hon. William F. Cody Known as Buffalo Bill the Famous Hunter, Scout, and Guide: An Autobiography.* Hartford, Connecticut: Frank E. Bliss, 1879. A facsimile edition was published in 1983 by Time-Life Books as part of its 31-volume series *Classics of the Old West.*

Chapter 19

49. Liberles, Robert. "The Jews and Their Bill: Jewish Motivations in the Controversy of 1753." *Jewish History,* vol. 2, no. 2, 1987, pp. 29–36. Springer, Berlin 1987. "These Ashkenazi Jews were funnelled by the railways of Europe to its North Sea and Baltic ports, and entered England via London, Hull, Grimsby and Newcastle."

Chapter 20

Note 14: The Imperial Theatre. The theatre was in existence: 15th April 1876 - 24th November 1907. In 1882, Lillie Langtry appeared at the theatre in Tom Taylor's *An Unequal Match*. She managed the theatre from 1900 – 1903, acting in productions by Henrik Ibsen and George Bernard Shaw. The Imperial Theatre Orchestra is mentioned in Watson's story, "The Adventure of the Solitary Cyclist."

50. Edward Walford, "Westminster: Tothill Fields and neighbourhood," in *Old and New London: Volume 4* (London, 1878). The Institute of Historical Research. School of Advanced Study, University of London. http://www.british-history.ac.uk/old-new-london/vol4/pp14-26

Chapter 21

Note 15: The Prince of Wales. His life as the Prince of Wales led him to become an astute diplomat. He was not cloistered from the world and was open to modern views. He became King Edward VII in 1901. During his reign, his strong condemnation of prejudice and his views were notably progressive for the time. His Royal Majesty reinvented royal diplomacy, became the first reigning British monarch to visit Russia. Edward VII modernised the British Home Fleet and reorganised the British Army. He fostered good relations between Britain and other European countries, especially France, for which he earned the title "Peacemaker." Ending centuries of Anglo-French rivalry. The Edwardian era heralded significant changes in technology and society. Edward VII achieved this and much more in one decade. "He was, in fact, the most popular king England had known since the earlier 1660s." – J. B. Priestley.

Note 16: Murray is mentioned once in Doyle's canon, in *A Study in Scarlet*. Watson's orderly holds a special place in our hearts. The story goes that these two brave gentlemen served in the Second Anglo-Afghan War which began 21 November 1878. Murray's heroic rescue of Doctor John H. Watson at the battle of Maiwand on 27 July 1880 is well-known to Sherlockians and Holmesians. I think with the British feelings towards the Irish at this time, Doyle was also doing his best to raise one such gentleman to the status of hero.

Chapter 22

51. Nespor, Cassi. "Medical Treatments in the Late 19th Century." Melnick Medical Museum, Youngstown State University. Youngstown Ohio, 2013.

https://melnickmedicalmuseum.com/2013/03/27/19ctreatment/

52. Thomson, William H. *Notes on Materia Medica and Therapeutics: taken from lectures delivered.* William H. McEnroe, ed. New York: Trow, 1894. Print.

53. Bell, Dr Joseph. "A Manual of the Operations of Surgery." Alberta, Canada: Okitoks Press, 2017 (originally published, Edinburgh: Oliver and Boyd, 1892.) Master Surgeon and distinguished professor of medicine at the University of Edinburgh, President of the Royal College of Surgeons of Edinburgh, and personal surgeon to Queen Victoria in Scotland. He was Arthur Conan Doyle's inspiration for Sherlock Holmes.

Chapter 23

54. Prim, Justin K; Gilbertson, Al. "An Afternoon with London's Oldest Gemcutters" Exploring British Lapidary Tradition with Charles Matthews Ltd. GIA Laboratory Gemological Institute of America; Institute of Gem Trading, Bangkok, 2019.

55. "MSaat Nefesh" [Gift of the Soul] was Mordechai Zvi Mane's poem. (1859-1886) Russian Jewish poet, author, artist.

"We should be ruled by the surrounding quiet calm
That ascends without waking
The solitary, silent mountain peak
Upon which the poet resides.
Alas, who will give me the wings of an eagle!
I also have a struggle to overcome
Like any other human being.
I would like the freedom to come and go."

Chapter 24

56. The kosher laws emphasize that life in its totality is a sacred endeavour. The advantages: health benefits, humane treatment of animals, their unifying effect on a dispersed people can be seen as 'spiritual nutrition'. Chabad.org Library article: *What Is Kosher?*
https://www.chabad.org/library/article_cdo/aid/113425/jewish/What-Is-Kosher.htm

Chapter 25

Note 17: As to my use of the monstrous Texas vigilantes, The Knights of the White Camellia as the progenitors of my villain. They were a Ku Klux Klan group in Texas during the Reconstruction Era following the American Civil War. Holmes, of course, has knowledge of the Klan at the time of *The Keys of Death*. But Watson is ignorant of them until Holmes relates their history in the case of "The Five Orange Pips" which takes place in 1887.

Chapter 26

Note 18: Counter-stamped Currency. What Holmes tore off his villain's watch chain was an American half dollar counter-stamped with G.W. KLARKSON in relief within a rectangular depression. It is typical of silversmith hallmarks. Gerald Waverly Klarkson was a justice of the peace in Houston, an officer in the Confederate army and the Texas Militia during the Civil War. As a silversmith and true son of the South, he was provisioning the troops and counter-stamping his own currency.

Note 19: François Eugène Vidocq (1775-1857) French master thief, conman, masquerader, escape artist, and the father of modern police investigation. Creator of the *Brigade de la Sûreté* and credited with the introduction of undercover work, ballistics, criminology, and a record-keeping system for criminal investigation. He made the first plaster cast impressions of shoe prints. He inspired Britain's creation of the CID in 1842, and many others around the world.

Vidocq and the Empress Emeralds: The case that changed his life and the history of police investigation. Napoleon failed to recover the stolen jewels, so he hired Vidocq, a criminal, who solved it in three days. Sherlock Homes employs many of the skills that Vidocq created seventy years before. That the emerald was stolen again in 1880 was a fancy of mine.

Chapter 27

Note 20: The toast is an art form, especially among those who meet formally or informally to toast absent friends. Among the Sherlockian and Holmesian Literary Societies, it is a regular occurrence, and they are toastmasters. A toast might go on and on or it can be short and sweet. But most toasts have that marvellous gift of the gab that brings warmth to the heart and joy to the soul, through humour.

Chapter 28

Note 21: The Tudor rose is the traditional floral heraldic emblem of England and takes its name and origins from the House of Tudor, which united the House of Lancaster and the House of York. Following the 15th century's traumatic civil conflict known to us as the "Wars of the Roses," Henry VII adopted the Tudor rose badge conjoining the White Rose of York and the Red Rose of Lancaster.

57. "Langdale Pike ... made, it was said, a four-figure income by the paragraphs which he contributed every week to the garbage papers which cater for an inquisitive public. If ever, far down in the turbid depths of London life, there was some strange swirl or eddy, it was marked with automatic exactness by this human dial upon the surface." Sir Arthur Conan Doyle, Doctor John H. Watson, "The Adventure of the Three Gables," 1926.

James Hudson's Garden Journal

58. My credentials as a gardener are simple, for the past decade, I have managed a large giveaway garden, in Doylestown Pa. We raise organic vegetables to donate to our local food banks. We

are part of a large coalition of businesses, gardeners, farms, and schools organized to end hunger.

59. Jekyll, Gertrude. *Home And Garden; Notes and thoughts, practical and critical, of a worker in both.* London, New York, Bombay, Longmans, Green and Co, 1900. "Throughout my life, I have found that one of the things most worth doing was to cultivate the habit of close observation. Like all else, the more it is exercised the easier it becomes, till it is so much a part of oneself that one may observe almost critically and hardly be aware of it." – Gertrude Jekyll.

60. Tull, Jethro. "Essay on the Principles of Tillage and Vegetation." 1731.

61. Card, Adrian; Whiting, David; Wilson, Carl; Reeder, Jean, Ph.D.; Goldhamer, Dan. CMG Garden Notes #234 "Organic Fertilizers: Fish and Seaweed." *Master Gardener,* Colorado State University, Extension, 2015.

62. Krohn, Elise. "Creating Community Gardens Guidelines and Resources for Gardeners in the Pacific Northwest." Northwest Indian College, 2013.

About The Author

"The power of imagination makes us infinite." – John Muir

 *The Keys of Death* is the beginning. Gretchen Altabef's third novel takes place at the very start of it all. In that auspicious London year 1880, when twentysomethings Holmes, Watson, and Mrs. Hudson first meet. Sherlock Holmes is a young gentleman genius, friendly, of a philosophic, scholarly bent, and genuinely human. In Doctor Watson's timeline, this adventure predates and also coincides with *A Study in Scarlet.*

Ms. Altabef's fictional journeys grow out of her copious historical research. Both the history within Sir Arthur Conan Doyle's canon of Sherlock Holmes stories and the actual history of the day. To this, she adds the history of women in Victorian times. Plus a creative application of that imagination and intuition Holmes usually finds lacking in the Scotland Yarders. She shares with her main character a half-humorous perspective on the world.

This book is a diversion from Ms. Altabef's two 1894 Sherlock Holmes novels. *These Scattered Houses,* debuted as second in audiobook holiday sales for MX Publishing. *Remarkable Power of Stimulus* is the sequel with heart. The third book in this series is presently in the works.

A member of The Sherlock Holmes Society of London, The Adventuresses of Sherlock Holmes, The John H. Watson Society, The Sherlock Holmes Society of India, The ACD Society, and The Philadelphia Dumpster Divers, assemblage artist collective.

She spends much of her time catching up at the Baker Street fire. Keep up-to-date by visiting Gretchen Altabef's Writer's Blog at: https://featuresofinterest.com/

9 781787 058880